ALL THE THIN PLACES

AN ALTERNATE REALITY NOVEL

RADHIKA SINGH

Publisher's Cataloging-in-Publication

(Provided by Cassidy Cataloguing Services, Inc.).

Names: Singh, Radhika (Writer), author.

Title: All the thin places : an alternate reality novel / Radhika Singh.

Description: [San Francisco, California] : Radhika Singh, [2023]

Identifiers: ISBN: 979-8-9876664-0-1 (Paperback) | 979-8-9876664-1-8 (ebook) | LCCN: 2023904672

Subjects: LCSH: Virtual reality--Fiction. | Alternate reality games--Fiction. | Multiverse--Fiction. | Metaverse--Fiction. | Gateways--Fiction. | Friendship--Fiction. | Shared virtual environments --Fiction. | Loneliness--Fiction. | Metaphysics--Fiction. | Transcendentalism--Fiction. | LCGFT: Science fiction. | Alternative histories (Fiction) | Action and adventure fiction. | Romance fiction. | BISAC: FICTION / Science Fiction / Action & Adventure.

Classification: LCC: PS3619.I5744 A45 2023 | DDC: 813/.6--dc23

Thanks, for helping with this, to
    Appi, who loves stories
    Ari, who said go for it
    Nav, who read this first
    Karen Gray, who edited this

1

———————

Michael said I should be the chronicler of all our fates. I'll try. I chronicle events as they happen and as I remember them happening. I craft a narrative that crests and falls like the turbulent waves of the Pacific Ocean, always searching to break upon the shore. It would be better to say I'm following the road that leads to Michael even when it ends at the ocean, but at least that signifies an ending. This story, and indeed all our stories, do not have the luxury of conclusions. Even death is a beginning. This much I've learned from Michael. So, I'll start from the Now.

I cannot say this with certainty, except when *The Dissolving* starts, I feel clutched by eternity. I slip between the cracks of time to enter now-time, an endless expanse where I have no memories and no tools to make sense of the whirlpool of images swirling around me. I sense the world's edges collapsing as I, too, am furled into something unidentifiable and shout in fear and fury the meaningless words, "I am Tashi Wheeler!"

I

This is my best attempt to describe what happens to me during these intense periods when my "self" dissolves. This has been happening with alarming frequency, increasing from a few times a month to twice this week alone. From a scientific perspective, I've tried defining my entry and exit times from these experiences, which I've begun to refer to as *The Dissolving*.

Time is a fluid concept. Many years ago, in an advanced physics class in high school, I turned in a paper exploring the shifting nature of relativity as it affects how we experience time and reality. I wish I could have added my experience now to my physics paper back then, but of course, this is impossible. The future cannot communicate with the past—or, can it?

During *The Dissolving*, the passage of time, seamlessly flowing from past to present to future, marks my life in real-time. The flow of non-time is a non-flow that heightens the numbing eternity of now-time, which feels a bit like living forever in the hyper-realized present but without the equanimity of a Buddhist-inspired moment. Only when I've passed from now-time and back to real-time does *The Dissolving* end. When it does, I find myself conscious again and lying on my back, spread-eagled on my bedroom floor.

The thin band of exposed skin on my back between my T-shirt and pajamas meets the firmness of cold hardwood as it brings on the involuntary shiver, snapping me awake. How did I fall? My tumble pushed the blue wool rug away from the base of the bed to lie diagonally between the bedroom door and the bathroom. The pointed circle of reading light affixed to the bed's headboard casts a feeble glow on the floor below. I have no roommate or boyfriend to call for help, so I run through a mental self-help checklist. I gather my data: no pain, broken bones, or head injury. Okay, except for blanking out on the floor. I hoist myself up and reach out to the laptop on the bed, knowing instinctively where to look for answers.

The rush of blood to my head makes me dizzy. I wear the augmented reality glasses on the bed beside the laptop, where

I must have taken them off before falling. My index finger hovers above the touchpad as I take a deep breath and ask myself the question aloud. "Am I ready to enter the 'Verse again?" I know the answer, but it still feels appropriate to wait, if only for impulse control. Every month, the universe of three-dimensional virtual worlds focused on social connections is expanding, getting richer and more immersive, causing the rewiring of our brains as we spend more time inside the 'Verse. The jury is still out on this, but the research being published has never been clearer. We're cooking our brains. Slowly. Everyone knows this, as do I. "Yes, I'm ready," I say aloud and touch the touchpad. I'm inside the 'Verse.

My vision blurs and then refocuses on the holographically projected scroll of comments from the beehive of avatars swarming my head, my every eyeball shift tracking a new comment. These are responses to a post on one of my social media feeds in a virtual world I'm logged into. Some of my 23.8 million followers are still commenting on my last post, in which I shared my vision for gAIa's future. I raise my head to scroll up to reread my post again.

A new evolution in consciousness in the 'Verse where anyone can use Global Artificial Intelligence Algorithms (gAIa's) open source software to unleash creativity in Ka World and take one giant step into collective awareness!

This humdrum post has gone viral.

I read through the comments again, trying to work out the mystery of my fall to the floor. I ignore all the positive comments. Compliments on my intelligence, contributions to creating open-source virtual worlds, or being an iconic young woman CEO at 28. My eyes gloss over even those that include images of me smiling, with all my pearly whites gleaming as I held the "Best Entrepreneur Award" plaque at AI-kon last week. Instead, I spend more time on comments by trolls. Needless to say, I'm being trolled; it's the one legacy of the old Internet age that the 'Verse has never been able to escape, as ubiquitous as an ancient policy of control as, say, colonialism.

So my eyeballs linger on the fast-multiplying negative comments that seem to lurk in another alternate reality and appear to be why I'm trending.

- Tashi Wheeler skank too dumb to create Ka World!
- Tashi Wheeler is a slut. A slut's gotta be beaten up yo!
- Of course you got the award @TashiWheeler is a sic girl, #fakediversity, #girlbullshit #scamartist. fake fake fake
- @TashiWheeler must be fucking co-founder @TonyRice. If you want to play with the boys, you got to fuck the boys

"I'm not fucking Tony!" I shout aloud. The speech recognition in the smartphone types this up and posts it as a text bubble above my avatar and posts this comment across the hordes of avatars I keep among the many virtual worlds in the 'Verse. Then the trolls take off gibbering on that, generating tons more comments. My mistake! I need to keep my thoughts to myself. Well, now that I think of it, Tony and I did have a one-night stand back when we were in college, but that was years ago. We never slept together after we both co-founded gAIa. We have our differences and fights over where we think gAIa should be headed, but of course, we are both sensible, professional, and competitive with each other now. We're a good team, agreeing on the crucial necessity of keeping gAIa's code base open source. Tony is not the reason why I'm winning awards. None of these comments make any sense, but that's the gist of the commentary.

I should have known that my entry into the predominantly male club of ex-gamers would cause resentment. I'd stepped directly onto the toes of the creators of the chauvinistic gaming conference gAMERcON that morphed into the symposium to showcase artificial intelligence applications (AI-kon) in the 'Verse. However, this level of misogyny and vitriol directed at me under the guise of anonymity still takes me by surprise. The anger snowballed after I won the award for best AI startup of the 'Verse. Last week, after I successfully demonstrated the deployment of gAIa's open-source code into a self-driving car's instructional model for a new virtual world, I believed my award was hard won. But judging from these comments, I'm nothing but a pretty face, a mixed-race diversity pick, and a girl to be dissed. As I continue eyeballing through the flood of vile comments, I feel a heightened sense of awareness similar to prey sensing its hunter. To escape the trolls, I enter Ka World.

Without the haptic suit and augmented reality helmet with their built-in environment sensors and neurotransmitters, which I left in my office at gAIa, the reality-bending virtual reality environment I've created carries the distinct patina of artificiality. Still, every time I enter Ka World, I think about Michael. As always, he isn't here even though there are as many experiences that remind me of him. Michael always talked about thin places where the boundaries of two worlds intersected. A thin place could theoretically open a portal to another world in another dimension. He used a thin place when he often disappeared into Ka, a real world that he claimed existed in another dimension. In such a world, the concepts of time and space blur together, and endless possibilities coexist. This is how he described Ka to me, as a world where he claimed to have found the meaning of his existence.

When I created my own Ka World in virtual reality, I hoped I could use it to generate a thin place where the boundaries of my world, Earth, and the boundaries of the world into which Michael disappeared, Ka, intersected. This may be my attempt to communicate with Michael or find clues that will lead me to him. Unfortunately, I haven't succeeded because I created Ka World based on Michael's experiences inside Ka. So many tales can get lost in translation between a person's lived experience and the memory of that experience. Then, of course, there's the receiver of the repository of these tales who brings her imagination to the table. So yes, my virtual reality Ka World is not a replica of Michael's original Ka, it's close, but that might not be enough.

As I navigate my avatar, a crocodile, through a virtual reality swamp environment inside Ka World, I think about how much of Ka World is a pastiche of second-rate imagery and, at worse, mimicry, including my crocodile avatar, which is a motif that Michael said repeatedly appeared inside his Ka. In my beleaguered attempt to recreate the pure bliss states from all those tales Michael told me about his experiences in Ka, I've exhausted the limits of my imagination inside the virtual reality world of my creation. Unlike Michael's positive experiences inside Ka, my experiences navigating Ka World leave me feeling dizzy and disoriented within minutes of logging in.

Even wearing only the augmented reality glasses, minus the sensors, I get the sudden hot flashes alternating with cold chills and a film of perspiration on my upper lip. I imagine the rapid firings of the neurons in my brain making my heart palpitate. My breathing is shallow. I sense the edges of my vision folding. Perhaps what I experienced before as I lay passed out on the floor is happening to me again. If I let this information overload continue, I am in danger of succumbing to *The Dissolving* that caused me to remove my augmented reality glasses in the first place, moments before toppling from the bed to the floor and getting caught in the clutches of now-time. I don't want to relive *The Dissolving* again. The lack of self is not a pleasant sensation at all. I force myself to blink twice to exit Ka World and then blink again to close all the other open virtual worlds one by one to avoid the unpleasantness from happening again. During *The Dissolving*, I think I've been experiencing the same thing

Michael had talked about all those years ago, something he called "Digital Vertigo."

I would love to compare notes on my dissolving experience with Michael. But Michael, like a whirlwind that swept through my life in high school, is a memory of the past. Michael, who disappeared without a trace in my senior year, set my friends and me adrift. Michael, who, like my brilliant childhood, is no more.

Little wonder, then, that I spend the rest of the night trying to conjure up images of Michael, something I have not permitted myself to do ever since his empty casket was lowered into the ground as a final joke against the world he had railed against for so long. The depths of the Pacific Ocean never released his body, where he had presumably jumped from his father's sailboat, which he had stolen to sail away one stormy night. These are the facts, but the truth leads elsewhere to a place in another dimension, to a world in another reality, to Ka.

I thrash from side to side as if I was fending off the same watery grave and awake with the comforter bunched up into an unrecognizable mound and the sheet twisted into knots.

It is early morning, and I'm tired and sleepy, but I get ready for my usual seven-mile run on the Embarcadero. As I lace up my running shoes, I let those thoughts of Michael, freshly seeded and watered by nostalgia, grow anew.

Melancholy was never my friend, even though it was Michael's constant companion. Occasionally, sweet happiness would pierce through darkening clouds like the dawning sun, and I would fall in love with him all over again. In these incandescent moments, Michael was riveting, as were his ideas on the meaning of life no less, and delivered with a dose of self-deprecating humor, all the more alluring to a shy high school girl who did not as yet profess any opinions of her own. Michael drew me toward him like a moth to a flame, and I drew closer and closer, unaware of the heat or the impending pain.

❧

"New dawn, new day, to wash my sins away," I say aloud as the revolving glass door of my apartment lobby on the first floor empties me into the street. In the distance, yellow sunlight is surrounded by gray. Somewhere along the twisted streets, golden light slowly burns the fog away, unwrapping buildings like crinkly candy paper to reveal decorated gables, projecting cornices, and roofs with overhanging eaves. The teals, mint greens, and peachy pinks of these unwrapped buildings remind me of the confections on display at the Ferry Plaza Farmers Market in the Ferry Building, which beckons to me and draws me closer.

I think, if Michael were here, he would have liked to run with me and offer some new insight into San Francisco's architectural heritage, like the exact names of each gaudy color slapped onto the famous painted ladies or the process by which the Golden Gate Bridge creates the weather system that pushes fog up and around itself, cloaking it in magnificent mystery. But instead, I run alone because I am the one who is still afraid. Michael talked about such majestic mysteries of leaving this world and stepping into another world that he called Ka, which, as he liked to explain, was the land of pure concept where everything began. A singularity that was akin to a black hole where the laws of physics broke down and did not apply. Where imagination reigned unfettered. At least, this

is what I understood from the retelling of his experiences in
Ka. He said he had gone there many times but had never
found a way to remain there permanently. Maybe he did find
a way, after all, to slip between the cracks of time and enter
Ka forever, this place he sought with a single-mindedness ever
since I came to know him.

Where I run, cracks fan out in jagged lines as if resisting
the thrust of shifting land below. My feet bounce on the
cement, and I tread subconsciously on the crevices that run
like veins through cement blocks thinking maybe I, too, could
slip between them and find myself in Ka like Michael. But I
don't fall and continue running sure-footed on my usual route
down the Embarcadero, my mind shifting through the intertwined memories of Michael and my old friends.

2

I reach the Farmer's Market outside the Ferry Building, which marks my turnaround point. Usually, I'd turn around and start running back to my apartment building, that triangular shard of glass jutting into the edge of the city's skyline. I'd shower, wash and blow dry my hair, then head to gAIa's office, four city streets to the right of where I live, even on a Saturday.

My routines never vary, come rain or shine. This is not out of habit but out of necessity. Before Michael disappeared, he used his administrator privileges to delete all the social media history on our private virtual world that was shared among five close friends in the 'Verse. He then shut down this virtual world that he had created. Afterward, it felt as if neither Michael nor I nor any of the other three members of our close group had ever been friends. It felt like we were a hive mind with Michael as the leader, and with him gone, so was the common thread that bound us together.

My friends stopped talking to me the day after Michael disappeared. Double loss for me. No Michael. No friends. Alone now, I've started chronicling my virtual lives with an intensity that borders on obsession. It does seem to me that the more trails I leave in the virtual worlds I visit in the 'Verse, the more I feel that while I'm going through the motions of breathing, working, eating, or sleeping, I can't tell for sure if I'm truly alive. It's an odd sensation, more like a sixth sense that makes me doubt my interactions in the real world where I wonder if I'm real, or if the physical world is real, or if my virtual followers are real, or if I've slipped into that edge of consciousness where in an Aha! Moment, I'll glean the correct answer—either I'm alive or not! Therefore, routines are necessary touchstones to feel the physical world and tether me to it.

Even so, despite my routines, for a brief moment daily, triggered by a smell or a fleeting glimpse of something or someone, I still wonder with the same intensity as I wondered for the very first time if Michael hadn't left clues to lead the way to the place where I was meant to follow.

Like now, when the glint of metal over which a passing shadow of a seagull reveals an image, which I perceive as mystical, but my brain perceives as serendipitous.

It is not an image but a pattern of crocodiles on a rectangular sheet of silver-gray metal. The tessellated shapes alternate between light and dark gray, appearing as pixelated dots close up as if the artist applied pointillist painting techniques to metal. When this metal square reflects sunlight, fluid luminescence ripples across its surface, which makes the crocodiles slither as if these creatures are pulsating to crawl out from the flatness of their two-dimensional world and into my three-dimensional one. I shudder because my heart is filled with a vague unease. Then, in my mind's eye, I see Michael doodling in the margins of his notebook in physics class. I see him drawing the repeating motif of tessellated crocodiles by applying light and dark strokes of a blue ballpoint pen on ruled paper. Then, he flips the page and repeats the pattern again.

The deep guttural grunt of a cormorant swooping in to land a few feet away erases Michael's image from my head space. Startled, I look up and meet the eyes of a stranger, a man whose penetrating gaze unnerves me enough to take a step backward. I notice that the metal sheet rests against a stack of other metal sheets bound together with yellow nylon cords placed vertically on the flatbed of a red pickup truck parked between two orange cones in a "No Parking" zone.

When I look up again, the man is still staring at me. I'm not used to locking eyes with strangers or anybody else, for that matter. Michael used to say that the eyes are the windows to the soul, and he had the most direct gaze of anybody I knew. Except now, this stranger looks at me like Michael did, and it unnerves me. The stranger has a thick shock of salt-and-pepper hair, a long beak nose, and a rugged face that something titled Men's Outdoor might feature on its cover. He looks like a hunter out in the wilds of Montana who might even be handsome were it not for his severe bearing and intense, unsmiling gaze. But his stare can only enthrall me for so long because all around me, the Farmer's Market bustles on Saturday morning.

The fruit vendors have been here since 5 a.m.; by 7 a.m., the fruit is moving fast. After the chefs finish buying produce, as soon as the first trucks arrive, the remaining fruits, vegetables, and flowers are available for latecomers stocking up on groceries. Then, there are runners like me who breeze past dog walkers and tourists with selfie sticks taking pictures with their backs to the murky green water. Out on the water, seagulls and cormorants bob in slow motion till one cormorant jerks abruptly, twisting its head, and pecks at the skin beneath its feathered wing as if to dispel the spell of artifice to snap back to reality. Emboldened, I walk toward the truck to get a closer look at those tessellated crocodiles, which blur into round holes up close. A paper label stuck to the bottom right corner reads:

BulletArt on Metal
Richard Thornton
Price on Request

~

A tingling sensation crawls at the base of my neck. I get the sense that I'm being watched. I whirl around, meeting the eyes of the same stranger who, even now, is holding me in a stead-fast gaze. I feel ashamed as if I've been caught trespassing, and I want to turn away, but he starts walking toward me. He moves with unique grace, both languid and purposeful, and when he reaches the truck, he asks, "What do you want?" His voice is raspy, like a cigarette smoker.

The question takes me by surprise. Posed by anybody else, the question could lead to a pleasant conversation, but from this man, it sounds like he's seeking a clue to an essential part of me. I want Michael to come back, but I say nothing. He doesn't accept my silence. "What do you think about it?" He means the artwork, of course. His voice sounds mellow now, but his hooded eyes are the color of a stormy sky at dawn, suggesting the kind of man who has lived a long and varied life and gained some wisdom along the way. Perhaps I'm projecting my experience of being bad at life and blowing an ordinary encounter with an artist out of perspective because I've let thoughts of Michael run amok like a relapsed addict. When I shake my head to warn myself to get my life back on track, naturally, the man thinks I'm commenting on his artwork. "It's not for everybody," he says.

"Oh no, I didn't mean that. I like it. It's lovely," I say, finding my voice. I think I shouldn't have used the word lovely. The pattern isn't lovely because the metallic holes that poke through the metal look like tiny violent implosions. This man doesn't seem to be the kind of artist who makes lovely things.

"What do you like about it?" Again, the directness of the questioning leaves me stumped. I don't know what to say. He's asking about art when I'm drawn to the experience. I don't know much about art. Unlike Michael, who saw the world in colors and shapes and who once stood for hours staring at the little parallelograms of afternoon light thrown by the slanted blinds on a dark wooden school desk, I'm often blind to the natural beauty of the world. It was Michael who first introduced the word into my vocabulary. Tessellation. The covering of an infinite geometric plane with a pattern made of shapes without gaps or overlaps. Michael introduced me to the tessellated drawings of M.C. Escher, an artist whom he deeply admired, whose drawings explore the concepts of time and space that I would not have had the chance to know myself.

The man in front of me is waiting for an answer. He has practiced the art of standing still, or maybe he is a man who looks at things with care or with infinite patience, a quality I associated with Michael. I feel I owe something to this man from Michael's tribe. I say, "It's great. These shapes are powerful, and I thought I saw the crocodiles moving in the play of light. It reminded me of somebody I once knew." That's all I will volunteer. I feel like I'm back in high school where I was expected to provide critical commentary but turned in something superficial, a weak attempt to tackle a subject whose surface I've barely scratched. I sense his disappointment as his gaze switches from me to a distant object. A keen sense of anguish sweeps over me when I'm no longer the center of his attention. It's a feeling I haven't felt since Michael left. Then, with a sudden, violent cry, he shouts, "Ollie!" He breaks out in an agile sprint in the direction of the water, disappearing behind the Ferry Building. On impulse, I break into a run, following him, drawn by the cries of "Ollie! Ollie!"

Ollie is a German shepherd whose wet fur and trailing red leash betray the fact that he's been where he's not supposed to be. With a sprightliness that belies his age, the wiry man stomps his foot on the leash. Ollie turns, greeting the man with such happy excitement that I'm sure he'd never receive such a welcome elsewhere. Man and dog reunited, come home. That would have been the logline for a script, except that the dog sees me. He leaps with infinite energy toward me and yanks the leash from underneath the man's foot. I, unprepared for the greeting, shriek. The man catches the leash before the dog reaches me and pulls, but not before I get the spray of saliva mixed with cold water on my hands and face. Wiping my face, I mutter an apology, given that I am the one who followed without encouragement. "I'm sorry," I say.

"Whatever for?" the man asks. He seems surprised. "Ollie's still a puppy two months shy of a year. I had to run because he got loose from the truck. They don't allow dogs in the Farmer's Market. He's been mucking around in the water they throw out after the flower buckets get empty. Dogs have a sense of people. He must like you," the man says.

I don't know why it's important to me to be the person dogs like, but that must be why I feel like my heart is expanding. So I smile and start walking closer to them.

"C'mon," he says and pulls Ollie away toward the direction of his parked truck, and then they both disappear from sight. I feel angry. Like how I'd feel if a friend left without saying goodbye or how I felt after Michael left. This is absurd, I tell myself. I manage to shake off the feeling as I run back.

My smartphone buzzes the moment I step into the apartment's lobby. I held the 'Verse at bay for this long, and now its lure is strong. I feel out of breath as I step off the elevator on the 34th floor and enter my apartment. It's not because of the run or the floor-to-ceiling windows that always stand between me and the dizzying heights. It's because it requires immense mental and physical effort not to check the social media posts and alerts for various interactive experiences that connect me to the virtual worlds in the 'Verse from my smartphone.

I once knew a girl in high school who created her own language to write private thoughts in her diary so nobody else could read it. "Privacy is the key," she used to say. She meant that nobody else except her had the key to decoding her writing. Her name was Ember, and she was my friend. Then, after Michael deleted all our social media histories and shut down the virtual world, we stopped being friends. Years later, I found new followers across virtual worlds in the 'Verse. I'm aware I can't call these followers my friends.

Ember no longer uses social media and doesn't even have an avatar in the 'Verse. In her last email to me, she wrote, "You're the influencer who needs influencing." I asked what she meant by that, but she never replied, and I was too angry to chase her down. So what if we had been friends once? This didn't mean we'd remain friends for life. Anyway, I'm stronger now. I don't need friends when I have my work and virtual worlds in the 'Verse, so I tell myself. Now, the desire to find out what the trolls are saying pulls me toward my laptop lying in the corner of my rumpled bed. As the 'Verse beckons me, the alarm on my bedside table goes off. That means I should have finished showering and making my bed by now. I would have if I didn't stop to chat with the man and run after him and his dog! As I turn the alarm off, I remind myself of the routines that tether me to the physical world.

I finish washing my hair in the shower and begin the elaborate sequence of blow-drying my hair. In the mirror, both my parents peer back at me. I have my mother's thick and long black Asian Indian hair, heavy-lidded round eyes, and my father's Irish snub nose, ruddy complexion, and wide lips. So even my face belongs to two different worlds but manages to exist in one. Then, something I've been trying to work out for so many years in Michael's absence dawns on me and clarifies why I created Ka World in the 'Verse. Maybe it's not wrong to think of parts of the 'Verse that contain virtual worlds as thin places where the boundaries of two worlds are close enough for you to touch. There's the physical world that I inhabit, Earth, and the other world in another dimension that Michael inhabits, Ka. Between the two lies a thin place in a virtual world inside the 'Verse. Earth has its own laws, as does Ka. Michael described Ka as a world of pure concepts where the laws of physics do not hold, and neither do social norms. I have sometimes briefly glimpsed this other world by being in a thin place in a virtual world, inside Ka World, for example. How else to explain the lost time, the fear of dissolving, and the vertigo of information overload if not for the perception of another world that I can glimpse but can't get close enough to so that I can cross over?

I once took a trip to Peru in my freshman year of high school. Michael and Ember were in my group, along with two other boys named Ash and Nachiket. We stuck together because we were friends. But the thing is that we met people who believe that countries have souls as well as histories, or that the Earth has ghosts that remain in one place, or that the mountains of the world are living spirits, or that trees have rhizomatic networks in their roots that let them communicate with other trees so that trees have feelings and no two are alike. Of course, what you believe depends on your perception of reality. Being in a thin place can alter your perception of reality. So I think that the person who can best tell the difference between the shifting realities of these thin places, which are far more common in the virtual worlds of the 'Verse than most people think, has a shot at being good at life. I wish I had a shaman to guide me along the shifting nature of reality in the thin places I've found myself in when I'm in a virtual world. Someone who could read the primitive emotions of your soul and guide you to a better place. Now wouldn't that be helpful?

In my mind's eye, I see the tessellated crocodiles quivering on the metal sheet, and I think of Michael, and I hope he really did find Ka after all and is living there now happily ever after. The realization that I miss talking to Michael hits me again. One afternoon, when we were in Andahuaylillas, Peru, I took such a long time framing a question for Michael that it came out in one long exhale. Talking to Michael, I took long, deep breaths. Maybe that's why I felt alive. Now, it feels like I'm holding my breath, waiting to exhale.

3

Two days after my last experience, I get *The Dissolving* again.

~

In gAIa's office, I'm riding the elevator down from the fifth to the second floor when I feel the edges of my vision folding in that brief sensation of weightlessness. I become fluid, blurring into approaching now-time. My smartphone slips to the floor. Seconds before merging into the land of no memories, I turn my face to the side to protect my head from the fall.

~

Tony says, "Go home." Red splotches rise on the smooth cheeks of his pale face. He blinks rapidly, perhaps because of stress or to counter the dryness from the contacts he wears. Then he wrings his hands, I think, both in worry about me and in consternation over the upcoming meeting with investors on our schedules this afternoon.

My jaw is sore, and I'm dizzy from the rush of blood to my head as I sit upright in my own chair, in my cubicle, back on the second floor. I must look confused because Tony says, "I waited for you, and when the elevator door opened, I saw you lying on the floor with your face turned to the side. I touched your face to make sure you were breathing, and you stirred and said, I know what this looks like. Don't call 911."

I'm back in real-time, and I remember walking up here with Tony, but I have no idea how I ended up on the elevator floor. What a vague concept time is. My entry and exit from now-time probably lasted the duration of the elevator ride. Whether it was a short ride or a long ride, I do not know because time ceases to exist in *The Dissolving*.

Tony says, "You're freaking me out." Then, as he paces the floor in front of me, he solves the problem. Noticing the augmented reality helmet with the built-in neural mesh on my desk and the haptic suit draped like a limp torso over the chair behind me, he asks if, before the elevator ride, I had worn the augmented reality helmet and the haptic suit to play Ka World?

I crane my neck sideways to glance over my shoulder. The haptic suit's black torso is splayed over the chair, its limp arms grazing the seaweed-patterned carpet like the body of a drowned man spit out by one sudden receding wave onto a jagged rock. The suit is not my petite size because engineering bought it for a star engineer who is 6 feet 2 inches tall and male. However, because the material is soft and pliable, like a cashmere sweater, and also form-fitting like a wetsuit, I can easily slip into it over my clothes and pull the extra material up around my wrists and ankles. The sensors are mainly in the torso, anyway.

I turn to Tony, who is still looking at me for an answer.

"I wasn't *playing* Ka World. I was *immersing* myself in the virtual reality of Ka World. It's not a game," I correct Tony. I don't tell him that I seek to immerse myself into Ka World, this virtual reality world I've created, to get closer to Michael. When I'm inside the Ka World of my creation, I'm inside a visually stunning world saturated with bright primary colors.

My avatar is a crocodile that typically navigates a swamp environment.

gAIa's platform that supports Ka World has a built-in Mind Matter interaction algorithm that lets you unleash your mind's creativity. Based on thought alone, it can place you inside a location in Ka World. I have yet to expose this concept to anyone because Mind Matter interaction is still an uncorroborated theory, but I've built it into gAIa's platform as part of the virtual world's building code. That's why the rendering of Ka World can be slightly different for everyone because every time you log into Ka World, the world recreates an image of itself based on your desires. Therefore, there will always be subtle differences in the rendering of Ka World for each individual. Yet, as far as I know, nobody has been able to pick up on this. I certainly have not advertised this fact to anyone, least of all to Tony.

As I stay longer inside my Ka World, augmented reality makes me more aware of my crocodile body. I experience a disconcerting loss of selfhood precisely when I begin to feel discomfort. The sensors in the haptic suit mimic the sensations of wetness and sense of smell, and I can feel the sliminess of vegetation and smell the dank and decaying vegetable matter, but it is when I open my mouth to talk and hear the disjointed grunts that my heart races in panic. The neural mesh inside the helmet over my brain informs me that this is sensor activity, but my mind panics nevertheless. These sensors must have shut me out of Ka World as the information overload that flooded my brain threatened to bring on *The Dissolving* again. When I emerged from Ka World, I must have needed to rest my brain more, but I didn't. I remember tossing the augmented reality helmet on the table, extricating myself out of the haptic suit, and throwing it at the chair before walking toward the elevator. I remember checking social media on my smartphone inside the elevator when *The Dissolving* caught up with me.

Of course, I don't tell Tony about *The Dissolving* or my

theories about it. I can't tell Tony that I've created this Ka World based on what Michael told me about his experiences in Ka. Michael's Ka was real, real enough to him anyway, and he claimed it was a world that existed in another dimension. Mine is a fake virtual reality world based on my understanding of Michael's imagery. I can't tell Tony any of this, or even about Michael, for that matter. I want to say that Ka World is my attempt to communicate with Michael and that this communication has been unsuccessful. So far. I'm also aware of how far-fetched this sounds and how little Tony would understand. So, I nod and let him hear what he wants to know.

"Yes, I was in Ka World, and I stayed there for 10 minutes or so before I went down in the elevator," I say.

Tony is an easy read. The expressions on his face flow without guile. When relief calms his furrowed brow, I know where he will go with my admission. He's been trying to get me to go there with him for the past six months.

"This Ka World, or whatever you call it in its beta phase, is disorienting. Whenever I've interacted with it, I've felt increasingly discombobulated. First comes nausea, then the headaches, and that's just in the first ten minutes. No wonder you collapsed in the elevator. Engineering says these are known bugs, but I've been told there's a fix…," Tony says.

"It's not a fix…," I say, but Tony interrupts me.

"Please, Tashi." Tony joins his palms together, pleading with me. His voice is an octave lower and has a softer snap, like peanut butter on toast.

"You've got to let me let them turn Ka World into a regular game! You've got to let them add levels so players can *have* something to do that keeps them motivated to stay and play. If you have a goal, your brain will ignore nausea and headaches. They'll go away entirely because you're so focused on working through the levels till you get to a final something, a golden egg…," Tony says.

"A golden egg!" I scoff and raise both eyebrows for good measure.

"Redeemable for millions of crypto coins," Tony continues. "If you play to win, nausea and headaches go away. A virtual world's got to have meaning, Tashi, and you give it meaning by turning it into a game! Otherwise, it's just a poor little alien world without meaning and primed to induce dissociative mood disorders. We could get sued by the people who come for interactive experiences inside it! The fact is, Tashi, this virtual world of yours, I don't know why you created it, what you want to do with it, or why it's even called Ka World in the first place? Don't shrug like that whenever I ask you these questions. I'm telling you, Ka World doesn't do anything for the player. You're also not leveraging the brain's neuroplasticity to teach it new things. So please, let me let them turn it into a game," Tony begs. He then gets that same squinty-eyed look when he's forced to do something distasteful, like delivering bad news to investors or laying off employees.

I know how this looks and what's coming next, and because of this, I know I should be careful, but I choose to make a momentous spur-of-the-moment decision. It's the kind of decision Michael often made in his carefree way. But when I say, "I won't let them turn Ka World into a game," the decision feels like it's not mine to make anymore, and my choice doesn't matter. Instead, it feels like a dark tomb encases my heart. The word "leaden" pops into my head, which is how I feel sitting on the chair. My soul waits for a warming ray of sunshine to penetrate the stone shield, but the fluorescent lights in the office offer no warmth. Compared to the color-saturated virtual reality of Ka World, the physical world is dreary and gray.

Tony persists. "You know how games can be helpful, Tashi. They teach by example, they create empathy, they are explorations of cause and effect, they can make people work together collaboratively, etcetera. This is basic game design, and you agree to these principles. Hell, you wrote most of the original principles!"

I shake my head. "The technology that creates the experiential states in Ka World is too new. We don't know what it does to the brain, less so to the brains of young adults who tend to be super impressionable. There needs to be ethical thought before widespread usage. That's why I wanted to expose it to the open-source community, so there could be ethical debate and participation in this virtual world. You can't turn Ka World into a game. Not yet."

"You'll regret this," Tony warns.

"I don't care," I say, aware that I sound petulant. However, it is the truth. A world without Michael is no world for me. Given that I have not found any clues leading to Michael in the virtual Ka World anyway, Tony can do whatever he wants with it, but I won't let it go without a fight.

"The board wants to turn Ka World into a game you can play across the 'Verse. Why do you think they want to meet us today? gAIa's been losing money at a steady clip. An open-source platform like your Ka World that is free to download doesn't pay. So they want us to put up a paywall before anyone can download our platform, and they want to make Ka World a game that you can play to win. You have to agree to this, Tashi. Otherwise, the board will fire you. You won't be CEO of gAIa anymore," Tony says.

"As long as I'm CEO of gAIa, I won't let them turn Ka World into a game. Let it continue to be open source and let people understand this new technology before they start playing inside it. I won't change my position on this. They'll have to fire me first." I dig my high heels into the carpet, pushing into the patterned tendrils that remind me of seaweed, hoping they'll entangle my ankles and anchor me instead of letting me drift away into open water, which is where my life appears to be heading anyway.

Tony nods. "I will tell you that the board sent me to pressure you to capitulate. I hate to be the bearer of bad news, but they've already voted unanimously to fire you if you say no to turning Ka World into a game."

"I know," I say.

"Alright, I'll inform the board. What are you going to do, Tashi? gAIa was your life. God knows I'm sorry. I'd love for you to take a break. You're burnt out. Take a break and come back. We'll find something for you to do when you come back." Tony offers me an olive branch, but I don't feel like taking it. What I do feel is the pressing need to take a break.

"Six months, maybe a year off from work, and not sure I'll be back," I say. It's a relief, finally, to acknowledge how I'm feeling.

"You're a fighter, Tashi. You're going to be alright," Tony says, blinking rapidly as he walks away.

In my mind's eye, I see the smooth swells of green water lapping at the edge of the concrete pier, the cormorant bobbing up and down and twisting its head in sudden anticipation. I catch the reflection of a cloudless sky in the glint of metal, and the tessellated shapes that register on the inward eye portend the calm before the storm. Given that I've become prone to spur-of-the-moment decisions, I lean toward the desktop and type "Richard Thornton Bullet Art on Metal" in the search box. After some digging, I find the man with the hooded eyes and the penetrating gaze again.

4

———

The road to Richard's studio leads deep within the Santa Cruz mountains, where the land transitions from woodland to forest. Cell service is patchy like the dapples of light playing across the windshield of the yellow Volkswagen Beetle as it makes the slow climb in the setting sun, whose light turns from orange to peach, then pearl gray.

I am driving again after nearly four years. City living isn't conducive to driving, so the yellow Beetle has remained in the underground parking below my apartment, waiting for this opportune moment to get fired up. When I tried starting it in the garage last week, the battery was dead, and I had to find a car mechanic off of the 'Verse and schedule a service call to replace it. The woman who came out for the service call said the battery wasn't the only thing that needed to be replaced because a whole host of problems had developed in the sitting car, from transmission fluid leaks to a cracked drive belt. The car had to be towed to a shop for a tune-up, where it stayed for three days.

I took advantage of the downtime to clean the apartment meticulously and obsessively post the resulting gleaming surfaces on my social media feeds in the 'Verse. My mother also called. She must have read the intentionally vague text in a company press release, so she wanted to confirm the news. "Is it a leave of absence, or are you fired?" "Both," I told her. She said maybe I did need a break after all, and I could always come home, but I said I was planning a road trip. Anyway, here I am now, driving on this winding road, and after all the work on the car, an easy familiarity with both the car and the long road settles in.

The car was a high school graduation gift from my parents, who hoped this would lure me to stay with them in Palo Alto while attending Stanford University nearby. I have no siblings, and my parents didn't want to feel like empty nesters yet, so they wanted me to continue living with them at home for as long as possible. That I did so had nothing to do with getting the car and everything to do with Michael's disappearance and the implosion of all my other friendships.

Watching the sky change colors as I drive unravels the spool of muddled thoughts. I let the thoughts flow and follow where they lead. I have nothing else to do anyway, and sometimes it's interesting to notice the spaces all the thoughts take up inside your head. When a thought reaches its end, like a period at the end of a sentence, it vanishes and invites another. That old story again, the old making way for the new, like everything else in the cycle of life, seems inexhaustible and, for that very reason, exhausting. Thinking is both pointless and necessary. My thoughts lead me everywhere and nowhere, likely a dichotomy for most of us on the planet, but at this moment, the weight of fragmented thinking feels like a terrible burden only to me.

My friends' families, mine included, are wealthy. Tech money. The families didn't know each other. They just happened to send their kids to the same private high school. I knew so much about my friends but not nearly as much about their parents. Possibly that's how everyone is in high school. At least my friends and I didn't think of the older generation as interesting people, given that they're the ones who've left us with a bunch of crap to take care of, like climate change and plastic pollution.

Other than their being doyens in the tech industry, our parents didn't have much in common. They didn't hang out at school fundraisers or parent socials. Perhaps this was because they kept themselves overscheduled, or maybe it's because it's hard to make friends as you get older. I should know. I haven't made any real friends since high school, and at 28, I've already become set in my ways. Not being able to live with a roommate, for example, or continuing the endless routines that tether me to the physical world is a setup for spinsterhood, as my mom likes to joke. It's not that I won't date. I do, but none of the guys are interesting enough to last longer than a one-night stand. *Nothing compares to you, Michael.* I'll take my chances at booty calls till my body is too shriveled up, by which time I suppose this interest, too, will wane.

My parents, busy with their all-consuming work, don't force the boyfriend issue, which is good. Otherwise, I would never have been able to stay at home during my college years.

How close my friends were when we were young! Closer than normal. Our group of five was like an extended limb of one body, one organism. I know how hokey this sounds. That's why I haven't ever talked about my close friendships to anyone because no one can understand that phantom ache in me for a fifth missing limb, this psychic connection to a group of people. In high school, we could read each other's minds and finish each other's sentences. Our school motto was: Know Yourself, Give Yourself. We did. Wholeheartedly. To each other but mainly to Michael.

~

Yet, one thing was evident to me, even at fourteen. I am unlike any of my other friends.

~

I am not like Ember, whose ethereal beauty reflects as a surprise in the eyes of every person who chances upon her and, in that first sighting, thinks how rare her beauty really is. Ember has an aura of mystery because she writes an open diary in an invented language whose code only she knows. Her real name is Riveko Ikeda, but she changed her name to Ember when her dad brought her to the United States when she was ten.

The way she answers in physics class is when the substitute physics teacher calls her Riveko from the roll sheet. She says to the surprised substitute, "Please call me Ember. Riveko died in Japan." When I press her later, she says in her mildly disinterested voice, "When dad brought me here, I felt that my 10-year-old self, my Japanese self, had died in Japan. Before coming here, I burnt all the childhood photographs I could find in the family albums that were never digitized, so they would never tell the story of a loving, happy family. There was no such thing anymore. It didn't exist. Therefore, those photographs shouldn't exist because they were wrong. When I burnt them, I felt my old self drifting away like embers. So I chose the name Ember to keep the memory of my old self being burnt as I was being reborn."

Ember, whose new self is irresistible to many boys and a few girls who gaze upon her from a distance because they are unwilling to come close to their idea of perfection. Still, I've seen the sadness in her dark eyes that sometimes rushes over her in a tidal wave of longing. Like when she stops abruptly on a sidewalk and stares for a long time at the fog enveloping a gnarled California oak. Then, slowly removing the small Nikon point-and-shoot camera from her jacket pocket, she looks through the viewfinder to shoot one perfect picture. She shows this to me; an image of a solitary tree marooned on an island of rolling mists. Ember's photos, like Ember herself, can appear otherworldly.

Unlike Ember, I am built solid, like a pine tree that sends its roots deep into the ground and stands steady.

Neither am I like Ash, who wants to become a doctor so he can join Médecins Sans Frontières and crisscross the globe dispensing urgent medical care in the world's war-torn regions. There are no doctors in his family, so he would like to be the first.

Ashley Adams is short and skinny and carries an EpiPen in his backpack in case his countless allergies rear their unexpected ugly heads. He once pulled up his shorts and plunged the thick EpiPen needle into his thigh to ward off approaching anaphylaxis because he accidentally brushed against a peanut at a non-nut-free table at lunch. Ash has light brown hair that falls to his shoulders and kind green eyes that trust everyone easily because he is incapable of deceit. He is an old soul who believes the world can be made better. "The peoples will help the peoples," he says, calling the grammatically incorrect phrase his mantra. On weekends, Ash visits the assisted-living facility near his house. He calls on each resident, inquiring with the same exuberance about their health and well-being as a resident doctor in the making. He often gets texts from his elderly friends asking when he's coming to visit again because they forget he's still in school.

Unlike Ash, I must admit that I have no passion or calling

for service or anything else. I like science and do not quite dislike math, and I can write clean code for the Computer Science elective. However, using these interests to predict a STEM career is a result that is only plausible because it is weighted by all those checked boxes of interests that have built up before. Unlike Ash, I am still a work in progress, unsure who I want to be.

Nor am I like Nachiket, who enjoys the thrill of old-fashioned treasure hunting in the GPS-enabled activity of geocaching.

Tall, angular Nachiket Pandey has bushy black hair and intelligent dark eyes fringed with thick long lashes that make him look dreamy. He dreams of finding a million geocaches, hidden containers containing trinkets, memorabilia, and logbooks that have meaning only to those diligent enough to seek their coordinates. When he finds his 8,000th geocache he says, "There must be millions of geocaches scattered like bird-seed across the planet's surface. It would be so neat if I could find a whole million!" He gets me interested enough to create an account on the geocaching site, but not so interested in actually going outside to hunt for a geocache myself. He says, "Once you start looking, you'll notice that there's this whole world around us that nobody ever notices."

Unlike Nachiket, who tends to notice things others miss, I, like most people, tend to see the world and everything in it exactly as it presents itself to me.

Nor am I like Michael, who seeks this Shangri-La named Ka with a single-minded determination. He wants to enter this fabled land ripe with myths and the riches of the human heart. He is interested in the connections of the human spirit, these unseen threads that bond groups of people and tie them into manifesting singular destinies. So he built, for our personal use and private pleasure, a virtual world inside the 'Verse where our avatars can bond and forever be together. This is a secret encrypted world shielded from prying eyes. A metaphorical bubble inside the 'Verse where the five of us, Ember, Nachiket, Ash, me, and him, seek solace and refuge from the turbulent waves of our beating teenage hearts. This is where these bonds grow stronger, where we become a hive mind with Michael as the leader. But, there is also Ka, ever present in our psyches because of Michael.

There are stories embellished with each person's retelling of how Michael disappears and reappears from Ka, which can mean either of two things. One is that Ka is entirely a figment of Michael's overactive imagination, and the other is that Ka is really a world that exists within another dimension, which we cannot see. The latter is true, say Ember, Nachiket, and Ash, over our heated debates about the validity of a world we cannot see. Yet, the others have seen Michael disappear and reappear from Ka. It is like vanishing into thin air and materializing again. How can you not believe your own eyes, they ask? It has happened. Take our word for it. There are eyewitness accounts, and we are eyewitnesses. Therefore, Ka is a world that exists. I am the only one who brings my doubts to Michael and the others. Why have I not seen this world? Why have I not seen Michael disappear and reappear from Ka?

Michael has no definite answers for me and only asks that I believe. He talks about the Mind Matter interaction theory about how human consciousness can influence quantum states. He thinks this is the key to Ka, to getting us to another world that exists in another dimension. He tells me this when we meet in the empty science lab at school, and then he takes me behind the racks laden with the lab equipment that shields us from prying eyes when he kisses me. His tall, angular body embraces mine, but my head nestles into the bony cavity at his throat. His dark brown curls shield my face, and looking into the green eyes clouded with flecks of gold makes this fabled land of Ka seem all too real.

When he talks about Ka, he is incandescent, and we become the luminous trails in the night sky emanating from the bright burst of an exploding firework. But then, there are times when I sense his deep melancholy. Dark moods threaten to overcome him because he pines now for another world where he claims to have found the meaning of his existence. Then, he brings out his sketchbook and starts sketching pages upon pages of tessellated crocodiles, alternating dark blue and white, the scratching sounds of ballpoint pen creating grooves in the paper. Some people want to be scientists, doctors, photographers, or geocachers. Michael wants to be a seeker who strives for an ephemeral world that does not exist in this dimension. Meanwhile, in frustration, he sketches.

Unlike Michael, I am content to remain inside the orbit of a fascinating young man who holds the secrets to unlocking the universe. Unlike Michael, who leads, I follow as I capture his every move in an attempt to create a path that will always lead to him.

I'm lost in the winding unpopulated roads in the Santa Cruz mountains. My smartphone has no signal. Given that my sense of direction has never been great, I begin to retrace my route to where I recall some cellular service. If I'm lucky enough to find that spot, I can download the map to Richard's house. I take a U-turn on the winding road, but when I come across a fork, I cannot remember which direction I'd taken. I take the right turn for no reason other than a hunch. I figure cell service has to penetrate some portions of the Santa Cruz mountains, given its close proximity to the Bay Area. As I drive aimlessly, little bits of memory light up the synapses in my brain.

A balmy fall day, the kind where a turquoise sky emits squint-worthy sunlight and a mild breeze dictates no-sweater weather. A thin film of dampness forms under my arms, but I still wear my mother's alpaca cardigan, which is the exact color of the sky. With my green jeans, the color of the school grounds, I camouflage myself into the first week of my freshman year. The girls I walk behind are the same ones from English class, which let out a few minutes earlier. As they walk in unison, they don't bother to look behind to talk to me. Instead, I meld into shrubbery beside the fat bees buzzing around long lines of lavender plantings that separate the school greens from encroaching woodland. Given this anonymity, as I walk I bite the ragged skin behind my already-bitten nails. Behind the cafeteria, the lavender ends at the base of a grassy knoll. At the top of the mound is a solitary cherry tree hanging on to dark burgundy foliage. Below, a tall thin boy lies on his side with his head propped by one hand, reading a book. There is something uniquely pastoral about this scene. The boy has curly brown hair that shields his face, and he seems oblivious to the gaggle of girls leading up toward him. He might live in another century, captured within a picture frame, centered by a tree and framed by blue sky and soft green grass.

The girls call out, "Michael! Michael!"

The boy runs a hand over his hair to brush the curls away from his eyes, looks up, and smiles. I get that same electric sensation when I'm on a beach in Hawaii watching green water break into white foam over black lava rocks, at the moment when the salty spray of wave breaks tickles my face.

I hear a languid voice in my ear. "What kind of girl are you?"

I drop my nail-bitten hand from my mouth, turn, and then can't help staring. She is the most beautiful girl I've seen up close. Porcelain skin and long dark hair, symmetrical features, with the deepest black pupils in slanted eyes and a slightly disinterested gaze as if she's seen everything many times before. She's my height and wears a white T-shirt over ripped blue jeans.

"Are you one of those?" she asks, looking at the girls who've now surrounded the boy and are openly flirting with him. He's talking to them, but I can't hear his voice over the girls' voices.

The girl says, "They want Michael to join their debate club because he's so smart. They think they're smart, but they only know how to answer every question with three robotic responses, (a) to hypothesize; (b) to delve in; (c) to summarize. So, I'll ask you again, what kind of girl are you?"

"Not one of those," I say, and she manages to look both at me and through me simultaneously and says, "Let's go rescue my Michael then, shall we?"

She doesn't ask my name but tells me hers. "I'm Ember, by the way. Would you like to meet my friends?"

Did Ember know then, when she called him "my Michael," how I'd steal her boyfriend from her? Me, Tashi Wheeler, boyfriend stealer. Or why I never told her or the others when I lost my virginity to Michael on that fateful trip to Peru. I told him to keep it a secret not only because of all the taboos around underage sex but mainly because I didn't want to hurt Ember. I didn't technically steal him from her because they were no longer a couple. They were amicable friends, yet I'd still catch Ember glancing his way when she thought no one was looking. Also, I was treading the murky water of getting together with your best friend's ex.

I wonder now, what else our close-knit group kept from each other? *But we could read each other's minds!* Now that I think about it, we read each other's habits instead of each other's minds. Michael used to say he was like the solitary blue whale traveling alone who found this small pod and decided to stay. Maybe that's how it was for all of us. We were traveling alone and happened to find each other. Ash and Nachiket and Michael and Ember and me. *Ember never slept with Michael but does she know I did?* My mind erases this question before I can keep turning it over and over, afraid of the answer, and welcomes an easier memory.

5

———————

I get some cellular service around dusk. It's still spotty, but at least I can download a map and find the directions to Richard's house. As it turns out, I'm lost somewhere in the middle of a mountain on a road that leads to a dead end. I'll need to start retracing my way back so that the Beetle can begin climbing up the mountain again. It starts to rain, and the cold smell of damp earth filtering through the car's exhaust reminds me of that time in Andahuaylillas, Peru, which is the defining moment that bonded all of us closer together.

∼

Andahuaylillas. In the rain, its narrow cobblestone streets shine glossy gray. Briefly following a cloudburst, rain falls in a steady mist before stopping. The hacienda with its large rectangular building with the sprawling low roof of clay tile, gray stone, and white plaster, and its dormitory-style rooms with doors painted bright blue. The glance that leads from the lush green foliage surrounding the courtyard toward the expanse towering beyond leaves me dizzy. Rising up in vertical formations, their peaks hidden behind a drifting veil of clouds, are the stony Andes. For a few brief seconds, I feel weightless as I sense the heaviness and solidity of a world that disappears behind the clouds as quickly as it appears. The sensation of seeing a mountain vanish upends me. At this moment, the thought of biting my nails feels curiously distasteful, and I push my hands into my green down-filled jacket.

"Mystical. Magical. This is where you can embark on a journey for self-transformation." I startle at Michael's low voice beside my ear.

"Easy now," he chuckles. "We're planning to sit around the firepit tonight. Come sit beside me and stay till after lights out, won't you, 'cause I'm already in love with you," he says, winks, and disappears into the low arch of another blue doorway.

Is he serious or joking? I don't know, but I've already decided to sit beside him around the firepit this evening.

That time in the creeping shadows of dusk, the five of us, Ember, Michael, me, Ash, and Nachiket, sit in a circle around a firepit. The fire still needs to be lit. A steady westerly wind blows through the gaps between our bodies, and we sink into our jackets. The thin air smells of sap and aromatic incense lit by a shaman who has wandered off somewhere while we wait for him to begin the ceremony. I try to make small talk, but everyone is moody, so I keep quiet. We sit in silence as the temperature drops lower as night falls. It gets darker. I glance back at the soft glow of light emanating from the lower floor of the large rectangular building and think we are the only idiots in the class to sign up for the evening's cultural activity that involves sitting outside in the cold. Everyone else chose to stay nice and warm inside the lobby of the hacienda, lured by Wi-Fi and an ancient arcade machine.

A stout man wearing a headlamp over a black beanie, with a ruddy complexion and wide smile, hurries over and says he's going to find the shaman for us. This is Danny Yupanqui, our host and guide during this school trip to Peru. Danny switches on the headlamp and disappears in the direction of the mountains. Danny probably didn't expect any of the visiting kids would choose to sit outside in the cold. That might explain why he seems unprepared for what's supposed to happen and when. More time passes, but nobody says anything about leaving. Then, the floating light of a headlamp draws nearer, announcing Danny's arrival with the shaman lagging behind.

Danny says, a bit theatrically, "This is my good friend Don Itzal. He is the shaman who will perform tonight's ceremony." In the narrow circle of light cast from the headlamp, the shaman's face appears weather-beaten and wrinkled like cracks in sandy leather. The shaman is a short old man, but his dark eyes radiate a vitality that makes him look youthful. He wears a multicolored wool knit cap that hangs down the sides of his ears and a dirty, stained black and gray poncho. Dark trousers and huaraches peek out from underneath the poncho. Unlike Danny, who wears a navy parka and hiking boots, the shaman seems lightly dressed for the cold. He also stands still, like the immutable Andes sheathed in the darkness behind him. When I look at the shaman framed by the dark Andes, I get the sense of looking at something inexplicably old, and a thought pops into my head: these silhouettes in the darkness must have witnessed countless shamanic ceremonies that have drawn tourists like us to a place trapped in a timeless loop.

Danny says the shaman speaks Quechua and no English, so Danny, who speaks excellent English, will serve as the translator. The shaman utters his first few words in a deep guttural voice. Danny says, "He wants you all to stand up and walk toward him but keep the circle." We do as we're told. The shaman uncovers a dark cloth bag from underneath his poncho, digs inside, and removes a small white cloth, which he unfurls before spreading it on the ground beneath our feet. Wind flaps at the corners of the cloth and hoists one side up like a sail. Unperturbed, the shaman rummages around inside his bag and places five brightly colored squares on top of the cloth, one in each corner and one in the center. "Sugar candy," Danny says. The shaman extricates a glass bottle containing a dark liquid from the seemingly bottomless bag and speaks. "He wants you to hold out your hands, and he will put a few drops of aromatic oil in your palms, and then you should rub them together. This is for cleansing," Danny says, making a rubbing motion with his hands. The oil feels warm in my hands, and as I begin rubbing them, the warmth spreads all over my body, enveloping me in a pleasant smell of pine and eucalyptus. I find myself relaxing even as I sense something ancient awakening around us. Then, the shaman reaches out for Nachiket's hand and holds it while holding Danny's hand. Danny says, "We must hold hands to link the circle."

When Michael takes my hand, I feel a pressure point under my right shoulder blade tingle, as if something invisible is exerting a slight push. Still, it feels pleasant, like the pressure of a thumb. Michael's hand feels warm and soft, but when he brushes his thumb over the tips of my ragged nails, I have a sudden urge to withdraw my calloused fingers. Michael squeezes my hand so I stay put. I can't help but wonder if Michael can feel the difference between my hand and Ember's, which he also holds, and whether her slender hand feels more delicate than mine.

The shaman begins to sing a sorrowful song in a mournful voice, which makes me sad. Danny says, "He is calling upon the spirits of the mountains to witness this ceremony." The shaman stops singing and starts speaking. Danny says, "Now, he wants everyone to introduce themselves to the mountains, and if you can, please, also explain the meaning of your name. For example, he says his real name was Demetrio Quispe. That is what his parents called him. But after he was initiated into his sect, his master gave him a new name and a segment of his own robe as his initiation ceremony. In fact, the gray part of his poncho is the segment of the robe his master gave him. His master also gave him his name Don Itzal, which means shadow. The naming of a person or thing is very powerful. What this means for Don Itzal is that he can tread lightly among these mountains like a shadow without any fear of retribution. Now, Don Itzal would like you all to please give the meanings of your names. You can speak in any order."

Ember says, "My real name was Riveko Ikeda, but like you, Don Itzal, I took on a different name. I call myself Ember, which means dying ashes."

Nachiket says, "My name is Nachiket, and it has meaning in Hindu mythology. Nachiket was the name of a young boy who gained self-knowledge from the god of death so he could realize the soul's nature and the universe's ultimate secret."

Michael says, "My name is Michael, and it is meant to be a reference to Saint Michael, the archangel who is present at the hour of death and tasked with bringing souls to judgment."

Ash says, "My name is Ashley, which means ash tree grove, and my friends call me Ash, like burnt ash, but I don't think my name means anything at all."

The shaman shakes his head and speaks, and Danny says, "The moment you name someone or something, it is significant. You name a person or a thing so you can know its soul. It seems to Don Itzal that the four of you all have names that have to do with death, and you should take this to be a good thing because it means that you will not fear death. It also means that you all are closely bonded together."

Michael, who has been reticent all evening, now expresses a sudden delight in the affairs of the night. "Of course!" he says and swings our hands with the force of the thought that occurs to him. "Look at our parts in this world's play. Ember is dying coals, Ash is the one who remains after burnt coal, Michael is the angel who presides over the dying, and Nachiket is the one who is free from death. That leaves us with Tashi. Come now, what part will you play, Tash?" he asks, turning to me. His pupils are dark pools as mysterious as the night. I wish my name meant something special like the rest, and I'm afraid what I say won't make me fit into the play at all. "Go on, Tash," Michael urges.

I say, "My name is Tashi, and it means good fortune in Tibet, which is where my parents met on a backpacking trip. So when they got married, they thought that if they had a girl, they would name her Tashi to remind them of their good fortune."

"Hey Tash, you get the part of the fortunate outsider," Michael says and squeezes my hand, which makes the heat rise in my face.

The shaman turns his gaze to me, which is unsettling, so I drop my eyes to the colored pieces of candy lying on the white cloth instead. Michael extracts his hand from mine and breaks the link in the circle. "So, you are the fortunate one. Good fortune," Danny says. I raise my head, unsure how to respond to the shaman, and manage to say, "I suppose so."

Moving on, the shaman instructs Danny to tell us to pick up a colored candy from the white sheet, one at a time.

Ember picks up a blue candy and flips it over. "A casa," Danny says, looking at the child's drawing of a multicolored house with a garden inside a white picket fence. The shaman speaks, and Danny translates, "It means you will be someone who will take care of the family, maybe become a homemaker and raise talented kids." Ember flicks her long hair behind an ear with one hand and tosses the candy back onto the white sheet with the other. I glance at her, but her face is hidden in shadow. Try as I might, I cannot imagine Ember married with two little kids and living in a house with a low-slung roof and a fenced garden.

Nachiket picks up a green candy and flips it over to reveal the picture of a red fox in the middle of Christmas trees. "You are someone who will protect nature and animals," Danny translates for the shaman.

Ash picks up a yellow candy, and when he turns it, there is

a picture of a deep red heart. Danny says, "Don Itzal wants you to know that you will be someone who will be involved in a deep romance, and you will have to fight between life and death for matters of the heart." This draws laughter and applause. It's easy to imagine Ash as someone who wears his heart on his sleeve. Ash gives a goofy grin and tosses the candy back onto the cloth.

Michael picks up a caramel-colored candy, turns it over, and shows everyone the picture of a blue whale. The shaman pauses mid-sentence and glances in the direction of the mountains as if he is waiting to hear something before he resumes talking. Danny translates, "Whales possess a deep and ancient intelligence, and some cultures hold these creatures in deep regard because they are powerful beings with the knowledge to cross dimensions. Whales are comfortable with being in thin places where the boundaries of two worlds, water and air, meet. You must be someone who seeks the knowledge of the thin places, so you can cross over into another world."

Michael says, "I'd like to be Jonah in the belly of the whale, or maybe I'd like to reappear like Ishmael and narrate a story like Moby Dick. But what I really want, Don Itzal, is to cross over into Ka. How do you think I could do that?"

I have no idea what Ka is, and I think I must not have heard him say it correctly, but his face, ghostly white and serious in the glow of the headlamp, sends a chill down my spine.

The shaman shakes his head when Danny talks to him. Danny says, "Don Itzal can't help you with this." The shaman stares into the darkness toward the mountains in deep contemplation.

Everyone seems a bit uneasy after the metaphysical explanation of Michael's blue whale, and they've forgotten about me. I bend down and pick up the last candy, a scalding pink color, and on its back is an outline of a desktop computer sketched in plain white. I feel deflated. I don't know what image I expected, but I hoped it would lend itself to a vague or mysterious interpretation. Of course, there is nothing vague or mysterious about a desktop computer, so when the shaman speaks, I pretend I'm not disappointed with Danny's "someone good at office work" interpretation.

"I think there's a different meaning, Tash," Michael whispers, his breath warm in my ear. "You can be the chronicler of all our fates."

"There may be room for interpretation. Maybe it means meaningful computer work?" I whisper back, thinking he's joking, but Michael isn't smiling. Instead, he shakes his head at me and says nothing more.

Meanwhile, the shaman concludes the ceremony as he whispers our names, collects the candy pieces, and wraps each candy in cocoa leaves. He starts a low chant as he folds the white cloth into a tight bundle with the pieces of candy enrobed in cocoa leaves and our whispered names. Danny says, "Don Itzal will bring your names for safekeeping and bury this deep within Pachamama, Mother Earth, so you can walk safely among these mountains." And with that, the ceremony is over. The shaman bows to us, thanking us for attending, and we thank him for letting us participate in the ceremony. Then, the shaman retreats into the darkness, and Danny lights the fire.

6

____

A lone with my thoughts, I continue driving into the deepening darkness. I think about the shaman in Peru and marvel at his simple ceremony's lasting effect on each of us. The shaman's prophecy for me as someone who would be good at computer work did end up coming true. After all, I did manage to become the founder of the most popular company in the 'Verse! Did his prophecies also come true for Ash, Nachiket, and Ember? I don't know because they stopped talking to me soon after Michael disappeared. What I do know is that Michael's sugar candy with the picture of the blue whale and the shaman's subsequent prophecy affected Michael deeply because he started yearning for Ka with single-minded intensity. I try to jog my memory and remember the details. What happened after the shaman had prophesied for each of us?

~

After the shaman leaves, nobody wants to head back indoors. We keep our circle as we sit on the low wooden benches around the fire that sends sparks into the night sky filled with so many stars and cloudy clumps of the Milky Way that it looks like a virtual rendering. The fire is roaring now, and I can feel the heat on my face as it loosens the stiffness in my body. I ponder over what the shaman said. I wish I, too, had a name that meant something specific like good fortune over death and not the fortune cookie non-specific version because then the question becomes good fortune over what? Now, if I had a name like the others with an element of death in it, I'd fit into this tight-knit group. Instead, no such reference in the meaning of my name is yet another thing that sets me apart from the rest and makes me acutely aware of my status as an outsider.

Danny warns us to come back inside when the fire dies down. I wait for Danny to leave and then turn to Michael, who strikes a meditative pose, spine erect, legs crossed at the ankles, and hands folded in his lap.

Since there's this thing that's been bothering me, which nobody has asked Michael to explain, I ask, "What's Ka?"

Michael unfolds his hands and places them behind the wooden bench, straightens his legs toward the fire, and seems engrossed in watching a succession of tiny orange flames travel upwards, licking the edges of a log.

Nachiket says, "You'll be happier if you don't know. Once you find out, there's no way of unknowing what you know." He pulls at the cowlick on his forehead, something he does when he's thinking. This avoidance tactic annoys me. "What exactly do I not know, and why aren't you telling me? What's Ka, Michael?"

Michael says, "It's a place, Tash, just like this. Except it doesn't exist in this world, it's one of those worlds you can't see."

I'm curious as hell, but the feeling of being left in the dark, of always searching for trails left by breadcrumbs that vanish the moment I glean something about the inner workings of this group, makes me feel overwhelmed. On the verge of tears, I stand up to go, but Michael grips my arm and pulls me back to sit beside him.

"Sit down, good fortune. I should tell you everything. You're as much a part of this group as anyone else, and therefore, you have a right to know. If anyone thinks Tashi doesn't have a right to know, speak now or forever hold your peace." Michael looks around at the rest of the huddle, and nobody speaks up.

Michael says, "Listen up then, Tash. I'm going to tell you a fairytale for the ages."

But first, he asks me a question. "Do you want to tell everyone what you told me when you saw these mountains for the first time? Bear with me, Tash, 'cause I won't be able to explain it to you otherwise."

I hesitate and look around at our group, at the serious faces that appear soft and ethereal in the firelight, waiting and expectant. "I said that seeing the mountains gave me vertigo. Especially thinking of that farmer who has to till his fields at the highest terraced level at 10,000 or whatever feet up the mountain. Everything here is vertical. All the living, farming, and working are performed vertically... I guess I'm used to a more horizontal context of the world," I say.

Nachiket gets up, walks over to Michael, and hands him a folded piece of paper, which surprises me. Michael takes his time unfolding the paper as he continues talking. "Yes, context. Now isn't that something? The context of your world is horizontal, but the context of the world for the people who live here is vertical. Did it ever occur to you that there might be many more contexts of the world that you're unaware of? For that matter, there might even be worlds that exist, but you cannot see them because you don't have the right context to see these worlds? Can you wrap your head around that?" Michael holds out the paper toward me.

Nachiket, who still stands towering between Michael and me, sticks his hands in his jacket pockets and says, "That's Ka."

On the paper is a pencil drawing of interconnected flat black-and-white shapes. Then, as my eyes adjust to the low flickering light, the shapes seem to creep outwards from two-dimensional flatness into three-dimensional creatures. It is a shock when these creatures register in my subconscious as crocodiles.

Michael says, "This is an example of trying to show you a world that you cannot see for yourself. These are the same tessellated crocodiles that I've seen in Ka. At first, I wasn't sure what these were or what they meant. Then, I came across them again on spring break when I was on vacation in Denmark. I was browsing this old bookstore and saw a book of prints by M.C. Escher. When I opened the book to a random page, there they were. These exact same crocodiles were set in a picture that was a real scene I could've sworn I'd seen in Ka. I couldn't believe it. At that moment, I felt that Escher must have gone to Ka and seen these crocodiles there. I've finally figured out how to get these tessellated shapes right by imitating his genius with my pencil drawings. I copied these shapes from a print called "Reptiles." Have you seen it?"

I shake my head. Having never heard of this artist before, it's highly unlikely I've seen his prints.

Michael takes out his smartphone from his jacket pocket and swipes the screen to show me a picture he's saved in his images. I take the phone from him and rotate it in my palm to make the picture appear larger. This is a picture of a surreal world. There is a depth to the detailed black-and-white scene, where interconnected shapes emerge from a flat void into fully formed crocodiles that crawl and climb their way over objects, including a book, mortar, and a dodecahedron. All of which, Michael points out, is hard to draw on two-dimensional paper. The crocodiles walk over random objects before jumping off from the top of a mortar to fall back into flatness, where they merge once again into interconnected shapes. The cycle of emerging and vanishing crocodiles makes me feel unsettled.

Michael taps his index finger on the surface of the phone. "He's showing you a world that can't exist and shouldn't exist, except that it does. This is Ka, Tash. It's the land of pure concept, the place beyond time where the past and future are circular. This is the image of Ka I carry in my head. It's the place I've been privileged to visit and the only world that makes sense to me. This world you and I are in now doesn't make sense. It has too much of everything and answers to nothing. To understand who I am in this world and what I'm meant to be, I must go to Ka because all the answers are there."

"Answers to what?" I ask.

"To life, liberty, and the pursuit of happiness!" Michael's serious face breaks into a wide grin, and the shine in his eyes makes him even more irresistible.

Michael doesn't speak for a while, and neither does anybody else. Then, Nachiket walks back to sit in his spot. I can hear my labored breathing in the thin air as I process the tale Michael tells me, even as my mind races with questions. "What do you mean by this world having too much of everything?"

"Like too much information for one. We're living in an age of distraction, and I have this problem, more so than most people, where I can forget none of it. It's like I'm plugged in all the time, consuming everything, forgetting nothing, and sometimes I have so much information overload that I get digital vertigo. It's a physical sensation that makes me feel turned inside out. I've experienced digital vertigo many times and only come away with a dull headache. But, this one time when I experienced digital vertigo, I was also physically in a thin place, and the next thing I knew, I found myself in Ka. It felt like I was in a place where I was outside of myself and yet connected with myself in a really true way, where even though what I saw should not have made any sense, everything fell into place. I grasped the meaning of my existence. It's as close to rapture as I've ever felt," Michael says.

I glance around the group to see if they're buying this. They are. Ember's head is tilted toward Michael. She leans forward, her arms between her legs and her fingers interlaced.

She is listening with interest. Ash and Nachiket aren't joking either, and Nachiket, in particular, is trying to read the range of expressions on my face where I'm sure he can read bewilderment.

There's the next set of logical questions for me to ask. "This place, Ka. Where is it, and how do you get there?"

"It's not a permanent place, at least not in the way we think of permanence. I've only managed to go there a few times. I think you need to physically be in a thin place where the boundaries of this world and Ka's intersect. Even then, it comes and goes like an altered state of consciousness," Michael says.

"And the picture of these crocodiles, is it supposed to prove that you've gone to Ka and come back?"

Michael shakes his head. "You want me to show you proof of the truest thing of all. There is no such proof. I can only ask that you believe like me. I yearn for Ka because I believe. The truest thing for me is to know my true self, and when I'm in Ka, I can begin to grasp the meaning of my existence. But if you're looking for eyewitness accounts of my comings and goings from Ka, I suppose you should ask the others because they have seen me physically disappear. It's like you step into a portal to another world. It's the only way I can describe it," Michael says.

"I've seen Michael disappear into Ka," Nachiket says.

"Me too," Ember pipes up.

"I've seen it happen, too," Ash says.

"What? Disappear? Like into thin air?" I ask, my mind racing, unable to form full sentences.

Nachiket says, "Correct, he took a step into thin air and vanished. The first time it happened was at school behind the cafeteria underneath the cherry tree on that little hill. We were all sitting under the tree when it happened. Michael got up and took a step, and for a brief moment, he was there in front of us, and then, in the blink of an eye, he disappeared. We tried to follow him but couldn't reach him. Meanwhile, the spot remained the same for the rest of us; nothing unusual. I had counted ten minutes by the time he came back."

"Came back?"

"Materialized, if you prefer that word, a few steps away from me. It was as if he materialized from thin air. Gave me a scare the first time he did that!" Nachiket says.

"How come you couldn't go there?" I ask Nachiket, who shrugs.

Michael says, "I'm not sure. None of the others have been able to visit Ka, but they've all seen me disappear and reappear from Ka many times. I think you have to be invited to enter Ka, and when you're invited, you have to hear the call and overcome a mental block to enter into its sacred space. So far, it looks like I'm the only one who's been able to go to Ka, but I can't go there anytime. It happens of its own accord."

"How do you know this place is called Ka?"

"Because it's the first thing I see when I enter that world. I find myself in front of a rusty iron gate with the letters K and A in the trellis work. This gate has always appeared to mark my entry into that world. That's why I call it Ka."

"What does it feel like to enter Ka?" I ask.

"There's a whoosh of wind that feels like it's coming from inside me instead of from outside, and that wind picks me up and propels me forward with increasing speed. It feels like every atom in my body is vibrating at a higher frequency. That's why I said you have to overcome a mental block because, Tash, it feels a little bit like dying."

7

———

In the car, driving in the deepening darkness toward Richard's studio, I think about what Michael meant when he said that going to Ka felt a little bit like dying. He refused to tell me anything more because, he said, it was an experience that couldn't be explained in words. I wonder, if he's in Ka now, would he have the words to reach back out again?

I also wonder if there was a moment right after Michael's disappearance when Ember, Ash, and Nachiket also disappeared from my life? It is hard to pin down an exact moment in time because theirs was a gradual fading away. My memories of them are like scenes from a movie from someone else's life. It's interesting how you can classify some events in time to signify eras. I can classify the events in my life as those that occurred Before Michael Disappeared (the BMD era) and those that occurred After Michael Disappeared (the AMD era).

In the BMD era, I knew everything about each of my friends, including which out-of-state colleges they were applying to. As I drive at dusk on this winding road, it occurs to me that Michael had insisted that I apply to colleges within the Bay Area. I remember feeling uneasy at this exclusion. I was always on the group's periphery, never quite a part of it. The fear of missing out overcame me and left me feeling upended. I had gained late entry into this group, while the others had been friends since middle school. I, a newcomer in high school, had always felt like I didn't fit in as easily as the rest because I didn't share their old stories. I wasn't artistic like Michael, ethereal like Ember, high-minded like Ash, or outdoorsy like Nachiket. So I always felt that no matter what I did, my friends would always be more interesting than me.

There was also something else. All of them, except for me, had seen Michael enter Ka at least once, this land of pure concept where anything, even the branching of your life into what it could or could not be, was possible. I was the only one who had somehow never received the invitation to see Michael disappear into Ka.

It is dark enough now for the car's headlights to turn on automatically. I'm beginning to feel that the winding road has a mind of its own. For a moment, I feel transposed as if I'm not driving, but I'm being pulled forward, as though I've entered a magnetic field. In the deepening darkness, the scents of pine and bay laurel filter through the car's exhaust as Michael's face pops back into my mind. He caresses my brows with his fingertips, tracing over them with a soft press that charges my body. I'm a conductor of electric current. Standing this close to me, his heavy mop of dark brown curls casts its shade over my burning face in the midday sun. His pupils are cool green with lighter gray flecks. I see myself reflected in them in miniature and think he must see every-thing through lenses splattered with ocean foam. When he curves his thin lips into a half smile, I forget my anxiety as he says, "You stay back, Tash, so you can be the chronicler of all our fates. You've always been my good fortune. You're my anchor. You'll pull me up when I go far away, won't you?"

During that time I grokked everything Michael said. It didn't feel odd that while everyone else applied to out-of-state colleges, I applied to those colleges in-state and closer to the Bay Area because Michael's insistence seemed like benevolence, an act of grace, something like eternal love where one does what the other wants, no questions asked. Like a fairy tale.

It's only now, in hindsight, that I can replay that conversation and question why. Why did he ask me to stay back when everyone else had left? Why did he say I should be the chronicler of all our fates? What did he mean when he said I was his anchor? How was I expected to pull him back up when I didn't even know where he'd gone?

In the early years of the AMD era, these questions messed with my head a lot, leaving me adrift and alone. Ember, Ash, and Nachiket would either take forever to reply to my texts or emails or give vague excuses about being busy. I couldn't put my finger on it, but there was something odd and stilted about our interactions. It felt like they were avoiding me, and at that time, it felt like a gut punch. I couldn't meet them anymore in the virtual world we had interacted with before because Michael had taken that down before he disappeared and, with that act, wiped our histories clean.

I busied myself with college. But on the weekends, I'd throw a sleeping bag and tent into the trunk of the Beetle and take long road trips, rather like now, to clear my head and to think. I took coastal routes on meandering highways to nowhere in particular but subconsciously heading toward the redwood forests. I'd try to follow the routes that had cliffs on one side and foaming ocean on the other. Sometimes I'd cross sections of flat farmland, and the windshield would be splattered with fertilizer dust and bugs. Then, I'd stop at a gas station, wipe off the windshield and retrace my way toward the redwoods. There was never a clearly delineated forest line, but a gradual fusing of dust and filtered light as the Beetle moved into an outcropping of the first set of trees, which became stands of redwoods deeper in. A bit before dusk, I'd start looking for a spot to camp for the night. Sometimes, I'd get lucky at a state park and find an empty campsite. If not, I'd look for inns and bed and breakfasts and usually find a cozy room for the night. Once or twice I slept in the car. I thought a lot about Michael during these road trips. Alone, I let the pain and anguish of losing Michael, and my friends, wash over me like waves of nausea, and I learned to hold my breath while bracing for the impact of that shuddering wave.

I keep thinking about Michael's disappearance (I refuse to call it death), replaying the incident and all its details in my mind. My parents gave me this car a week before graduation. That same week, three days until graduation, Michael disappeared. The only plausible explanation the authorities could devise for his grieving parents was death by drowning. They said he had taken his father's sailboat that was docked in Sausalito out to open sea, all alone, in stormy weather. They said he sailed in the choppy waters under the Golden Gate Bridge when he fell overboard, likely at midnight when the storm was at its peak. The Coast Guard found the sailboat near the Golden Gate Bridge the next morning with no one on board and no missing life jacket. Therefore, he wasn't wearing a life jacket when he fell overboard. Michael Hayes died by drowning. Case closed. Except, it didn't make any sense to me. There was no way Michael could have drowned; he was too good a swimmer. Every summer, he would swim the breath of Donner Lake in Tahoe, plus he was both an excellent surfer and diver. When he was diving off the coast of Belize on a family vacation the summer before he disappeared, he logged a deep dive at 170 feet. He was as natural in the open ocean as a whale that routinely sinks to deep depths and emerges like a leviathan to breathe again. The death by drowning statement is so incongruous that even now, thinking about it again, I can sense the lie in my bones the same way they sense the cold.

~

Lost in my meandering thoughts, I've forgotten to turn on the heat, and now there is a perceptible temperature drop inside the car. I turn the heat on and make a dinner of the two energy bars I put in the cup holder as an afterthought. I munch on the chewy peanut-flavored bites as I concentrate on the road ahead of me, still winding in the dark void beyond the reach of headlights.

At nightfall, I reach Richard's studio, pulling up onto an unpaved section of road, which reveals itself only because the cellular network reawakens in time for the map app to chart a new route on my smartphone. The tires make crunching noises as they tread slowly over forest debris, and when I pull to a stop on an incline in front of a low-slung house, tiny winged bugs get caught in the yellow beam of the car's head-lights. I hear quick yelping barks even before I turn the engine off. As I get out of the car, a light switches on at the far end of the porch revealing a series of steps jutting into the rising earth and leading up to the porch above. This is a house incised into a mountain. The barking is incessant and appears closer behind the door as I approach the base of the stairs.

Darkness hugs the sides of the house and becomes deepest behind the parked car. There is no light other than that emitted by the house, and I draw closer instinctively. Like a moth to a flame, I can't help thinking as the crunch of each footstep echoes in my head, increasing the trepidation I feel as I climb till I stand, waiting, at the door.

I can't locate the doorbell in the dim porch light, so I knock twice on the thin wooden door, and the hollow raps draw a frenzy of barks. My palms are clammy after the long drive. I wipe them on my jeans, stick my hands inside my jacket pockets, then take them out again and clasp them in front of me. I stand tall and take a deep breath, hoping this will make me presentable to the person who opens the door. Now I am anxious about how I'll be received at 9 p.m. instead of the original appointment time of 4:30 p.m. I am hours too late, thanks to my meandering thoughts and the capricious navigation of the map app on my smartphone. I know why I've come here, but it might be hard to explain this to Richard, this artist whom I've sought out to test my theory, which at the moment feels like a crazy hunch. I'm here to understand the clues that Michael is putting out in my world for me to unearth. Didn't he say that words had no meaning inside Ka? If he did manage to reach Ka forever, then perhaps the only way he can reach me in my world is through images that remind me of him.

The door opens with a grating sound as if swollen wood is being dragged across the floor. The man I've come here to meet stands in front of me, holding the collar of a German shepherd who is bursting to leap. Perched on top of his gray head are reading glasses with red frames. He looks tired and perplexed to see me standing outside. I realize that if there is someone I can talk to about Michael, it must be Richard. I resolve to tell him why I'm here to see his artwork of the tessellated crocodiles again.

Richard speaks first. "The studio closed at 5," he says. His voice sounds weary, and I'm sure he's tired. I'm tired too. The long hours sitting inside the car have caught up with me now in small waves, but I must state my case because I don't want to go back and come another day. I begin the speech I've prepared in my head. "Hi! I'm Tashi. I'm really sorry for disturbing you at this late hour. I *had* made an appointment with you to see your artwork of the tessellated crocodiles in the afternoon, but I got lost coming here. I couldn't find cell coverage or get continuous map directions on my phone. Please hear me out. I know what this looks like. I'm not crazy. I can explain why I need to be here at this late hour, but it's a long story."

Richard seems to be caught off guard. He stands still with furrowed brows as if he's working out something in his head. Neither of us moves, and only the dog is straining to break free from Richard's grip on his collar. Then, as if the final piece of the puzzle falls into place, Richard's bushy brow smoothens, and there is a softer glint in his eyes.

"You're the girl who stared at my crocodiles and then ran after me at the Farmer's Market," he says.

I nod in relief. Given that my craziness has been well established, my odd behavior of turning up at his doorstep at night might get me a pass too. "Hey, Ollie," I say, and Ollie goes wild with excitement and wags his tail, welcoming me with his barks.

"I suppose you should come in," Richard says.

I follow Richard into a narrow hallway that opens into a wide room. The low table, two armchairs, and sofa look like they're made from reclaimed wood and bear the handmade charm of an artist who works with wood. The sofa is covered in a deep red tweed fabric with blue piping, and a muted red and navy kilim rug pulls the room together. Behind the sofa is a brimming built-in bookcase that spans the wall and touches the ceiling. The effect is cozy and tasteful.

Ollie is still straining to break free from Richard's grip. "You should sit down, or I'll need to put him in another room. I can't keep restraining him like this," Richard says.

I tread across the rug and sit down on the sofa. Richard sits on an armchair facing me and admonishes Ollie to sit down. Ollie listens the second time, but the curiosity is palpable on the canine face. I know he'll leap toward me the moment Richard stops holding his collar.

Richard strokes the dog's neck, calming him down. "I'm still training him, but I've been a bit lax about it. I live alone, and we don't get too many visitors this late," he says.

"I wish I could have kept our earlier appointment time this afternoon, but I got lost coming here, and this trip was, is, very important to me," I say.

"Well, whatever reason you have, you must wait till the morning. I can't take you to the studio so late at night," he says.

"Oh no. I really need to see your work with the tessellated crocodiles. Please, it won't take long. I'll leave after seeing it. Please believe me, I really did come all this way to see your artwork and I do have a story to tell you why," I say.

"I admit I'm intrigued, but you don't understand that the studio is half a mile down an unpaved path behind the house. Even if I could, I wouldn't go there in the dark. Perhaps if I was younger, I would have taken you there now and opened up the studio. But it is a space in an abandoned warehouse, and there are too many things to trip me up, even on good days in broad daylight. Frankly, my dear, I'm too old to walk you there in the dark," Richard says.

"Of course. I understand. I'll come back in the morning. Can I please park my car here? I'll sleep in the car tonight. I know it sounds weird, but this way, I'll be here first thing in the morning, and perhaps you can show me your artwork then. I promise I won't take too much of your time, and I won't bother you anymore afterward."

"You'll sleep in the car?" Richard asks. I can tell he doesn't quite know what to make of me.

"Yes, if I can park here. I've done it before," I speak with a steadiness in my voice that belies my frayed emotions.

Richard sits still, but I glimpse a glimmer of recognition in his eyes.

"If you want, you can stay in my wife's cottage tonight. It's right next to the house. She liked to work there at night, and she sometimes slept there while working on her paintings," Richard says.

I can't believe this change of fortune. Maybe that's why Michael called me good fortune after all. Thinking that this is another sign that I need to follow, I say yes, thank Richard for the kind offer, and say I hope his wife doesn't mind.

"Fiona, my wife, died five years ago. I don't think she

would have minded you staying at the cottage. I recognize her kindred spirit in people like you," Richard says as he gets up from the armchair. He removes his hand from Ollie's collar, and Ollie doesn't leap at me but stands obediently beside his master.

"Thank you for your kindness," I say. I feel a rush of relief and gratitude toward this man I know nothing about.

I follow as Richard leads the way outside. Ollie, who is no longer excitable, tags along. The thought that Richard has trained his dog too well occurs to me. Perhaps by placing his hand on Ollie's collar, Richard indicated wariness, a signal to watch out for this girl who entered their house. Now, Ollie seems content enough to follow alongside his master.

Richard picks up a flashlight and a key from a nook in the narrow hallway before opening the door. Again, the door protests. He switches on the flashlight, and I follow him down the steps to the right of the house, where he illuminates a gravel path leading to a small square structure. We reach it in a few steps, and Richard tells Ollie to sit outside as he turns the key in the door and opens it with a smooth swish. Ollie sits down to wait as Richard disappears inside and turns a light on. The cottage is cozy with a shabby chic décor. The door opens to a room that contains a small bed with a wooden headrest and a plump mattress with a light blue duvet. A white desk and chair are next to a door that opens to a room, empty except for three canvases turned to face the wall with their exposed wood frames set at an angle leaning against it. This room has a large window and a concrete sink for a wash basin. I'm guessing this is the room his wife used as a painting studio. To the left of the bedroom is a small door that leads to an equally small bathroom equipped with a tiny shower stall. There is no kitchenette. I find myself thinking I could live here.

"Fiona would be glad to find it being used. I clean it once in a while, and whenever I've had visitors on occasion, I've put them up here. The room heater is under the bed. You should turn it on, and it'll warm the room up in a bit. You're welcome to stay here tonight if you'd like, and you can come up to the house tomorrow morning and tell me why you're here," Richard says and hands me the key.

I'm glad to have this space that is so clean and welcoming to spend the night, and I express my gratitude to Richard. I follow him outside to get my backpack from the car. Ollie moves along his master's side. Out of habit, I've packed toiletries and a change of clothes in my backpack. There's also a sleeping bag in the car as part of my planning whenever I take road trips alone. It starts to drizzle by the time we reach the bottom of the stairs. Ollie starts barking again. He shakes his coat, not liking the sharp cold droplets. My face feels prickly too. Richard hands me the flashlight and heads back up the stairs. He watches me from the top as I pop open the trunk and grab my backpack and sleeping bag. I'm not sure how effective the heater in the cottage will be because the nighttime mountain air in late fall gets cold.

"I can offer you breakfast if you can make it here by seven. I'm usually at the studio by eight. You can come to the studio directly if you're not an early riser. You'll see the path behind the house when it's light enough," Richard says.

"I'm an early riser too. I look forward to explaining everything to you in the morning," I say as I snap the trunk shut. I watch Richard turn and enter the house, and then the door closes behind him, and the porch light switches off. I stumble in the darkness before remembering to switch on the torch. Then, I retrace my steps in the soft light back toward the cottage that stands like a halfway house at the edge of the unknown.

8

———————

Sometime between 12:30 and 1:00 a.m., I'm awakened by the sound of rain falling on a tin roof. I lie motionless inside the cocoon of the sleeping bag atop a soft mattress. I don't miss the chill of the forest floor or the woody debris inserting its sharp edges into my dreams. Instead, a calm warmth envelopes my rhythmic breathing in the gentle rise and fall of my stomach. The rain sounds like pebbles bouncing off the roof. A whole spray of tiny stones hits at once, and the downpour continues for a while, but it doesn't bother me. The more closely I listen, the more I like the falling rain, which sounds like the drum line of a high school marching band. Sometime later, the sound of the drum line turns into the sound of pebbles bouncing off the roof again, and I drift off into a deep and peaceful sleep.

Then around 5:30 a.m. I'm awakened again by the buzzing of the alarm on my smartphone. It buzzes at my right ear, and I unzip the sleeping bag to reach my arm out so I can pat my hand on the soft bedspread till it touches a cold metal surface.

I unzip the sleeping bag further so I can bring the phone closer into my cozy lair. As I swipe across the screen to silence the alarm, a cacophony of pings heralds a flood of alerts and notifications. As my bleary eyes adjust to the squinting brightness, I can't help thinking that the sounds of these notifications are like the sirens in The Odyssey, beckoning me toward the virtual worlds in the 'Verse. To avoid the call of the sirens, Odysseus stuffed his ears with wax and had his shipmates lash him to the mast, which is how he survived to tell his tale. I, of faint heart and with no recourse to ancient Greek methods of bodily entrapment, let myself be summoned virtually by the swipe of an index finger.

Even though I'm not wearing my augmented reality glasses, once again, I lose myself in the outrage, fear, anger, and anxiety of the alerts and messages, and I begin to sweat inside the sleeping bag. A fleeting thought half formed in the land of sleep takes shape in my mind, and I latch onto it as an escape route out from the 'Verse. The thought presents itself as one question after another. If a virtual world can feel real enough to participate in for most people, including me, then why can't a world like Ka be real and palpable to Michael? If I can enter a virtual world with the swipe of an index finger, then what's preventing me from entering Ka?

Michael used to say that our world had too much of everything. He meant that our world had too much information that was presented without any context. In his telling, Ka was the world of pure concept where everything had context and, therefore, meaning. It was where he had found the meaning of his existence.

No such luck for me, the girl who lies inside a sleeping bag atop a perfectly made bed. Being in this strange space reminds me that if I'm to find meaning in my actions, which brought me to this cottage, I better get ready and present myself again to Richard, so he can show me that picture of the tessellated crocodiles that has captivated me. I'm unsure whether seeing the images will reveal the magic clue that provides me with answers to Michael's disappearance or leads me to Ka. Still, this long shot is all I've got to work with for now. So I rise to ready myself for the day.

~

The cold chills my bones the moment I get out of the sleeping bag. Last night, I didn't find the heater under the bed, and I was too tired to search for it. Now, as I don my jacket, I again search for the heater and find it when I open the accordion doors of the small closet. It's the small metal rectangle standing on the last shelf, wedged between tins of paints and a box containing brushes and tubes of oil paints. I pull the heater out and plug it into a socket under the desk. The fan starts with a whir, and warm air pushes out toward me. I stand in front of it until the warm air radiates enough heat for me to get uncomfortable enough to step away. In the small bathroom, I leave the shower on till the water runs hot, and then I step inside the scalding spray till my skin turns red and the steam fills my lungs.

Afterward, feeling clean and rested and wearing the fresh set of clothes I brought in my backpack, I do random chores like rolling up the sleeping bag and tidying up the bed. There is nothing else to do except sit and wait for a good time to go and knock on Richard's door. I figure a 7 a.m. door knock is more acceptable than a 6:30 a.m. knock. What to do in the half-hour downtime? I think about going outside for a short run, but it's still dark, and the ground is sure to be wet from last night's rain.

The phone emits a ping. It's Tony texting to ask if I can be available sometime today for a quick chat because he wants to run something by me. A part of me wants to know what is so urgent for Tony to text me this early in the morning, but another part of me, the tired and weary part, seems unwilling to deal with whatever can of worms Tony opens up. With

Tony, it's always a can of worms, those slimy, slippery problems that he thinks are other people's jobs to get rid of. Besides, Tony shouldn't be reaching out to me, given that he agreed to boot me out of the company. I sigh because he knows I'll always be emotionally invested in gAIa. He knows I can't resist solving gAIa's challenging engineering problems. In fact, I miss it already.

I text back, "I'm on a road trip. Cell service is super bad. Have it now. But patchy. Leave voicemail. I'll get back to you when it's better."

White lies. I'm on a road trip, but on the periphery of the Bay Area, and while cell service was patchy in the mountains, it is excellent near Richard's house.

Three dots appear on the message window as Tony types something long and convoluted. I don't feel like reading it yet. Not after I've heard rain falling on a tin roof and the ensuing silence in its aftermath. I switch the phone off and put the now useless device into the pocket of my jacket. I tell myself that Tony and his world can wait as I walk into the next room and switch on the light.

The room appears large because it contains nothing except three canvases that rest against a wall. The floor is unfinished concrete. It might even be the foundation of the cottage. A large unadorned window set into the wall facing me reflects the darkness outside. This gives me an eerie feeling of being inside a glass house. There are no curtains or blinds on the window. This may be intentional. Perhaps Richard's wife wanted to work in natural light. I can test this hypothesis when the sun rises. It's easy to picture a woman painting on a canvas on an easel set in the center of this room in the area that has the most splotches of scuffed paint. Thinking about this image makes me feel better.

The canvases face the wall and are set vertically alongside

each other. Their exposed wooden frames are lettered and numbered in red paint. I'm curious about these canvases and walk over to read the small red block letters painted with a fine brush on each wood frame. From left to right, on each canvas, I read Daybreak 1, Daybreak 2, and Daybreak 3. I can't find the artist's signature on any of these.

I turn Daybreak 1 around to face me. It doesn't look anything like a painting because there is only a pale wash of color on the canvas. My brow crinkles as I'm faced with this unexpected abstraction. Then, the layers of paint seem to pull through the canvas presenting a three-dimensionality of texture, and now the hues of pearl gray have perceptible shifts of increasing brightness till the effect is of seeing something grow from darkness to light. I feel a noticeable change in my mood. I'm a little less anxious and relaxed. I turn Daybreak 2 around to face me and see even more brightening in the hints of grays turning into a pale wash of yellow, an unfurling of shades of peaches and pinks turning into a golden glow. I turn Daybreak 3 around, and the abstractions of color become immediately recognizable as the yellow streams of sunlight, the azure of the sky, and the brightness of wispy white clouds.

The three panels together contain no pictures, only hues of paint. Yet these paintings tug at my heart in a way that moves me to speechlessness. At this moment, I have no thoughts, and I don't know how long I stand there staring at these paintings in a meditative mood, my eyes drawn again and again to the slow unfolding of dawn into a day. Daybreak. I had often wondered what could make Michael so transfixed when confronted by the unexpected beauty of the world. Or, how for instance, he could stand for ages staring at the parallelograms of light thrown by slanted blinds on a wooden school desk. Standing in front of these paintings, I am transfixed in the same way, humbled by the presence of nothing but the color on these canvases and stupefied as to how forcefully a lack of imagery conveys the image of hope at the rise of a new day. Gently, I turn each canvas to face the wall again, and when I step back, the light in the room has a different quality. The windows are no longer black but gray, and I can see the shapes of bushes, trees, and outlines of elevation outside.

9

Richard asks, "So tell me, my dear, why are you here?" He sits at the dining table, sipping from a steaming mug of black coffee, and casts his penetrating gaze at me. Ollie sits panting at his side, licking his chops, and drooling at the smell of food on the table. Richard has served breakfast as promised, but I'm surprised at the rich spread. In his tidy kitchen, the rough-hewn wood table with its many dents and scratches holds a feast for the hungry traveler. This man knows how to cook herbed scrambled eggs with ham, fried baby potatoes, and a freshly baked loaf of sourdough served with a pat of hand-churned white butter with flecks of gray truffle salt.

"You're the fortunate one indeed, Tashi," I think as I eye the dishes, the need to satiate my ravenous hunger deeper than anything else I feel. "Will you forgive me if I eat first?" I ask.

Richard nods as I tear a chunk of sourdough bread and smother it with butter. In my mouth, the dense sour crust and the chew of soft gluten combined with the rush of salted fat fill a need in both my belly and my heart. My cinched eyes and blissful face must express my gratitude because Richard laughs. This makes Ollie jump up and start barking and wagging his tail. I laugh as I load up my plate with eggs and potatoes, eating the hearty food with an enthusiasm I hadn't thought possible.

When my hunger abates, and I can finally have some of the coffee and let a third serving rest on my plate, I say, "Thank you for doing this when you didn't have to do anything. You could have turned me away last night. But instead, you chose to let me sleep in your wife's cottage. Because of that, I had a good rest and feel refreshed today. And thank you for providing this excellent meal, which is much better than any meal I've had in a Michelin-starred restaurant. God! I've never been this hungry. I only had two energy bars and a bottle of water all day yesterday. This is heaven!"

"I'm glad you like the food. I like to cook, but I don't always have company. You looked hungry last night, but I only thought I should have offered you milk and cookies after I'd gone back to bed again. You surprised me by turning up so late in the night when I wasn't expecting anyone. Sometimes I have students who visit me and stay over in the cottage, but none have shown up unannounced at night. As you can see, I am much more hospitable in the morning." Richard has a twinkle in his gray eyes because he is smiling at me. He might be the type of person who is open to possibilities. So, I tell him. Everything about Michael. Everything about my friends. Everything about me.

Richard listens without interrupting me as I tell my digressive and circuitous story. I need to share this with someone else, and Richard has the patience to listen to a tale for the ages. After I finish talking, we sit in silence for a while. A weight shifts in my heart, and for the first time, I sense that the future can be reconciliatory. I finish the breakfast remaining on my plate, treasuring the feeling of lightness in my chest after this storytelling. Richard tips his chair back as if he's contemplating something, and then he pushes it back and gets up from the table with firm resolve. "I'm going to take you to the studio. Hopefully, you will find what you are looking for. But first, I have to clean up here."

I help Richard clear the table while taking notice of the simple joy of tidying up. Richard only instructs me once to put the dishes in the dishwasher instead of washing them in the sink. The dishwasher is to the far left of the farmhouse sink, customized to resemble an oak cabinet, which is why I assumed there wasn't one there before. When I'm done, I follow Richard outside. Ollie bounds ahead of us. We're halfway down the stairs when I realize that Richard didn't lock the door behind him, but when I remind him, he says he stopped bothering with locked doors a long time ago. This is interesting because his wife's cottage was locked last night, but I keep this to myself. He must be the kind of guy who needs to take care of the cottage to honor the memories of his wife and keep her sacred space alive.

The sky is bright blue with wisps of clouds, but the trail behind the house is muddy from last night's rain. My running sneakers, like Ollie's paws, are coated in mud an inch thick. Richard, who wears hiking boots, seems the most suited for trudging through squelching mud in the path with pockets of water collected in the deep treads of a truck's tire tracks. I start walking off the trail on the patchy grass and slippery clay, but I walk precariously along a ridgeline. The understory drops a few feet below me into a valley, then rises to meet the tree line above. Now I understand what Richard meant when he said he couldn't take me to the studio at night. The dense thickets of manzanita and coyote bush lining the path have wandering roots that jut from the ground, ready to trip you up if you're not careful, like now, when I'm looking up and almost twist my ankle on a gnarled root, taut and springy like a tripwire.

Ollie runs off, barking in the bend ahead. Around the bend lies a red barn with a gable roof and a cantilevered carport with a red pickup truck underneath. All around the barn are piles of scrap metal, scattered rusty poles, carriage wheels from another century, car parts, and other assorted metal shapes twisted beyond recognition or conceivable purpose. All this junk strewn around reminds me of the staged landscaping of a Hollywood set, ready for the rolling cameras to shoot a scene for a western. I reserve my thoughts about the safety of some of the larger metal poles positioned precariously atop each other and follow Richard as he slides this unlocked door open.

Daylight floods the cavernous dust-filled space inside. Richard has been working with wood. Wood shavings are everywhere on the cement floor, and sawdust is on the large wooden racks, tables, and low benches. The scents of patchouli and terpenes from timber logs fill the space. I notice that the metal scrap from the outside has also made it inside the barn. I step over timber and an assortment of metal pipes as I follow Richard, who appears to be on a scavenger hunt for the metal sheet with the tessellated crocodiles.

Compared to the cozy tidiness of his house and cottage, his studio seems to explode in chaos unfolding in slow motion. This is a highly entropic environment. Therefore, it takes Richard a while to find what we're both searching for. He disappears behind a wooden rack, from where I hear an Aha! He then emerges with a stack of metal sheets. They're bound together with the same yellow nylon cord I'd seen when he had parked his red pickup truck between two orange cones in front of the Ferry Building in San Francisco. I walk over to help him, but he shakes his head as he hauls them to a high work table and hoists them atop. He unties the nylon cord. The first metal sheet is the one I've come here to see. He blows across the metal surface, and motes of dust rise in the air around him. Telling me to wait, he wanders off to get a rag and then proceeds to methodically wipe the surface of the metal. When satisfied, he places the sheet on the floor, letting it rest against the leg of the wooden table. With the sunlight streaming in from the wide open door, the metallic surface shines like it's under a spotlight.

I squat a few feet away, watching the light reflect across the gray metal, noticing how the dot-matrix pattern goes from dark gray to steel gray. I realize now that the dark gray areas are painted over for the separation of light and dark to become pronounced. Viewed from this perspective, the dot-matrix of tessellated shapes do appear as crocodiles, but they don't invoke the images of Ka imprinted in my mind. When the images that captivated me while I was running seemed to pulsate and move, they registered at that moment as a reminder of Michael. As I watch the interplay of light move across the metal sheet again, I am unmoved because the pattern is sterile. I realize the dot-matrix was created by firing bullets at this metal sheet, and nothing now hints at the numinous or the magical inside this barn.

My hamstrings burn from squatting low, so I scoot closer and sit cross-legged on the sawdust-strewn floor. I pull the metal sheet toward me, feeling its cold metallic surface. "Aluminum?" I ask. Richard nods in reply. I turn the sheet to its back, feeling the distinct ridges of the bullet exits with the pads of my fingers. I hope this tactile contact triggers an emotion or an image about Ka to make this excursion worthwhile, but nothing pops into my head.

"What made you want to shoot bullets into metal?" I wonder aloud.

There is laughter in his eyes when they meet mine. Richard leans an elbow on the table and answers while looking down at the top of my head. "I was enamored with a .22 caliber rifle when I was younger. I never wanted to hurt any creature with it. Fiona told me to use the rifle to create a work of art. I made quite a few of these bullet artworks in my twenties. This one is from that time. I don't work with the rifle anymore. I work on sculptures on commissions that make me use all this wood and scrap metal. I've been trying to clear this barn to get more space for a large commission. I can't start on it till I clear out this stuff and get this open space free of clutter. I tried to clean out some of this stuff last week when I came across some of my early work, including these metal sheets. A friend of mine wanted to see if she could buy them for the new restaurant she started in Half Moon Bay. She's also a chef at this restaurant and buys produce from the Farmer's Market in San Francisco, so I told her I'd drive up there with the metal sheets to save her a trip to see me. That's why I had parked outside the Ferry Building when you saw me that day. She bought a few of these, but luckily, not the one you came here to see."

I lean forward to rest the metal sheet against the leg of the table again when I notice a word etched in the metal above Richard's looping signature near the bottom left corner.

"Zeitgebers," I say aloud.

"Fiona named that one. She thought these crocodiles were zeitgebers, time givers. Fiona used to say that the crocodiles reminded her of another world. She liked to think they belonged to a different world where they entrained the circadian rhythms of the creatures of that world. When Fiona first proposed this name, she said sunlight is the most important zeitgeber in our world. So why wasn't I willing to conceive of another world in which these tessellated crocodiles were the zeitgebers? Certainly, they have a rhythmic rise and fall, so I liked that idea, and that's the name of this artwork."

"I saw three paintings in the cottage that really moved me. They were abstract splashes of color, but they reminded me of day breaking. But they are unsigned. Did your wife Fiona paint them?"

"Ah, the Daybreaks. Yes, Fiona painted those while she was sick and battling cancer. She didn't want to sign them. She said they weren't hers to sign. She was in a lot of pain, and the opioids and other pain relievers would make her hallucinate. She believed she was painting a portal to the future, or it could also be the past because she believed in the concept of circular time. That what lies ahead has also lain in the past and that we will eventually meet the footsteps of our ancestors. My wife had an overactive imagination. She had grown up in Ireland on her grandfather's farm. When she was a little girl, she often found herself in a thin place at the boundary of her grandfather's farm and the surrounding woods. I have never experienced anything like that, but I liked hearing her talk about her experiences in these thin places. They're not as uncommon as we've been trained to believe. Fiona used to talk about seeing glimpses of another world as tessellated shapes when she was in a thin place."

"She actually called these places 'thin places'?"

"Indeed she did."

"Did she ever try taking you to a thin place?"

"No, my dear, I'm not wired that way. I can't see things that don't exist in my world, but I'm also not dismissive of people who claim to have seen strange things I haven't. Maybe that's what attracted me to Fiona and made me fall in love with her every day of the fifty-five years we were married. We just had different ways of being in the world. But enough about me, we should be talking about you, who has her entire life ahead of her but is sitting inside my barn trying to figure out why she's lost. So tell me again, why are you here, Tashi?"

I hesitate to answer, but Richard is patient, willing to wait as I gather my thoughts. After a while, I say, "I came here looking for a clue to find out what happened to my friend Michael, but now I'm not sure I'll even understand what that clue will mean even if I find it. I'm trying to think of these crocodiles as zeitgebers entraining Michael's circadian rhythms inside another world, inside Ka, and this thought frightens me. I really can't make sense of these images. When I'm experiencing *The Dissolving*, and the world's edges start folding around me, I see the pictures of the world fragmenting into interconnected tessellated shapes. I'm scared because I always tend to blank out right after this moment."

Richard picks up the metal sheet from the floor and puts it back on the table. I rise and dust the sawdust from my jeans. Richard contemplates the metal sheet in silence. "Maybe you cannot make sense of these images because you're experiencing the act of seeing something as it transpires through time, and it doesn't seem to have any meaning." Then, after a slight pause, he continues. "We see the world in discrete images, but we're able to build those images into a continuous experience of meaning. This is what creates our reality. So the next time you experience this thing you call *"The Dissolving,"* and you start getting overwhelmed by the flood of images, you should embrace the act of looking instead of being afraid. Only when you have fully looked at something will you be able to have a continuous experience of it. This may be what your friend Michael was able to accomplish. He was able to get a continuous experience of these images from which he was able to construct the reality of the world he called Ka."

I say, "I'd like to buy the Zeitgebers." Richard nods and quotes a price, which isn't cheap but isn't a gallery price either. I ask if he accepts credit cards, and he says checks are preferred. Except, I don't have a checkbook on me. So Richard says, "You can mail me a check later, but the Zeitgebers are yours to keep." He leaves me beside the table, goes outside, and calls for Ollie. I hear barks, and soon Richard is back with Ollie trotting by his heels. Ollie ignores me, goes to a water bowl below the table, and greedily laps his refreshment before flopping beside it. Richard says, "He'll keep chasing squirrels all day if I let him."

I want to sit with everything Richard said about the Zeitgebers and process that for a bit. I'm no closer to finding Michael, but I feel more open, relaxed, and present within my body. I haven't felt this way in all these years of the AMD era. This prompts me to ask Richard if I could stay and watch him work because I think he won't mind. Richard says, "You're welcome to watch me work. I don't like company when formulating an initial idea because the concept and image are tender and fleeting, and I need to pay full attention to them. But right now, I'm working on a commission whose concept and form I've already articulated. So I welcome the company because this part of the creative act will be repetitive and methodical."

Richard walks halfway across the barn and sits on a low stool beside a long wooden pole stripped of its bark. The pole rests on two raised planks at opposite ends to give it the necessary height so Richard doesn't have to stoop to work. On the pole, he's carved out a thick hump in the middle ending in a natural rise from the wood splintering into two thick branches. Now he runs his gnarled hands over the smooth log, the barest shade of tan. For a moment, he is as still as a statue, his face bowed as if in prayer. Then, he quickly removes the red-framed reading glasses from the pocket of his gray flannel shirt and puts them on. He reaches for a paring chisel lying on a low work table beside him, and then he starts maneuvering it across the tail end of the log, where it splits into two. Little curls of wood shavings land on his lap or fall, swirling to the floor, mingling with floury sawdust.

Instinct makes me pull out my smartphone from my jacket pocket to click a picture of the artist at work. I am shocked that the smartphone has not been switched on since early morning. There have been no pictures taken, social media updates, or text messages sent for more than four hours. I turn the phone on, and while waiting for the Home button to come up, I realize I haven't bothered charging it at night. This feckless behavior is almost worthy of its own post. I have half a mind to send it out when Tony's bizarre text is the first notification that grabs my attention as the phone switches on.

"Call me back when you get this. Something odd is going

on with Ka world. Engineering can't figure out a fix. I can't share details here. Strange things. Please call. Better still. Let's meet."

I'm curious as hell, but a feeling that's been submerged under the waves of my subconscious bobs up now like a gasp of fresh air and causes me to do something counterintuitive. So instead of replying to Tony's text, I ask Richard if I can stay in his wife's cottage for a while. "I'll pay rent, of course, per night or however you'd like to charge. I need to think about a few things, and it's so peaceful here."

Richard blows on the section of wood he's been chiseling, and floury dust rises around him. He puts the chisel on his lap and pushes the glasses up on his head.

"You want to stay here? For how long?"

"I don't know. A week or a month? Long enough to get a few things worked out in my head or reach some sort of resolution. I was hoping I could take it a week at a time. I really don't have much else going on at the moment. Can I help you in any way? I could create a new metasite for you, build up the business and the social and virtual aspects to make it easier for people to find you and your work inside the 'Verse. You can get so much more exposure. When I was searching for you in the 'Verse, I only found one unconnected node, and it has one picture of you. You're not even uploaded as an avatar in the 'Verse, and you belong to no virtual worlds. So, if you'd let me, I'd love to set that up for you. I'm really good at this stuff."

Richard chortles. "I bet you are," he says, and his face is serious. "Please don't do any of this. Whatever peace I have accumulated will evaporate. I've been down this road of immense exposure before and ended up in rehab. I had to pay a company to wipe out my virtual presence. They do that stuff these days for a lot of money, but you must know who you're dealing with. They came highly recommended, and they have delivered what they promised they would do. So, no, thank you. My students and clients know how and where to find me.

It's enough for me. You can stay in the cottage if you want and have your meals with me. I've said before that I welcome your company. But please, keep your phone in your pocket, tucked away from me."

I nod quickly. "How much will you charge per night?" I ask, wanting to change the subject. I understand now why he was so difficult to find online. He must have paid big bucks to get his online presence wiped clean. He must have money to do that and afford this large estate with acreage around it. He lives close to Silicon Valley, and properties with sweeping hill views like his are ripe for second vacation homes. I know because some of my friends' parents had getaway homes like this in the Santa Cruz mountains. Ember's dad and Ash's parents had weekend homes here. Sometimes, Ember and Ash stayed in the Santa Cruz mountains when they logged into the virtual world Michael created specifically for us. Our private virtual world was always available to us; one of us was always waiting, ready to talk. I have such a sudden onset of nostalgia about my friends, especially Michael, that I miss hearing what Richard says.

"Huh?" I ask.

He repeats. "You can stay free of charge."

Odd man who leaves me flummoxed. I'm not used to dealing with people who don't view transactions in monetary terms. Not in the AMD era, anyway.

"I don't want to keep imposing on your hospitality. Is there something I can do in exchange?"

"Well...I need an assistant who can help me clean out the studio. I can use the help. I'm too old for the heavy lifting and cleaning. Look at this place. It's filled with sawdust. You can pay me back by sweeping this up," Richard says with a twinkle in his eyes.

Sweeping Richard's studio floor is infinitely better than sweeping up Tony's can of worms. So I say, "I'm delighted to be your assistant, and I'll be honored to sweep this floor."

Also, voicing my interest in this newfound position, I ask, "What are you working on, by the way?"

"A totem pole with a humpback whale."

I think, *A whale!* What are the odds of finding clues when the world is filled with coincidences?

"Speaking of which," Richard interjects. "As part of the commission I've undertaken from the Monterey Bay Aquarium, the big one I've been trying to clear out this space for, I need to build a giant sculpture fashioned out of all the junk found in the bellies of whales that have been washing up dead on the shores of the Pacific. I learned yesterday that a 70-foot blue whale washed up dead on Mori beach in Pacifica. I will head up there tomorrow with a team of marine biologists from the Marine Mammal Center. They're going to cut open the belly of the whale for science, and I'm going to be there to salvage anything inside. In the past, I've found a lot of plastic, and that has presumably also been the cause of the whale's death. I want to bring back whatever I find tomorrow. If you'd like, you can come with me, but I must warn you that if you're squeamish, then you shouldn't come. This work is not for the faint of heart."

I feel lightheaded as if the universe is flooding my senses with clues that are still beyond my capacity to decipher. First, the tessellated crocodiles, and now a whale. I promised myself I'd follow all the clues on the road that led me to Michael, even if they ended at the ocean. So I hear myself saying words I could not have imagined myself saying a fortnight ago. "I'm not squeamish. I'll be there with you as your assistant when they cut open the belly of the whale."

10

Pacifica, built on eroding cliffs overlooking the Pacific Ocean, is a city shrouded in the morning fog. There is a faint glare of sunlight, an imperceptible pale wash of the flesh of a lemon. From the vast, wrinkled surface of a gray ocean, a 70-foot adult female whale has emerged from unfathomable depths to this final resting place on a windswept beach. She looks like an outcrop of slick black rock from a distance, so massive that the surf breaks into foam upon impact.

A score of people, researchers from the Marine Mammal Center, mill around the beach spreading along the length of the carcass. Richard stands in the middle of a huddle, easily recognizable by the full gray head of hair. Like the others, he wears a yellow jacket, rubber hip waders, and elbow-length rubber gloves. The researchers don't want novices around, so Richard asks me to wait till I'm called.

"Where?"

"Anywhere. Somewhere on that bluff where the wind doesn't carry the stench."

He's wrong about the wind. The stench of putrid flesh smells like rotting durian fruit borne by the wind, even on the high bluff where I stand overlooking the operation below. The wind whips my ponytail into a frenzy. On the horizon, the black line of a storm nears. The team must work quickly on the necropsy. They've carted in all the ancient tools, the flensing knives modernized with carbon steel that cuts through thick black skin and blubber, and the meat hooks that slowly peel it back to reveal Pepto Bismol-colored flesh. The tide is rising, and the water around the carcass is turning pink. An orange excavator positioned on the beach moves into operation. There are 300,000 pounds of whale flesh to deflesh, cut into blocks, and haul away to be buried in the sand. The ocean won't claim its own. The storm won't push the carcass back into the ocean. The residents of this coastal city won't want the stench of rotting durian fruit wafting into their homes on an ocean breeze or see an enormous decomposing carcass when they stroll on the beach.

Is death the final indignity to the body? Michael once said that death was consciousness deciding to move into another dimension, leaving behind organic flesh that felt neither pain nor humiliation. Where is this whale's consciousness now, I wonder? Did it get sent along another dimensional journey after the group of Hawaiians performed their ceremonies for this dead whale last week, praying for this mammal and her entire species? A sudden pang of loneliness tightens in my chest like a taut wire. I wish I could stand on this windy bluff watching the defleshing below with my friends from high school. In my mind's eye, nostalgia shines a lens on those halcyon summer nights when we would chat in our private virtual world with Ember waxing poetic about the mysteries of life and Michael guiding and prodding us to explore the unknown and unchartered expanses of our souls. Instead, I stand surrounded by a crowd of curious onlookers armed with selfie sticks and camera phones. And even though every pound of flesh being hauled by the excavator below is cataloged through the camera lenses of so many smartphones, I feel I alone bear lonely witness to the surreal scene below.

I spot Richard breaking away from the group working on

the left flank of the whale's carcass. I hurry down the bluff to see if he needs me.

Richard says, "It's slow going because they have to be careful not to cut through the bone because they eventually want to reconstruct the skeleton. Most bones they'll boil in vats of sodium peroxide, and the largest bones they'll painstakingly clean by hand. You might see the skeleton of this whale in a museum in two or three years. It's a long process of reassembly." Richard sounds weary and looks cold. The wind slaps his hair and reddens his cheeks. He hides the gray eyes behind sunglasses, so I can't tell what he's thinking. I follow him to a line of black plastic tubs containing fresh water. There's a long hose attached to one of them. Richard extricates himself from the elbow-length rubber gloves, hip waders, and yellow nylon jacket, tossing every item of protective clothing on the sand and rinsing it off with the hose before tossing each one into its separate tub.

He says, "It looks like the storm will hold till they get the job done. It looks like the whale died from a ship strike. They said it would take them another hour to get to the stomach. This is my third whale necropsy in two years. What a horrible thing to witness and such tiring work for an old man. I told them I'd be back in an hour, and if they got to the stomach and found something there, they should deposit it in a tub. They'll need to do that anyway to catalog everything."

Perhaps it is the carcass's stench, the excavator's relentless rumbling, and the pools of pink froth slowly spreading out into the ocean that make him unusually loquacious. He didn't bring Ollie with him, which is understandable given this sensitive environment. You don't want a dog bouncing up and sniffing around a dead whale, no matter how well-trained he might be.

"I'm going to rest in my truck. I have to make a few calls from my smartphone." He makes it sound as if using the smartphone is an undertaking more massive than the necropsy of a whale.

I wonder what I'll do for an hour, but I say, "I'll be here when you are."

I suppose I could start posting about the dead whale on social media, but the feeling that I'm desecrating the memory of Michael that, in my mind, is linked to this dead whale prevents me from doing so. The problem of how to spend an hour without posting anything online leaves me with a deepening sense of anxiety. I've already been to my apartment in San Francisco this morning and packed a carry-on with enough clothes to last me two weeks. I grabbed my hiking boots, laptop, a backup power supply, and all the granola bars I could find in the kitchen pantry. I've even had an early brunch at the coffee shop on the first floor of my apartment building because I knew I wouldn't have the stomach for lunch after witnessing the whale's necropsy. I've checked off all the tasks I set to accomplish, and I should be feeling good, except there's this nagging chore at the back of my mind that I've been avoiding. Now that Richard's left to make a phone call, the nagging thought creeps to the forefront, becoming the only unchecked item on my mental to-do list. I call Tony.

11

Tony asks, in a tone that foreshadows the announcement of my leaving, mentioned almost in passing as "stepping back from the day-to-day activities," and buried in the third paragraph of a company press release is an event from a past so remote, it's forgotten already. "You took your time. I've been waiting for your call. Where are you?"

"On a beach, watching the necropsy of a whale."

Without missing a beat, Tony says, "You must be in Pacifica then because a whale's washed ashore there. It's everywhere in the 'Verse. You can watch a real-time feed. But…I haven't seen any posts from you recently." The distraction in his voice implies that he's checking my social feeds while talking to me.

"I've been moving up and down the coast, and connectivity hasn't always been good."

"You've been taking the break seriously." He sounds surprised.

"Isn't this exactly what you asked me to do? Anyway, I don't recall being given any incentives to stay."

If Tony detects the bitterness in my voice, he chooses to ignore it. "Listen, Tashi, I can't say this over the phone. If you're still in Pacifica, I can drive there to meet you in person in 20 minutes."

"You'll drive?"

"Yes. I should debrief you in person."

"I'm only available for the next 40 minutes."

"I don't need much time to detail the problem. You'll need days to think of a solution if one exists at all. I don't know if I should even call it a problem. I don't understand what it is yet."

I hear the whoosh of wind over the phone. "Are you already driving?"

"Yes."

"It smells terrible here, and the necropsy is still underway. I must warn you if you're squeamish not to come," I say, echoing Richard's words.

"There's nobody else I can trust right now, Tashi. It's a can of worms, and you're the only one I know who can deal with a can of worms like this one. You say it stinks? I'm going to park on the street closest to the beach. We'll sit inside my car with the air turned on and the windows rolled up."

Tony isn't wearing contact lenses. Instead, he sees the world through the thick lenses of tortoise-shell framed glasses. His pink and gray checked shirt is rumpled, and the creased shirt tails hang out over gray cargo shorts with frayed hems, though this might be by design. Anyway, he looks like he hasn't been sleeping much.

The smell of rotting durian fruit lingers inside his black BMW convertible, even with the top up and the windows closed. He rubs the bridge of his nose with his index finger and thumb. "It stinks like the can of worms I've opened," he says.

"What have you found?"

"It's what I haven't found that's problematic. A man is missing, Tashi. Or rather, a man has disappeared. In any other circumstances, a case like this would primarily be a police case involving a private detective, a modern-day Sherlock Holmes, who would then proceed to solve the mystery of the disappearing engineer. Did I say he was an engineer? Well, I'm telling you now who he was. Except, and here's the kicker, I'm the one who saw the man disappear, vanish into thin air in front of my eyes.

What complicates the matter is that I can't go to the police with an eyewitness account like this. They wouldn't believe me. I doubt anybody would believe me except you, Tashi. Actually, believe is not the right word. Curious is more accurate. You might be curious to solve this problem because, you see, the engineer disappeared when he was playing Ka World."

The smells of new leather and vomit infiltrate my lungs as I take quick, shallow breaths to modulate my voice, so it sounds normal. "This guy who disappeared, what was his name?"

Tony seems relieved to provide tangible details. "Karthik Pitchai. No, you didn't know him. I hired him six months ago so he could turn Ka World into a gaming platform."

"You went behind my back!"

"I'm sorry, Tashi. Yes, I didn't tell you about it. You can't blame me. You were so resistant to turning Ka World into a game, and I was under tremendous pressure from the board to generate revenue or show explosive growth in daily users. That's why I hired Karthik because he knew how to incorporate game theory into virtual reality worlds. Do you remember the haptic suit you were wearing while playing Ka World before you fell in the elevator?"

I nod. "That was embarrassing. In retrospect, it feels like a fall from grace."

Tony, who's always been selective about the information he needs to hear, filters out my comment. "I bought that haptic suit for Karthik," he says.

"How come I never saw this Karthik around at gAIa?"

"Because he'd come into work after 9 p.m. I didn't tell him to be extra secretive. It was how he was wired to work. Anyway, he succeeded in turning Ka World into a game based on intent. Two weeks ago, he called me back into the office at 10 p.m. to show me how the game worked."

"What exactly is a game based on intent?"

"Think the law of attraction meets virtual reality location tracking. We called it KA World, with the letters K and A capitalized. Eventually, he said, there would be a verb for people playing KA World. KAing. Karthik put a lot of thought into usage patterns. He made Ka World available on a test server and found that the trial version was downloaded 500,000 times in one day, proving that people are hungry for intent-based games. He claimed that playing Ka World turned your thoughts into reality. Have you heard of the Mind Matter interaction theory?"

A shiver runs down my spine. Of course, I've heard of the Mind Matter interaction theory. I'm the one who created an algorithm for this theory and added it to gAIa's code base because Michael used to talk about it all the time. Michael used to say there was a technology waiting to be developed in the 'Verse that could leverage this theory and use it to expand consciousness into other dimensions, other worlds. In my simple-minded way, I created the virtual Ka World based on this theory, but as far as I know, this has never worked. I have not told anyone how or why I created Ka World based on the Mind Matter interaction theory. I feared I'd be made a laughing meme stock in all the universes in the 'Verse. So I'm visibly shaken when Tony brings up this theory and even more so when he admits another engineer intuitively understood this theory as the underlying layer to Ka World. I want to know what the engineer did with this theory without showing much interest.

"Vaguely. It's a dubious theory, uncorroborated as far as I

know. Remind me again, what is it?" I mask my curiosity behind casualness.

"It's a far-fetched theory that posits that human consciousness influences quantum numbers. Karthik believed in this theory and wanted to channel users' intentions to influence random exploration in Ka World. Playing Ka World would allow people to break out of their predetermined reality and influence a random outcome in Ka World with their minds. You might like it if you play it. I could play it with you."

I ignore his offer to get me to play it, but I'm curious as hell. "How would that work in a game?" I ask.

"When you first log in to play Ka World, your avatar appears, and you are told that you can achieve enlightenment by answering a question. Then you get an AI-generated question. The question can be anything. For example, where would you like to go today, or what do you want to do? Now, if you said, in response to the first question, I'd like to go to an underwater canyon in the Bermuda triangle, you would then be prompted to focus your intent on your answer for three deep breaths. I know, this is all timed by AI, but soon you'd be transported to an underwater virtual reality canyon whose coordinates were in the Bermuda triangle."

"Less like a game and more like virtual reality location tracking."

"Don't be so dismissive. Underwater in that canyon, your avatar could die from any number of scenarios, including a lack of oxygen or a shark attack. These scenarios are based on AI algorithms that constantly force you to evaluate your survival strategies. If you survive this reality you created with your answer, you get to move up a level. You would then get another open-ended question, with another reality created based on your answer. Eventually, the goal is to unlock a golden egg, the final reality level after which you'd be enlightened."

Tony ignores the incredulous look on my face and continues talking. "Anyway, that evening, Karthik called me in because he wanted to demonstrate his latest update in the platform code. He told me that the code he introduced into Ka World blurred the line between consciousness and technology. He called it a "thin place," for lack of a better word.

I thought he was being facetious. I told him it's only a virtual reality game, so let's not get grandiose ideas about it. He said, "I'm not joking," and then he wore the haptic suit and logged into Ka World. I heard him say, "I want to disappear." I remember bringing my hand to my mouth to stifle a laugh at his pretentiousness, but my mouth hung open in shock because Karthik had disappeared in front of my eyes. A moment before, he was standing in front of me, and a moment later, he had vanished into thin air. I couldn't believe my eyes. I had goosebumps all over and chills down my spine. Then I thought that this was a trick and that Karthik and a few other engineers were in on it, and they were playing a joke on me, and they would all come out now laughing. No such thing happened. That evening, there were a few other people inside the office working on a different floor. I asked each of them if they had seen Karthik, and some said they had seen him come in but hadn't seen him afterward. I searched for him for hours inside the building but could not find him. I even tried logging into Ka World with a backup haptic suit in desperation. I said, "I want to disappear," in response to a question that asked me where I wanted to go, but I only ended up inside the panoramic expanse of a desert. After I logged out, I thought that the incident with Karthik had never really happened. I figured I'd made it all up because I was so stressed over getting Ka World to function without any software defects or that I had played Ka World a lot, which messed with my head. I went home thinking that Karthik would turn up the next morning.

Two days passed, and there was no sign of Karthik. Then, on the third day, his girlfriend contacted the office. She said she hadn't seen him since that night when I had seen him disappear, he had not come home in the morning, and she had contacted everyone who knew him, and now she was worried. Security called the police, and they came to the office and talked to everyone who had seen Karthik that night, including me. I answered truthfully that the last time I had seen him was when he was playing Ka World. Even the haptic suit was missing. They checked the badge swipes for everyone who entered and left the building and found out that the only person who had never left was Karthik. Then they said that he might have taken the haptic suit and exited from a window on the first floor that did not have a security camera. He might have staged his disappearance. But they could not establish a motive because the evidence was inconclusive. Therefore, this investigation was going to remain an open missing person case. But I know what I saw, Tashi. On the one hand, I don't want to believe it because it is simply not possible. On the other hand, Ka World may have evolved beyond our wildest imagination."

Rage washes over me like a cresting wave, pulling me out with no tether to land. I hit the dashboard with the palm of my hand to ground myself. "What exactly were your intentions? I told you I didn't want you to turn Ka World into a game. This is such a new technology, and we know it messes with the brain. That's the reason why I wanted to keep the code open source. I wanted people to figure out how to use it. I wanted the debate and ethical thought around its usage. It's all I ever post about online when I talk about gAIa. And what you've gone and done is worse than a can of worms, Tony. Move fast. Break things. That's the worst mantra in our culture to live by, but you love it. You abide by it. Well, a man has disappeared. You don't know how. You don't know where. And now, there is yet another technological platform that has grown beyond our control. Let's avoid repeating the same old mistakes. So bring it down. Bring down the entire platform that supports Ka World."

Tony's eyes blink rapidly behind the thick lenses. He says, "I can't. That night before Karthik disappeared, he had also pushed his code update live, and since then, Ka World has been downloaded 2.3 million times. We're finally showing an explosion in the number of daily users. We're talking about a $6.5 billion IPO next month. I'm going to be a billionaire, and you, Tashi, will be worth $700 million at least. You can't seriously expect me to say no to that."

"You can't possibly be worth more than me. We have almost the same number of shares."

"You lost almost a quarter of yours when you walked out. Chose to walk out. And let's just say that facilitated a different arrangement."

The fury must show on my face when I say, "It stinks in here." I get out of the car and slam the door shut.

Tony rolls down the window. He says, "Stay angry for a while because I know that's how you process things. But you can't stop the inevitable. I come to you as a friend."

"You will always have enough money, Tony. Bring down Ka World," I implore him.

"You know I can't do that."

"Can't or won't?"

"I know you're angry right now, but I also know you believe the strange tale I've told you. At least I feel better having told you. I didn't know who else to turn to."

A waft of wind carries the briny smell of the ocean with the hint of something rotting underneath.

I say, "I'll be in touch." Walking away from the car feels like walking away from gAIa, from my own creation that I no longer recognize. Something inside my gut flutters, rising upward, bringing a feeling of expansiveness and fear. If that guy Karthik disappeared into Ka World, then perhaps I, too, could disappear into Ka that Michael talked about. Are they the same worlds or two different worlds entirely? It didn't happen to Tony when he tried it, though I wish he was the one who had disappeared. Why does it happen for some people and not others? As usual, I realize there are always too many questions with too few answers.

Tony calls out. "I can see you're intrigued. That's good. It means you're thinking about the case of the disappearing engineer."

I turn back, still angry with Tony for going behind my back, for cheating me out of my shares of gAIa. I say, "I've never had to care about money, but I certainly care about principles."

"I know. I wish there was a better way to resolve disagreements between founders. At least be in touch if you think of something. Please," Tony begs.

"I might need to borrow that extra haptic suit. Can you have it delivered to an address?" I ask, giving him Richard's address. I wait till he adds it to his smartphone.

There is palpable relief in Tony's voice as he finishes typing in the address on his phone and says, "Of course, anytime."

12

Richard says, "From the whale's belly, a rich harvest of human detritus." He points one accusatory finger at a black tub overflowing with trash that looks like dried brown seaweed piled high.

"She was starving?"

"Seems likely. We found 22 pounds of trash in her stomach. The final blow was probably an accidental strike from the hull of a cargo ship because her befuddled brain mistook one leviathan for another." Richard looks out at the storm on the horizon as he contemplates the whale's macabre ending. "Anyway," he says, turning sideways to counter the wind gusts, "can you also make a copy of the inventory before we haul this tub to my pickup? I want to try to reuse everything we've found." Richard walks over to talk to two marine researchers, presumably to ask them if it's okay to haul the entire tub away.

I lean over the lip of the tub. There's a hodgepodge of things in there. Beside the tub, on the sand, lies a clipboard with a sheet of grid paper enclosed in a plastic sheet. I read it closely.

Things Found Inside The Whale's Stomach

1. Greenhouse plastic sheeting
2. Two dozen plastic bags
3. Nine feet of nylon rope
4. Two long cut pieces of garden hose
5. Three plastic flower pots
6. One plastic spray canister
7. Multiple pieces of fishing nets
8. Blue plastic box with two cartoon green crocodiles
    on the lid

Number 8 is the curiosity I most want to see, but I have to wait for Richard to finish talking and come over to help me haul the tub away. Richard comes back. "They've finished photographing and cataloging everything, so we get to take this tub now. I'll lift here, and you lift that end. Ready? Let's bring this stuff home," he says.

At this time of year in the Santa Cruz mountains, night comes quickly without the interlude of twilight. I turn the car's headlights off after rolling to a stop behind Richard's truck on the flattened earth in front of his house. There is a chill in the air and a fresh sprinkle of rain on the ground.

Richard left the porch light on so a yellow glow encases the front door, enough to make out vague shapes in the darkness engulfing the house. I hear Ollie's excited barking pick up as a stooped Richard slowly shuffles up the stairs.

"We need to see what we brought back," I remind him.

He says, "I have to let the dog out. Can you leave everything in the truck? I'll drive it to the studio in the morning."

I hear the protesting creaks of the swollen door as it opens. Ollie's yelps and barking increase in intensity when he greets his master before being set loose to run outside. He gives me a few quick sniffs before running around the side of the house.

Since I first saw the blue plastic box with the tessellated crocodiles on the lid, I've become obsessed with finding out what's inside it. The crocodile motif is another clue that I feel I must follow to unravel the mystery of Michael's disappearance. So, ignoring Richard's appeal to let things be, I climb into the back of his pickup and shine my phone's flashlight into the tub. I can see the box underneath the section of the garden hose. I had placed it there for easy retrieval.

I hear Richard whistling for his dog to come back into the house. He leans against the door, whistles again, and shouts in his raspy voice, "Ollie! Ollie!"

"There is something important here that can't wait till the morning," I call out before Richard turns to go.

Richard seems taken aback to find me rummaging in the back of his truck, but he shrugs his shoulders. "I suppose you should bring it inside then. Whatever is so important, it can't wait till morning," he says and whistles again. This time, Ollie reappears and bounds up the stairs, and Richard coaxes him back inside.

I extricate the box from underneath the hose and climb down from the truck. The weight of the box rests on my palms. The box feels light, but it must contain something inside to give it this mass. So it seems fitting that I carry it like an offering, accompanied by the chirring of insects, into the house.

I expect the box to carry the stench of rotting durian fruit, but it offers the briny scent of the ocean instead. The ugly scent may be masked by the aroma of tomato soup bubbling in a saucepan on the stove or the wholesome fragrance of buttered sourdough sizzling on a cast iron skillet that Richard has set on a slow heat.

Richard insists we eat first, so I walk across the kitchen and place the box on the windowsill. I'm not impatient. Having waited this long to open the box, I'm willing to wait a bit longer. Maybe I'm stalling now because I don't want to be disappointed after getting my hopes up.

We eat in silence. It's been a long day, and we're both tired. When I stand up to clear the table after dinner, waves of tiredness wash over my body, and I think how nice it will be to have a hot shower and crawl inside my sleeping bag. But I'm drawn to the mysterious box, and I know I won't be able to sleep until I've discovered what it contains.

I say, "We're both tired, and I know you want me to go back to the cottage and leave you alone, but I want you to open the box. I need to see what's inside. I won't sleep until I do."

I bring the box from the windowsill and place it on the table in front of Richard. He reaches for the red-framed glasses resting atop his head, puts them on, and says, "Okay. Let's have a look at the object of your fascination."

I say, "See the tessellated crocodiles on the lid? I think it's the same motif repeating itself as a clue. You can call it a coincidence, but I feel this might be another clue that Michael is putting out in my world for me to see and feel something. Maybe. Possibly." I shrug because I am too tired to articulate this deep desire to reconnect with Michael. I know that I'm willing to try anything, including grasping at straws.

Richard peers at the tessellated crocodiles on the box's lid. He says, "Of course, any object can have an emotional pull. In my view, that is an idea worth exploring." He picks at the two tiny plastic clasps with his thumbnail and pops open the sealed box.

~

The rubber gasket around the inside of the lid is a tight waterproof seal. Out of an abundance of caution, the contents are taped inside a clear plastic bag. Richard picks at the tape, but it doesn't give, so he rips through the plastic and extracts the contents, spreading them out in a row on the table. There is a small black notebook, a plastic ballpoint pen, a gray metal dog tag, a round magnet with a picture of a humpback whale, and a postcard with printed words in the offset spacing of a piece of poetry or verse.

Richard rifles through the notebook. He says, "It's a list of names and dates written by different people. Take a look." He hands the notebook to me.

I know from glancing at the first page what this book is. I've seen such notebooks before and even helped Nachiket make similar entries in the notebooks he found.

I say, "We've found a geocache."

Richard's face betrays the question, so I have to explain it to him. "Geocaching is an activity that some people really love to do. It's like treasure hunting outdoors. The participants hide and seek containers, most containers are tiny, but some are mid-sized like this. Anyway, it's all done using a GPS receiver or a GPS-enabled mobile phone," I say. I quickly pick up the logbook and flip through the pages before putting it down again. I point to each item, so I can tell Richard what each item means. I say, "This is a logbook that lists the names of those who found the geocache and the date when they found it, and the ballpoint pen is for writing down the entries. This metal dog tag is most likely what geocachers call a trackable. It's a game piece with a unique tracking code that lets you track on a metasite, this object's movements anywhere on Earth. And, this magnet here could be a signature item, a geocacher's way of saying I was here. Interesting that it has a picture of a humpback whale on it. Hmmm. I'm not sure about this postcard. It might be a collectible or a signature item."

I slide the postcard around to read the words better. They read like a rhyme.

The flowers no one wants are weeds
speckled yellow in a sea of green
If they were all together in a sea of yellow
think how beautiful they will seem

∼

I flip the postcard over, expecting to see a meadow of flowers. Instead, there are goosebumps on my arms. It's a good thing I'm wearing long sleeves. Richard doesn't know the sense of hope and the dread I feel as I see the picture of a rusted wrought iron gate with the letters K and A clearly visible in the trelliswork, but he can read the stupefied expression on my face. He slides the postcard with an index finger toward him, peers at the picture for a while, and says in perfect concert with what I'm thinking, "That must blow your mind. I suppose you should look in the logbook again. If you think this geocache was found by your friend Michael, it must have his name there."

He's right. There, as the last logbook entry, written in the slanting cursive that is so familiar, is the name Michael Hayes and the date. An involuntary cry escapes from my mouth, and I manage to say in a strangled voice, "It's the date that Michael disappeared." My hands tremble as I snap the book shut.

I'm not sure how I missed seeing Michael's name the first time. Perhaps I was glancing at everything too quickly. Now, I'm reminded of Nachiket, who kept insisting that I should notice things other people missed when he took us geocaching, but I was too busy noticing Michael and being pulled into his orbit instead of paying attention to finding hidden containers.

As Richard picks up the logbook to verify for himself, I slide the postcard toward me again. The strong feeling that this postcard has Michael's fingertips all over it makes me run my fingers over it. I trace the outlines of the letters K and A, imagining my fingertips touching Michael's, and then I'm filled with hope and dread again. Hope because I've found a clue that can lead me to Michael and which resonates so strongly with me. Dread because I'm stymied again, not knowing how to follow where this clue leads.

Richard places his gnarled fingers over mine, stopping my tracing. He means it as a kind gesture, and his raspy voice sounds like the calm voice of reason. He says, "We all have an innate desire to find explanations for the inexplicable. Perhaps you should gather what you've found and find your three other old friends. Maybe this group will have the answers you're seeking. In my experience, grief can rip people apart, but given time, reconnections can happen over a shared loss. From what you've told me, I would think enough time has passed."

I nod because I know I can't get very far based on the clues Michael is putting out into my world. I need help. Maybe the answers lie with Nachiket, Ash, and Ember. Maybe I need to start with why they stopped answering my emails or phone calls the week after Michael died. I was so hurt by their betrayal that I never sought them out. But perhaps Richard is right. Too much time *has* passed. After all, it has been a decade since Michael disappeared, so perhaps I could make the old reconnections and seek some answers now. If this geocache is a clue leading me to Michael, then the best person to solve its mysteries would naturally be my old geocaching friend, Nachiket.

I thank Richard for letting me stay late. Then ask if I can keep the box and its contents. I say, "I'd like to show this to someone."

Richard ponders this for a while. Then he says, "Go ahead. I'm also interested now in all these odd coincidences. I'm open to thinking of them as clues. It would be good to tie them together and solve the mystery of your friend's disappearance. But you should plan on bringing these items back. They really belong to the Marine Mammal Center, and I need to find a way to add these to my sculpture since these are now officially part of the commission."

As I gather the contents and put them back into the box, I reassure Richard that I'll bring everything back. Then, I carry the box outside, stumbling a bit in the dark, till I reach the cottage and switch on the light.

13

At night I dream of Michael again. In my dream, I stand on a narrow path flanked by rolling fog that covers the sides and the end of the path. Then, in a wispy clearing of the mist ahead, I see a faint silhouette of a man. The curtain of fog parts suddenly and reveals bright sunlight. As I squint into the intense glare, the figure turns toward me, and my heart registers the unmistaken piercing gaze of his green eyes. I cry out, "Michael!" It takes me another moment to realize that the golden glow surrounding him is because of a hill that rises behind, every inch of which is covered by yellow-flowered weeds. "Dandelions," I gasp. Michael bends down to pick something at his feet. It is a dandelion turned into a puffy white ball. He blows at it five times till all the seeds float away. I run toward him, but the fog closes in and blanks out the hill, the dandelions, and Michael.

When I'm jolted awake from my dream by a loud pop, I'm befuddled to find myself lying in the sleeping bag on the bed inside the cottage. My mind is still reaching out for Michael when I hear another loud popping noise shake the remnants of my dream into wakeful action. I unzip the sleeping bag and jump out of bed as another popping noise comes from the roof above. I stick my feet into my sneakers and grab my jacket, shrugging into it as I open the door and step out into the chilly early morning. Above the cottage's roof is the expansive spread of a gnarled California oak. A surging breeze shakes the tree, and the oak drops a few acorns that clatter on the roof like popping corn. Mystery solved! I retreat inside, shutting the door to keep the chilly air out. I sit on the edge of the bed, not bothering today with routines such as rolling up the sleeping bag or taking a shower. If only mysteries were this easy to solve, I think. Of course, now my mind is drawn to the many unexplainable mysteries that I'm nowhere close to solving. The mystery of Michael's disappearance and the subsequent mystery of my broken friendships, or the recent mystery of the disappearing engineer at gAIa. I sense that these mysteries are all connected somehow. Yet, without resorting to wild leaps of imagination, I cannot solve any of them in good conscience.

My phone emits a ping. It is a long-winded text from Tony again.

They're calling Karthik Pitchai's disappearance a suicide. They say there are a million ways to disappear, jumping into the middle of the Pacific for one. It would be hard to find a body there. They're basing it on the improbable theory proposed by this Times reporter that playing KA World can cause people to experience dissociative brain states. This reporter suggests that Karthik might have been in such a state, possibly suicidal, when he disappeared. You know how this will play. It's a clickbait story that will balloon into something far bigger and worse.

Then, 20 seconds later, comes another text from him.

You can fix this. Find out what happened and what's really going on? What should I do?

Annoyance makes me type this reply.

I don't know.

Then, Tony types a plea disguised as a thinly veiled threat.

Please Tashi. I'm here to help you figure this out. But you're the one who designed this world. You're the creator. It has your fingerprints all over it. So don't be surprised when you get a call from that hard-nosed Times reporter. After all, he's only doing his job when he follows the trails leading to you.

I decide there isn't anything more I want to say to Tony. Anger makes me clench my fists till my nails dig into my palms. Of course, Tony would kick the can of worms down the road to the co-founder and creator, who left in a huff. What better person than me to take the brunt of the blame?

I walk into the room that contains the Daybreak paintings. I don't turn them around to face me, but I notice again how the artist left them unsigned. What makes a creator create something monumental and not put her name on it? Is it a lack of ego or something more transcendental? I decide to go with the former and set my ego aside. I pull out my smartphone and search for all the Nachiket Pandeys interested in geocaching.

There are too many Nachiket Pandeys who are interested in geocaching, but none of these is my friend from high school. Their pictures don't match. Then, buried in the middle of page three of the search results, a line of text leaps out at me. Between the highlighted search terms "Nachiket Pandey" and "geocaching" are the words "wildlife biologist." The thread of a connection floats in my head. It brings up a memory of the shaman in Peru, the one who called himself Don Itzal, who told fortunes from sugar candies. He had prophesied from the picture of a red fox on Nachiket's candy that Nachiket would become someone who loved animals and took care of nature. The same shaman had prophesied that I would be good at computer work. Perhaps there is an element of truth to his predictions, given that I've spent the last decade glued to a computer screen. I click on the search result that now carries the possibility of being related to my old friend, and when it opens in a new tab, I find I am not wrong.

~

It's a blog post for the California Department of Fish and Wildlife featuring an interview with "Nachiket Pandey, the wildlife biologist whose interest in researching the endangered Sierra Nevada red fox originated from his love of geocaching."

Has to be him, I think, as I read on with growing excitement.

There is no picture of him. Instead, there are two cute pictures of a slender, bushy-tailed red fox, one juxtaposed against a snow-covered tree line and another on the craggy granite cliffs that the caption says are in the Klamath mountains. Under the heading "How I Became a Wildlife Biologist," I read the following lines.

"When I was in high school, I always looked for chances to escape to the wilderness. I was very interested in geocaching and loved searching for hidden geocaches. I had a knack for seeing things most people miss. One day, I thought I glimpsed a red fox following me as I crept across rocky crevices near Manzanita Lake in Lassen Volcanic Park. I was searching for a geocache hidden there, but once I spotted this animal, I started searching for it instead. I had heard about the Sierra Nevada red foxes and knew they were endangered, although there had been few sightings. I must have been lucky to see it that day. I was drawn to learning more about this animal and how species like these put our own into context. I wanted to know how our two species could coexist again without one endangering the other. I decided that day to change my major from engineering, and I got a Bachelor of Science in Wildlife Management and later a Master of Science in Forestry. I've always appreciated the chance to do my work outdoors and research one of the rarest and elusive animals in the Sierra Nevada."

The pieces of the puzzle begin to fall into place. In the BMD era, I knew Nachiket was accepted to engineering school at MIT. This career change is extraordinary, but I have a sneaky suspicion that Don Itzal's sugar candy confection featuring a red fox and the subsequent prophesy by the shaman might have triggered the switch. I want to ask Nachiket if I'm right, but first, I need to find out how to reach him. Of course, there is no official address in the blog since listing this would have been inappropriate. I'm not sure I should bother sending Nachiket an email, given that he never replied to any of my emails or texts from the last decade. Then, I read something that catches my attention. "Pandey is with CDFW's Northern Region. Based out of Redding, he covers the Sierra Nevada red fox program for the Shasta and Trinity counties."

I know how to find him.

I leave at daybreak when the first pearly light washes over the trees and reveals the ridgeline behind the cottage. I recognize the translucent gray hues from Daybreak 1, the first painting that Richard's wife painted in the cottage. She must have been an early riser to capture this unearthly light. I know Richard to be an early riser too, so I won't risk going up the stairs to leave a note on the porch. I don't want Ollie's excited barks to break the early morning silence, this small window of time before the birds and animals have begun to stir. So I write a note on a yellow post-it and stick it on the windshield of Richard's truck, leaving the wiper across the note so it won't blow away.

I review what I've scrawled to make sure it's legible:

Gone for a few days
Keeping keys to cottage
Found an old friend

As an afterthought, I write my phone number in case Richard wants to reach me, and then I get into the Beetle and buckle my seatbelt. There are far too many clues that Michael has put out into my world for me to see. It's like a bread trail leading me first to Richard, then to Nachiket. "The time for secrets is over," I mutter under my breath as I punch in the directions on my smartphone to the California Department of Fish and Wildlife's office in the town of Redding in Shasta County. I can hear Ollie bark as I pull away from the driveway to turn on the road leading me on my quest.

14

———

Nachiket agrees to meet me at a restaurant close to his place of work. Our meeting seems so easy, almost prescient in its timing, even though I have contrived it. On the drive to Redding, I called the CDFW office and asked for Nachiket Pandey. I didn't expect the lady who answered my call would connect me right away to an extension or that I'd hear a familiar voice answer, "Tashi? Luckily you found me when I was in the field office. Although, I was hoping you'd find me sooner!"

Can it be that after all these years, it is really this easy to pick up where we left off?

Redding, located near the foothills of the Cascade and Klamath mountain ranges, is a city slowly sprawling outwards. We're supposed to meet at a restaurant for an early dinner. It's one of those Italian chain restaurants that serve American staple fares such as cheeseburgers, French fries, soups, sandwiches, and pasta. After being spoiled by Richard's home-cooked meals, I find it hard to appreciate the heaps of food on plates set before the diners. Maybe the tight knot in my

107

stomach makes it hard to work up an appetite. I order a beer instead of an appetizer while waiting for Nachiket to arrive. I'm fifteen minutes early and was half hoping Nachiket would be here too. He isn't. He was always a stickler for being on time, and I think he might not have changed in that regard. So, now I wait, sipping my beer, sitting alone at the table with my eyes peeled on the door.

After all these years of waiting, I can finally ask why he and the others abandoned me after Michael disappeared. As my body registers the cold fizz of the bitter-sweet ale in that first sip, I'm stunned at how easy it might be to get an answer and shocked that the question can be asked in the first place.

Nachiket walks in at the exact time he's supposed to. He doesn't wait for the hostess to arrive back at her station but strides inside like all those times when he would hurry to meet our group gathered together under the cherry tree behind the cafeteria when school let out. I think Nachiket has aged well in the last decade. I have forgotten how tall he is, but he is no longer skinny. His shoulders and waist have filled out in a muscular way. His face is no longer gaunt but filled with a lush hipster beard. The unruly hair that used to fly about in the wind is pulled back into a slick man bun showing the faint traces of a receding hairline. He wears a long-sleeved gray shirt tucked into green hiking pants, looking like someone who spends most of his time outdoors. The blog post correctly captured this image of him, I think, as he scoots the chair away from the table. Without skipping a beat, he plops in the chair in front of me and says, "My god, Tashi, I sure wish you'd come sooner. It's too late now to fix anything."

I laugh in shock at this proclamation. Beer spittle flies into his face, but I don't care. He swipes a hand across his beard, and I say, "It took me years to build up the courage to meet you in person, knowing that *none* of you ever bothered to return my phone calls, texts, or emails. And now I'm here, and you agreed to meet me, and this, *this,* is what you have to tell me? That I'm too late? I was so stupid to come here." I stand up, and my sudden movement causes the table to shake. The beer bottle topples sideways, spilling its brown liquid over the white tablecloth. Nachiket reaches to steady it as people sitting across from us shoot worried glances in our direction. I am almost past his chair, barreling toward the door, when he tugs my arm from behind and makes me walk back to him again. He doesn't loosen his grip on my arm and says, "Sit down, good fortune. I'm sorry I started it this way. Will you sit down, please?"

I stand motionless. Weirdly, Nachiket's voice sounds so familiar yet new. It reminds me of when Michael held my arm to sit me down in front of the fire and tell me about Ka. Perhaps that memory of Michael holding my arm and saying, "Sit down, good fortune," makes me twist my arm out of Nachiket's grip and sit in the chair facing him.

❧

I say, "I want to know, of course. How could I not after spending all these years thinking about why you all abandoned me after Michael disappeared? It messed me up."

Nachiket gets up and steps toward me to bend down, drawing me into a bear hug of an embrace while I'm still seated. He says, "I am sorry, Tashi. I am sorry it had to be you. I want to tell you the whole story. I do." He untangles his limbs from the embrace and, at that moment, looks as gangly and unsure as he once was.

He sits back in the chair, sighs, and says, "It's best to ease into it. The story, I mean. I've kept it together for so long. It was an oath, a vow, or whatever crazy thing we called it back then. I don't know why I went along with that stupid childish vow for so long. Over the years, I tricked myself into forgetting about it. But something changed last week, and I wish I had never made that stupid promise. Maybe I could have prevented it from happening. I'm sorry. Please give me a moment to collect my thoughts, so I can know where to start."

He looks lost and a little scared. I am still angry, but I can tell this meeting is hard for him too.

He says, "It's so good to see you. I've missed you. I have. You look good, Tashi. So… put together." He makes circular gestures with both his hands. "I've followed your rise, how you built gAIa, how famous you are in certain circles. You were always the one I knew who was the go-getter of the group, someone who would do big things! There was never any doubt."

I can sense that he is still figuring out how to tell the story. I'm impatient, but it also feels like a relief to talk to someone with whom I no longer have to pretend. So I go along with the easy feeling. I tell him how surprised I am to hear this because of the way he has steadfastly avoided me till now. I also don't recall ever feeling like I truly belonged when I was a part of the group. I tell him how it felt like I was always hovering around the edges, always trying to fit in when everyone else was more intelligent and interesting than me.

He shakes his head in disbelief, gives me a wry smile, and then says none of the others felt this way about me. He says, "I have to tell you, hugging you now felt like wearing an old sweater again! Although you smell different. Kinda sweet and fruity, yet sophisticated. You also no longer bite your nails. Look at that manicure! But when I hugged you, it felt like my old friend was back hanging out with me again. I've missed that connection with you and the rest of our group. It was a strong bond. Crazy what we had. I've never been able to explain it to other people."

I say, "Old sweater! You smell like mothballs."

He says, "What are you, thirteen?" With that, the tension breaks. We can laugh together.

He decides on something for us because the waiter has come twice to find out if we're ready to order. First, he asks me if I have any new allergies. When I shake my head, he says he is trying to be vegan now and checks if that's okay with me. I shrug and say, "Whatever." It does feel like old times. He always liked trying fad diets and bold, adventurous foods, dragging us to Japantown and Chinatown in San Francisco to try new cuisines while also geocaching in the area.

When the waiter leaves, I say, "Go on, tell me why you stopped talking to me."

Nachiket says, "It was Ash. He didn't want the three of us talking to you anymore."

I'm sure my face shows my bewilderment. I think aloud. "Ash? I never thought it would be Ash." I remember the last email that Ember sent me with the cryptic message, *"You're the influencer who needs influencing."*

"There were times when I thought it might have been Ember but never Ash," I say.

It's Nachiket's turn to feel bewildered. "Ember? No, she was on your side. Terribly conflicted about it, but it was necessary. It had to be done with surgical precision, and Ember and I did it at the time."

Nachiket waits for his admission to sink in. So, I nod for him to continue because I don't trust myself to speak.

He continues talking. "What you didn't know about Ash was that he had always had suicidal tendencies. As far as I know, this started in the middle of sixth grade. It might have been even earlier, but I wasn't aware of it until sixth grade. This was something that Michael, Ember, and I knew about, but we never spoke about it. Maybe that's why it felt like we kept secrets from you. We all liked you, and you were a close part of the group, but you weren't there with us in middle school. Also, somehow, Michael never brought it up, and of course, we all took our cues from Michael, so none of us ever mentioned it to you. I doubt Ash would have mentioned it on his own because it was a touchy subject with him and his parents involving years of therapy. By the time we entered high school, we had all forgotten about Ash's struggle because he was doing great and keeping well. Then you came into our group like a breath of fresh air, and the more pressing topics of conversation then shifted to Michael. Because it was

Michael now who had started experiencing digital vertigo and all those headaches connected to it. And simultaneously, he had started going in and out of Ka, which fascinated all of us."

"Wait!" I interrupt him while thinking this is how Ollie, the dog, must feel at the first scent of a bone. This is how it is with me at the mention of Michael's name. I have to latch on to it.

I say, "I didn't know Michael had so many headaches or that he experienced digital vertigo so often. I thought digital vertigo had stopped because he had started entering Ka."

"No, the headaches were always there. It was digital vertigo that preceded the entry into Ka. Didn't he say you had to have two things to enter Ka? First, you had to experience digital vertigo, and then you also had to simultaneously be in a thin place?" He looks at me for confirmation as if he doubts his version of the story.

What it feels like to me is two people swapping their own versions of the same story. I say, "I thought there was also another thing. You also had to be *invited* to enter Ka. I recall that none of us except Michael ever received the invitation to enter Ka. In my case, I'd never even witnessed Michael enter Ka, which somehow you, Ember, and Ash, had all seen him do numerous times. I don't know why I never saw it."

Nachiket thinks about this for a moment. "I wonder about that too. In the years we stopped talking to you, I wondered why you never saw Michael enter and exit from Ka. It made me think a lot about what it is that we had really seen. Did we all really see him disappear, or was it a mass hallucination because we were so desperate to believe in Ka? On the one hand, we were young, impressionable, and idealistic, which would explain everything. But, on the other hand, was there something in the suggestive power of our collective minds that made us see something that wasn't there? Or was it you who saw reality the way it was supposed to be seen? I don't deny we experienced something. But exactly what we all experienced together, I'm not so sure. But what I do know, we sure were an impressionable bunch!"

He stops talking because the waiter brings out plates of food. I find I have little appetite. Neither does Nachiket, who spreads his long bony fingers on both sides of his vegan pasta bowl and tries hard to read the expression on my face.

"Bon appétit," the waiter says and leaves.

I want to say that this is silly behind the waiter's back. You should have said "Buon appetito" instead, but then I think I'm being ridiculous because I have better things to be nitpicky about. It also doesn't make sense to keep talking about Michael's entry and exit from Ka since we are each looking at what we saw or did not see through our own lens.

I nudge Nachiket back to the present. "What does this have to do with Ash? Why did he tell you to stop talking to me?" I ask.

Nachiket startles from his reverie. He says, "After Michael disappeared, thoughts of suicide came back for Ash, stronger than ever. It worried his parents and therapist so much that they reached out to us for help the day we learned that Michael had disappeared. They didn't want to embarrass or involve you or your parents, even though Ash was bringing up your name because they knew what Ash was saying to them was impossible. Ash said that you, Tashi, were the one who had made Michael disappear, that you'd forced his hand this time because you so badly wanted to see him enter and exit from Ka. You had badgered the group a zillion times about not being able to see Michael's comings and goings from Ka for yourself. So, in Ash's mind, Michael had tried to force himself to go to Ka instead of being invited to enter Ka, and now Michael was stuck inside Ka and could not get out. So he blamed you squarely, Tashi, for Michael's disappearance. Then Ash told everyone he would kill himself if we ever talked to you again. There was no doubt in our minds that he would do it."

My face must be stupefied as I sit there listening because

Nachiket elaborates. "Of course, his parents didn't know what he was talking about, and they didn't know what Ka was, but they were right to be worried that he was having a mental breakdown. While Ash was kept under close observation at home, Ember had an emergency meeting with me. She said that Ash was fragile and you were strong. We had to make a choice. Ash needed our help to survive, while you, Tashi, could survive on your own. You would survive this. The only way this could be done, and I'm repeating Ember's words here, would be with a 'clean surgical strike.' We stopped talking to you the day after Michael's empty casket was lowered into the ground. I remember telling Ember that you'd come around one day seeking answers, and she said we'd deal with how to tell you when you came to one of us."

This knowledge, the now-solved mystery of why my friends stopped talking to me, shifts weight in my heart. It is a relief to finally get an answer. I take a deep breath, and the feeling stays with me. I should be angry, but I'm not. Maybe if Ash had chosen someone else to blame, I'd have done the same thing. It's always better to join the crowd than go it alone. Instead, I feel sorry for Ash. I thought he was so brave and strong when he plunged his EpiPen needle into his thigh at the school lunch table because he had accidentally brushed against a peanut. I looked on in awe, knowing I could never have done so myself. I remember his brown hair falling over his arm as he stabbed himself and the carefree laugh that followed when he extracted the needle with a yelp. I thought he was someone who would always choose to live life on his own terms. A worry flits across my mind. I ask, "Where is Ash now? What made you change your mind to talk to me?"

I'm surprised to see Nachiket's eyes well up with tears. He says, "That's why, Tashi, I said it was too late. He killed himself a week ago. He left behind a suicide note, an email, saying he had lost the will to live."

I find myself mouthing, "How did he die?"

I'm hoping he disappeared like Michael or that engineer

Karthik, somewhere into another world from a thin space. For it would be a consolation to know that somewhere in some plane of existence, Ash was, in a sense, alive.

As if anticipating this thought, Nachiket talks faster to dispel it. "I thought at first he too might have disappeared as Michael did. But no. He hung himself in his apartment and sent out a time-scheduled email alerting us, so there was never any doubt of finding his body."

~

There is nothing to say. There are too many things to say. Words are hard to come by. So we sit in silence, our meals untouched and uneaten.

Nachiket breaks the impasse. He says, "In retrospect, I chose a bad place for our first meeting. I should have met you outdoors instead of at this restaurant. Some things should be said in a more…sensitive environment. But I was so relieved and excited to finally meet you that I wanted to find the quickest place to meet."

I nod, still not trusting myself to speak. It's evident that after all this sharing of secrets, neither of us has any appetite.

Nachiket says, "Let's go." He leaves a wad of cash on the table, enough to cover our meals, and a generous tip for the waiter who arrives wringing his hands over our untouched meals. Nachiket placates him, says the problem isn't the food, and exits before the dumbfounded waiter can pursue the matter.

I think it's odd that Nachiket, who extolled the virtues of smartphone payment systems because they made life so much easier, of all people, would decide to use old-fashioned paper money. I no longer carry cash because the world has moved on to more innovative and easier ways to pay. I wonder what made Nachiket revert to being a hold-out Luddite. Perhaps he, like Richard, must have his reasons to avoid partaking in such technology.

I follow Nachiket outside to the parking lot. He walks to the far end, where his dust-splattered jeep is parked. It is covered with fine dust, coating it in a gray patina so I cannot make out its original color. Is it dark blue or light gray?

There's an orange haze in the sky because of the enormous wildfires burning in Oregon. Yet, the air here is breathable, and the wan light reflecting down on the asphalt masks the chill that will settle by late evening. I think how far removed this terrain is from the craggy cliffs that the Sierra Nevada red fox considers its habitat, based on the blog post interview with Nachiket I read online. I'm shocked that I say this aloud. My voice sounds strange, and I think it's easier to talk about something other than Ash. Thinking about Ash is one thing, but to express these thoughts aloud is another matter entirely. I doubt the rapid-fire synapses in my brain will produce enough energy to ask aloud, let alone answer the questions. "How do you talk about the death of an old friend? How do you know how his death affects you when you no longer know if he was your friend or enemy? Did you really know him at all, even when you felt you were so close and thought you were in on each other's deepest secrets?"

A wave of emotions washes over me. Earlier, I was angry about not knowing why my friends had stopped talking to me. Later, I felt relief because I finally had an answer. Now, I feel grief. A leaden weight rests on my chest, threatening to submerge me under this emotional flood, a feeling akin to drowning before the shock of the last deep gasp of air.

My sudden sharp breath shakes Nachiket out of wherever his thoughts have taken him.

He says, "I keep wondering if I should have broken the promise and told you earlier, would it at least have made you less miserable? Maybe it would have made a difference, or maybe it would have made no difference at all. I believe my not telling you contributed to Ash being stable and alive all these years. But then I think that it doesn't matter anyway because neither Ember nor I could have prevented this tragedy from happening. Ember was always in touch with Ash and was taken completely unawares by his sudden death."

I tell him, "Thank you for telling me."

He runs a hand over his face as if putting the past behind him. Then, he says, "You are correct about the Sierra Nevada red fox living in rugged terrain. I found a fox den deep inside a craggy granite cliff in the Klamath mountains. My team was able to position a camera there. It's a female with a litter of five cubs. They're in the safe zone from the wildfires for now. Hopefully, it stays that way. Would you like to watch the live feed? You can watch it at my house. If you follow me in your car, I'll show you where I live. Then, we can talk some more at my place. We have years to catch up on, and I can order some pizza for a late dinner. We'll probably be hungry by then."

He is extending the live fox-watching feed as a peace offering while searching the expression on my face. He's right about the years of catching up we need to do. I doubt we'd cover everything in one evening. There will be wide gaps, but the main pieces of our lives, like my quest to follow the clues that are leading me to Michael, like the geocache in my backpack that I need Nachiket to see, are the things significant enough to encompass the story of the last decade of our lives.

15

———

Driving in the Beetle following behind Nachiket's dust-splattered jeep, I think about the dark crevices of Ash's mind that he hid from me so well. How much of the world do we remake within our minds by firing specific neurons repeatedly, which become neural pathways creating a representational view of the world over time? My neural pathways have been etching synaptic maps, building on the clues leading toward Michael's final destination, Ka. It is an obsession made stronger by thinking. I know I am guilty of this. What made Ash's neurons fire in a direction that led him to the yawning abyss of despair? Did he think that by ending his own life, he would touch the bottom of his grief, the final destination on his synaptic map?

A thought occurs to me and fills me with a vague unease. There must be another reason why Ash thought I was to blame for Michael's disappearance. Why single me out and not Nachiket or Ember? If I remember correctly, both were equally willing to coax Michael into entering and exiting Ka on his own instead of waiting to be invited to enter Ka. They both thought that if they saw it happen enough times, they, too, would be able to reproduce the effect for themselves. I never saw Michael disappear and reappear from Ka, but I wonder how many times Nachiket and Ember did. I doubt I'll get a straight answer now from either of them. Memory is selective and prone to hyperbole when recreating the past. Perhaps Nachiket was right when he said he wasn't sure exactly what he saw, given that we were a bunch of impressionable teenagers willing to believe. Didn't Michael himself ask this from us? He had said, "*I can only ask that you believe.*"

What do I believe? I believe that Michael disappeared into Ka and that he's left me clues to reach him there. I am willing to hold onto this belief until I am proven wrong. However, I also believe that Nachiket isn't telling me the whole story of what made Ash think I was responsible for Michael's disappearance. Behind his apparent gladness to see an old friend again is yet another secret.

Nachiket pulls into the driveway of an A-frame log cabin set at the edge of flat farm country. I recall passing a sprawling white stucco hacienda with an orange-tiled roof a few minutes ago, a barn, and a horse corral with a few horses. I must have missed seeing any fields for the horses because I was lost in thought. I was thinking about Ash and the mysterious connections with this group of people who, despite their absences, continue to be strong presences in my life. So, I shake my head, turning my attention to this place Nachiket calls home. It's a log cabin behind which stretches a strip of flat green grassland and, beyond that, the dark blue thread of the lower Sacramento river. It is a wild enough place with a view of the river and the dry wind-twisted vegetation on the opposite bank. As gnats swarm at the water's edge, I am surprised it is already dusk. The Beetle's headlights switch on automatically as I pull to a stop behind Nachiket's jeep.

He stands on the narrow porch by the cabin door, waiting for me to get out of the car and walk up the three short steps. He watches me approach and rubs his bearded chin with mild panic in his eyes, probably because he's only now realizing how much he's overpromised.

"I forgot that it takes forever for pizza to get delivered out here because they always get the address wrong and deliver it to the main house a mile up the road. This cabin doesn't show up on the map. So I never get any deliveries here. Instead, I collect all my mail from the CDFW office or request big deliveries at the main house. So, food-wise, I have survival food stashed away, ramen and canned tomato soup. Will that do?"

I say that's fine and give him a grin hoping this will absolve him of his guilt as a host. It seems he isn't used to visitors, which in retrospect, makes sense because the cabin looks small outside. I'm glad I brought my tent and trusted sleeping bag in the trunk of the Beetle. My eyes are already searching for a flattened bug-free patch around the cabin to pitch a tent for the night when Nachiket opens the door and beckons me to enter. He steps inside to switch on the light, and almost immediately, a fat gray cat appears out of nowhere and hisses at me. I freeze in terror against the door. Nachiket wedges himself between the cat and me and opens the door wider with an arm while shouting an order to the cat. "Shoo!" The cat brushes its fat body against my ankles as it slinks outside. Nachiket turns to go in and doesn't mention the cat. I don't ask its name either as I cross the threshold. He knows how I feel about cats. Something about their glassy eyes and feral, slinking bodies set me on edge. Unlike the welcoming smells of Richard's house, Nachiket's place smells of dampness and cat.

The cabin is small, sparsely furnished, and dimly lit by a stark bulb hanging by a long cord from the center of the living room. A faded yellow sofa and a rattan armchair with palm-print cushions hug the length of one wall. On the opposite end, there is a comfortable gaming chair and a large table with a workstation, two monitors, and enough hardware underneath to power a small city. I notice an augmented reality helmet and haptic suit hanging on the chair. He is clearly not a Luddite, given his interest in exploring the sensory experiences of virtual worlds in the 'Verse.

Nachiket sees me eyeing the equipment and grins at me. Then, he says, "I bought this suit when you first created Ka World at gAIa. Ember and I each bought one at the same time. So, naturally, we were curious…because…well, first, it was named Ka World, and second, you had created it. You'll have to ask Ember what she thought about it. But, I wanted to see if it lived up to my idea of what Ka was supposed to be."

My heart quickens. My friends did not forget me! Even I can hear the wistfulness in my voice when I say, "If you both had been with me, I would have welcomed your inputs into building Ka World. We could have built it together."

Nachiket shakes his head. "I don't think so. We have neither the vision nor the follow-through, and the three of us together…well…we'd all have different ideas of what Ka was supposed to be. Sometimes I think that even though we were all in the same room when Michael described his experiences in Ka, we all perceived what he said differently. We each created our own idea of Ka."

I have to ask. "Entering my virtual Ka World, did it live up to your idea of Michael's Ka?"

"Yes and no." He is cagey.

"Do you like being in it? In my Ka World, I mean?"

He pauses to think about this, always thoughtful in his answers. "No. Because I was looking for someone who wasn't there. I was looking for Michael inside this virtual reality world you created. I was curious to see if you had created this world as a tribute to Michael. I thought I'd find some bits of him reflected in there. I guess I was relieved not to find anything. The experience of being inside Ka World is unsettling. It's early tech, and it does weird shit to the brain. I don't think I've lasted more than 15 minutes inside your Ka World. Maybe you can last longer now that gAIa has turned your Ka World into this crazy location-tracking game that promises to lead toward enlightenment! But I think the problems are still there. It's bad to push this new technology out to unsuspecting people. It always causes trouble in the long run. I'm sorry if you were expecting another answer."

His review stings deep inside my chest, but I manage to show no emotion and keep my voice on an even keel. "It can induce dissociative brain states. I never meant for it to become a game, which is what it is now. I wanted no part of that. I walked away from gAIa because I disagreed with pushing early technology on people. We don't know what can happen or how it can spiral out of control. I think it might already have."

He says he agrees with me but also needs to warn me. "Instead of trying to become more aware of what is happening to themselves, rather the masses will escape into false realities of virtual worlds in the 'Verse. Your Ka World is, at best, a distraction. At worst, an addiction to a false reality as people start using it to escape the problems breathing down their necks—climate change, pandemics, political violence, and poverty. You can't walk a fine line between creating something and turning away because it turned into a monster. They'll hate you for it."

"Explains why you're a Luddite," I say.

"I like to be present in one reality," he says.

On that somber note, Nachiket turns on the monitor and sets up the live feed for me to watch. I see grainy pictures of feral shapes and many glowing eyes, presumably the mother fox and her cubs. He apologizes for that. "It's dark now in the mountains. You can see them better in the early-morning light," he says.

He hasn't mentioned if I can stay at his place, and I don't ask because I don't want to spend the night in this dank cabin. There isn't room for the two of us here. One tiny bedroom to the left of the living room extends into a little kitchenette. I'd rather sleep outdoors than on the dusty yellow couch. The weather outlook is dry enough.

Meanwhile, I'm thinking of how to frame the questions I

still want to ask Nachiket. So I stand leaning on the small countertop watching him take out two dry packs of noodles from a small cabinet above the electric cooktop. He pulls down two cans of tomato soup, opens them with a can opener, and proceeds to put the lumpy red mounds into a wide saucepan filling it with a copious amount of water. Then, he says, "I'll throw the noodles in there when it boils. Tomato noodle soup. Voilá!"

I give him an encouraging thumbs up. I'm still trying to figure out when and how to ask my questions. Then, he starts filling me in on details about his life, some of which I've figured out already. He says, "I live alone. I suppose I needed an address in Redding, so this is it. I'm outdoors in a tent most of the time because I love being out in the field, and I come here rarely, only once in a few months, when I need to be in the office. I have a girlfriend, Leigh, but she doesn't like to come here. So most of the time, when I'm not in the field, I'm at her house. She is a working artist, a jewelry designer, and she has a nice house with a studio a little bit up north with a clear line of sight to Mount Shasta."

I say, "Leigh sounds fun," and then I ask about the cat.

He turns his back to me to stir the saucepan and says, "The cat came with the cabin. It's a wild thing. Knows how to get in and out on its own. It's a hunter too. You'll see some bird bones picked clean and feathers beneath the deck. I've seen him returning after a hunt, carrying a bird in his jaws and dropping it under the deck to eat later."

It's the appropriate time to change the subject. "What made you come back here now? You said you were waiting for me to call. How'd you know I was coming?"

He rests the wooden spoon against the rim of the saucepan and turns to face me. He says, "A week ago, I was backpacking through the Klamath mountains when it hit me that I needed to get back to Redding right away. When I could pick up reception, I switched on my smartphone and saw the urgent messages Ember had sent me about Ash. I read Ash's email that said he had lost the will to live. I didn't want to meet anyone then, so I turned back and spent a few more nights camping. I needed this time to process his death. Then, two days ago, I had a strong feeling that you were looking for me and that you'd find me, so I returned to the field office, hoping my intuition was right and that you'd call."

I ask if he really believes our group has a psychic connection with each other.

"Possibly. I always felt we shared a strong bond between the five of us that was pretty damn unshakeable when we were teenagers. I don't know if it's a sixth sense or what. Or maybe, it was me who was searching for you. If you hadn't found me, then maybe I'd have come looking for you because…maybe… Ash not being alive anymore made me think about our group again, about you, Tashi, and how we had locked you out. I've certainly never felt this same connection again with any people, and I've met many people. I think that when Michael disappeared, we all lost that connection."

I find myself saying aloud, "A hivemind with Michael as the leader."

He gives me a curious glance but doesn't say anything. The tomato noodle soup is now ready, and he turns it out into blue enamel-coated camping bowls with matching spoons and forks. I find that my appetite has returned. Nachiket says we can eat outdoors. The porch wraps around the house, widening at the back, where two camping chairs face the river in the moonlight. It is almost a full moon, reddish like the color of the heart on Ash's sugar candy. I carry both bowls and set them on the porch next to the camping chairs. Nachiket brings out a camping lantern and lights a citronella candle to keep the mosquitoes away. I can still hear their annoying whine, but they keep their distance for now as we sit down to watch the river and eat. The soup's taste, ramen flavored with celery and onion, is unexpected but wholesome. The citrus scent of citronella wafts in the air. Hungry now, we both eat quickly because canned soup tends to congeal in the cold.

The night is chilly, and we both sink into our jackets. There are a few stars, nothing like the clumps of the Milky Way I'd seen during my high school trip to Peru, but enough to remind me of it. I think about my group of friends, Michael, and my blessed life in the BMD era.

I ask, "Do you remember the shaman in Peru, Don Itzal, who told our fortunes from sugar candies? When I read that interview about you where you talked about switching your career from engineering to wildlife biology, I wondered how much influence the shaman's prophecy might have had."

Nachiket gives a wry laugh. He says, "I'll admit the thought did cross my mind. How much of the mind is open to suggestions? The suggestion of a red fox on a sugar candy as a vehicle for a prophecy can be pretty powerful. The thing is, I did see a red fox following me while I was out geocaching, and it did spark my interest in researching the animal. So, maybe the shaman's prophecy did come true after all."

"You do believe it?"

He shrugs his shoulders. "I think so."

I say, "The shaman's prophecy for me as someone good at computer work came true after all. I've been glued to a screen for the past decade."

Nachiket laughs. He says, "His prophecy for Ember came true too. She is married, has a little son, and lives in a house with a white picket fence like that casa on her sugar candy."

I cover my mouth with an exaggerated gasp. Nachiket's smile is the widest now. "It's true enough. Ember is a photographer, and she lives in Portland with her wife, who is an architect."

"She's a lesbian? I never knew. I thought…never mind…it doesn't matter now. She has a wife and a son? Who is the father?"

He shrugs. Ember couldn't get pregnant, he says. There was a surrogacy. He doesn't know the details.

He knows I'm surprised, but he won't give me more details about Ember. Instead, he says, "You should go and meet her. I think it will be good for her to see you now."

A flash of anger flares up in me. I say, "I don't want to see Ember. There have been far too many secrets between the two of us. She never told me she was a lesbian, and I always thought she was in love with Michael. Also, she shut me out of the group."

Nachiket shakes his head. "I told you, Ember thought it was necessary to shut you out because she was trying to save Ash from himself. And, while there might have been a moment when she was with Michael, I think as a teenager, you're unsure of your sexuality till you try it out for size. It was always pretty clear to me, even then, that she liked girls. I always thought it was you she liked, not just as a friend but as someone she had a crush on, to be more precise."

"Me?"

"Uh hmmm."

I'm too stunned to speak. My thoughts churn. A crush? Who has ever used that word since high school? Ember liked me and not Michael. How come I never picked up on it?

Nachiket says, "You were always so obsessed with Michael that you never even thought that anybody else could be attracted to you."

We sit in silence for a while. The whine of mosquitoes is sharper, although they resist the crisp, lemony scent of citronella. Not too long before one bites me. My thoughts wander, sparking memories. Ember's curious glance at me when I ask her about her life in Japan, the girls who follow her and giggle self-consciously when she walks past them, the moment when she asks me, "What kind of girl are you?" I replied then that I was not one of them, not one of *those* girls. Did she implicitly understand my sexual orientation at that moment, knowing I was straight? Who were *those* girls? Were they attracted to Ember but talked to Michael instead to get her attention? I never gave sexual orientation much thought in high school, even though I had plenty of sex education classes defining sexual orientation and gender since middle school. Sex is biological, and gender is a construct. This was as axiomatic as the postulates of Euclidean geometry. When something is so obvious, it can be easy to miss. When have I thought about Euclidean geometry in the whole scheme of things? Besides, Nachiket is right. My attraction to Michael was all-consuming. What other signals had I missed? Ash's soft face pops into my head. I think about his frequent emotional outbursts. How it was always Michael who could placate him. How once Michael put his arm around Ash, drawing him closer, mimicking Humphrey Bogart's deep voice, but using his own lines, "You wear your heart on your sleeve, kid." We all laughed then. The definition stuck. Ash was someone who always wore his heart on his sleeve.

I say, "The shaman prophesied something for Ash too. There was a picture of a red heart on the sugar candy Ash picked up. Looking at that, the shaman said Ash would be someone who would get involved in a romance, and he'd have to fight for matters of the heart. Did his prophecy come true?"

Nachiket shifts his weight in his chair and tucks his long legs toward him, crossing his ankles. He fidgets and clears his throat. "Tashi, this is going to be hard for you. I think the shaman's prophecy was true for Ash. He was deeply in love with Michael, but I don't think you realized how much. Michael tried to be a good sport about it and tried to continue being his friend even though Ash had openly declared his love for him since middle school. Michael was the one who told Ash that it was okay to wear his heart on his sleeve and feel comfortable in his own skin. But I don't think even Michael realized how much that encouraged Ash to fall deeper in love with him. I say this with some perspective now as an adult. When we were teenagers, it was so confusing."

I come back seething, "Ember is a lesbian, and Ash was gay, and I thought I knew everything about my friends. So much for a psychic connection to each other. Is there something you want to tell me about yourself that I didn't know?"

Nachiket gives a slight laugh, then shakes his head. "I wasn't attracted to anyone in our group. My head was filled with geocaching and Michael's descriptions of Ka. I still think we were a close-knit group. We couldn't have known each other's deepest feelings, but collectively we shared a bond. There is no denying that we felt like there was nobody else but us in the whole world. It made us stronger despite whatever was happening with each of us."

"Was Michael gay?"

"No. At least, I never thought so. Bisexual, possibly."

The river glows like a pale opal. The kind of place and time where you should sit around a campfire and spin a tale for the ages so that later you can unravel it and examine what's true and what's not. I say, "Ash singled me out for a reason. He could have chosen you or Ember to blame for Michael's disappearance. Why'd he choose me?"

"I think he was jealous of you and Michael. We all knew how you felt about Michael, you followed him everywhere, and Michael had not brushed off your interest as he had with Ash. So, Ash must have carried this grudge, and God knows how it mushroomed. When we all found out that Michael had disappeared, Ash was distraught. He said some incredible things about you and Michael. Threw around wild accusations about seeing you two making love in the laundry room of the hacienda we stayed in during the school trip to Peru. He said you kept this a secret from the group and forbade Michael from talking about it. Ember and I were convinced that this possibility couldn't be true, but we let him talk. He had convinced himself that you had a diabolical mind and some power over Michael, making him do things he didn't want to do. That you made him enter Ka when he wasn't ready."

Heat rises in my face as I remember how my body felt, expansive, elemental, under Michael's electric fingertips, the feathery touch on my skin opening it to new sensations. One memory opens the floodgates to another. How Michael and I snuck away in the early hours of dawn to the tiny laundry room behind the hacienda, a tight space filled with the rumble of industrial-strength machines that generated enough noise and heat for us to hide from the world outside and disrobe, lying down on mounds of heated sheets that covered our intertwined bodies like a cocoon. There was never any fear, no doubts, at least not from me. Afterward, I felt I had emerged into confident womanhood from the chrysalis of self-conscious adolescence. We were both laughing when we threw the mounds of stained bed sheets back into the wash. Being together with Michael like this was the purest thing I had ever experienced.

Nachiket turns his face toward me and watches the redness spread across my cheeks, belaying the truth of my thoughts. "My God! What part of that is true? The sleeping with Michael part or you forcing Michael to go to Ka part?" he asks.

I think I have failed my friends. Taking their trust for granted, I planted the seed of suspicion in Ash's mind. I did it to protect Ember because I thought she would be the most hurt. I never knew it was Ash who needed protecting all along. I look Nachiket in the eye and say, "The former is true. I thought by not telling any of you, I would avoid telling Ember because I thought she and Michael were an item at the time."

Nachiket whistles, digesting this information. "You never stopped loving him, did you?"

I shake my head.

He says it softly then. "I'm sorry you lost Michael and all of us at the same time. I didn't know till now how much we hurt you."

The tears that welled up in me now spill over. I cry for Michael, my friends, and my beautiful childhood that is no more. Nachiket touches my shoulder and keeps his hand there. I've turned my face away, but he knows I'm crying.

An imperceptible movement stirs at the corner of the

deck. The shine of yellow eyes. The cat is back, slinking its way to the bottom of the deck. I can't tell if it carries a bird back from a hunt. I think we are all animals, slinking back into the darkness to habits that, come daytime, we hide from others.

∿

Nachiket breaks the silence. "What really made you come here looking for me now?" he asks.

I wipe my eyes with the sleeve of my jacket. "I've been finding clues that I think are leading me to Michael. I found some new clues that led me to you," I say.

He raises an eyebrow, wearing his questions on his face.

First, I have to fill him in on the background. I tell him how I created Ka World as a way to reach Michael because my intuition is telling me that Michael is putting clues out in my world, like the tessellated crocodiles, so I can find him. I tell him how I've been experiencing *The Dissolving*. Whether it's the same thing as Michael experiencing digital vertigo, I don't know because I haven't had the debilitating headaches or physically disappeared or reappeared from another world. I tell him my theory about thin places being more common-place in virtual reality worlds. I tell him about the curious case of the engineer Karthik Pitchai, who disappeared while playing inside Ka world, and how Tony saw him disappear. I tell him how I think all these mysteries, *The Dissolving*, the thin spaces inside virtual worlds, the disappearances of Michael and now Karthik, are all linked somehow.

Nachiket scrunches his face and whistles. Then, he says, "Good fortune will find Michael in Ka."

"Yes…somehow…but I need your help."

He says, "Speak then, good fortune."

I roll my eyes at him. I lead with the shaman's prophecy for Michael based on the image of a blue whale on Michael's sugar candy. I repeat verbatim what the shaman said. "Whales are comfortable with being in thin places where the boundaries of two worlds, water, and air, meet. You must be someone who seeks the knowledge of the thin places, so you can cross over into another world for yourself."

Nachiket is impressed. "You remember it all? I'm reliving the shamanistic ceremony again because you repeated it word for word!"

Nachiket listens with an ear cocked to my side, deeply interested in everything I'm saying about the clues that led me to Richard. He's fascinated by the necropsy of the whale that I witnessed yesterday, even though it feels like a lifetime ago, and he latches onto the geocache found inside the belly of the whale. He understands now why I've come to see him.

16

———

The contents of the geocache, the small black notebook, plastic ballpoint pen, gray metal dog tag, a round magnet with the picture of a humpback whale, and the postcard with a picture of a rusted wrought iron gate with the letters K and A visible in the trelliswork, these lie on the table with the two monitors that Nachiket has pushed aside to make room.

Nachiket switches on a desk light clamped to a monitor, picking through the items. After a while, he says, "The container itself is not important though I can see why you were drawn to the tessellated crocodiles on the lid." He holds the logbook open to the last entry, tracing his index finger over Michael's handwriting. I can tell by how quiet he is that nostalgia is raking those scattered memories on the surface of his mind, making room to accept what lies beyond comprehension.

I whisper beside his ear. "He wrote this on the date he disappeared."

He can't trust himself to speak. Not yet.

I want to remove all doubt, so I slide the postcard toward him with an index finger. "And the letters K and A in a wrought iron gate just like how he described them." I flip the postcard to show him the rhyme.

He seems awed, his fingers trembling as they touch the postcard. I say, "I still get goosebumps every time I see this."

He reads the rhyme for a long time and then puts the postcard down. Emotions flit across his face. It's hard to tell what he makes of the rhyme. When he finds his voice again, he talks about the trackable instead. "I can look up this metal dog tag. If it's indeed trackable, then I should be able to track its movements and find the last coordinates. That might give us an idea where Michael disappeared." He tosses the augmented reality helmet and haptic suit from the gaming chair to the sofa and sits down, pulling out a keyboard tray from under the table. In a few minutes, he locates the trackable on the geocaching site, and then we both hold our breaths as he enters the coordinates into an Earth map. Immediately, the map throws an error message. "These coordinates do not exist on planet Earth."

"What the…" Nachiket's voice conveys frustration.

"Try again," I urge him.

He enters the coordinates five times, and the map throws the same error message each time.

"Do you think someone logged an incorrect coordinate for the trackable?" I ask.

He shakes his head. "Not possible. It's an automatic tracker."

Defeated, I slump on the yellow sofa that smells of the cat. I put my head in my hands, and the odor of cat piss recedes a little.

Nachiket says, "Here's an interesting thought experiment."

I raise my head and find his eyes blazing with a curious mix of candor and curiosity.

"I honestly don't know if it will work, and it might sound

far-fetched, but if you're willing to suspend belief like we did with Michael's entries into Ka..."

"Go on then, tell me." I snap at him with impatience. He winces, but I'm tired of the weight of the past that does nothing to mitigate the dread of the future.

He rubs his beard as he speaks. "Your Ka World has now been turned into this location-tracking game, right? This means that the gAIa engineers would have had to build a map of the 'Verse in which Ka World exists. I suggest you try out these coordinates inside the Ka World game."

I perk up, alert now, ready again like Ollie, the dog at the scent of a bone.

"Try. That's all I can do," I say.

Nachiket nods in agreement. "It's the one defining trait of our species."

I wear the haptic suit and the augmented reality helmet and login into Ka World. It's unrecognizable to me now. Instead of offering an open-ended exploratory virtual sensory experience, it's now a game you play to win. The thought of my creation being turned into something else unsettles me. Then I hear Nachiket chuckling in his deep voice behind my head. "Let me know when you achieve enlightenment."

"Shut up," I say, feeling like I'm 13 again.

Inside Ka World, my crocodile avatar projects itself inside an empty blue space. A breathy anodyne voice reads the text of the question that floats in front of me.

Where do you want to go?

"I want to go to these coordinates." I'm surprised at how

normal my voice sounds as I say the coordinates aloud. In my version of Ka World, before it was turned into a game, my crocodile avatar emitted a series of low grunts every time I opened my mouth to speak. I recall how disorienting that felt. I think they no longer throw you straight away into the deep, immersive experience. Much as I hate to give Tony credit, this slow acclimation to the immersive virtual environment is helping me remain longer inside Ka World. I don't feel the disjointed sensations, at least not yet.

The breathy anodyne voice reads the text appearing in front of me.

> Human consciousness can influence quantum
>   states.
> Tap into your unlimited potential.
> Take three deep breaths while focusing on your
>   destination.

"Here goes nothing," I think to myself as I think of Michael and take three deep breaths.

Everything goes dark for a moment till my eyes adjust to the darkness. A wave of coldness washes over me, followed by a strong force that pushes me aside. I begin to flail till I realize I'm in the deep watery depths at the boundary between indigo fading into blackness. Again, the strong force knocks me sideways. In the dimming twilight zone, I sense a dark leviathan emerging from the deepest depths and pulling up into the lighter void above. The depths churn in its wake, and I'm spun around like a wet rag inside a washing machine. I gasp, unable to swim to save myself. In that brief moment of weightlessness when I'm tossed upside down, I see above me in the dark purple void the vague black shapes of a school of fish forming the letters K and A and swimming inside the trellised pattern of a gate. I want to swim up and touch the gate, but the edges of my vision collapse, threatening to bring on *The Dissolving*. Nevertheless, I persist, and at that moment when a sliver of silvery blue light emanates from the gate, I find myself caught once more in the clutches of now-time, my sense of myself dissolving into nothingness, and I can no longer remember anymore who I am or what I have become.

Nachiket says, "You stayed plugged in for 30 minutes. Longer than I've ever been able to stay in. But it knocked you out for more than an hour. I've been worried about you, but you seemed to be breathing alright, so I thought I'd let you rest and come back out of it on your own. How are you feeling now?"

I'm feeling groggy. I'm lying down on the couch, still wearing the haptic suit, but the augmented reality helmet is back on the table. Nachiket helps me stand up and free myself of the haptic suit. The movement makes me feel dizzy, and I have to sit on the couch again.

"Headache?" he asks.

I shake my head. "I never get headaches before or afterward. I feel slightly dizzy because of the rush of blood to my head from sitting up. I think I experienced *The Dissolving* again."

He frowns, trying to process my terse descriptions of what happened to me, but the uppermost question in his mind begs to be asked. "Did you locate the coordinates?"

I nod and tell him what I saw and how I experienced *The Dissolving* at the exact moment when silvery blue light flowed through the gate.

He thinks about what I've said. Then, he squats on the carpet and peers into my face as if seeking to confirm his theory. "Perhaps Michael's digital vertigo and what you call *"The Dissolving"* are the same things. Maybe Michael also experienced headaches because he was overly sensitive. I don't know. But from what it seems to me, your descriptions of yourself dissolving into nothingness seem similar to Michael's descriptions of digital vertigo. This makes me think your and Michael's experiences were both brought on by information overload to the brain."

A wry laugh escapes me. My mouth feels dry when I speak. "Yeah, except I never physically disappeared beyond that gate I saw. Heck, I could barely reach out to touch it."

Nachiket gets up and stands towering over me. "Not yet," he agrees, as he helps me to my feet and leads me to the bathroom, where I can freshen up.

The bathroom is tiny and, lucky for me, doesn't smell like the cat has ever ventured inside. Perhaps because the door can be closed to feline wanderings. The space smells of pine, and as I splash cold water on my face, I feel my spirits lift a bit as I have an idea.

I call out while wiping my face with the hand towel. "Why don't you try it out yourself to verify what I saw?"

When I step out of the bathroom, I see that the thought has already crossed Nachiket's mind. He's wearing the haptic suit and augmented reality helmet and is logged into Ka World. I wait a good fifteen minutes before he removes the helmet and unzips himself from the haptic suit.

"Well?" I ask.

"The coordinates are there, alright. And they are in some cold, deep water. Has to be an ocean. I didn't see a huge leviathan, but I did see the school of fish and the letters K and A. I couldn't touch the letters. Didn't want to, I guess. I was starting to feel pretty nauseous at that point, so I stopped. I'm not sure we're meant to touch it. Has to be another way to enter it. When do you get asked the next question?" he asks.

"You need to survive for a certain amount of time in this environment. But, you have to learn to adapt first," I say.

"The experience…is so disconcerting. I don't think I want to try again."

Something nags me, so I have to ask. "What's your avatar?"

"The Sierra Nevada red fox, of course." He gives me a curious look to see where I'm going with this.

"Of course! The fox won't survive in water, let alone in an ocean. Neither can a crocodile. We'll need to reconsider our avatars as we go in," I say.

He thinks about this for a bit. Then he says, "I think you can figure out a way for your avatar to survive in alien environments. You can send your avatar in a submersible, for example, and I'm betting there's a way to unlock the gate as you play along. But that's not the point. If we're going to stay with this leap of faith and think about how to physically disappear from this world into whatever brave new world awaits us beyond the gate we both saw inside Ka World, then we'll also have to suspend logic. So I think, Tashi, you should try to go in yourself and not send an avatar."

"And how do you suppose I do that?"

He chuckles. "That's a question for the ages, isn't it?"

It's late, and the emotional toll of today, the long drive, and the trip inside Ka World leave me exhausted. Nachiket understands without my having to say that I prefer to sleep outdoors, so he offers to help me set up my tent on the porch at the back of the house. He does most of the work. I only have to tell him which flap the stakes are in, and he chuckles and says he doesn't need those because there will be no wind tonight. I feel like an idiot for mentioning the stakes in the first place because where would you hammer them into a porch anyway? He unfurls my sleeping bag inside the tent and doesn't put up the rainfly. "Dry conditions tonight, plus you'll see the stars as you fall asleep," he says.

I'm surprised he wants to sleep indoors on a night like this. He says he often sleeps in a sleeping bag on the porch, but tonight he has paperwork to catch up on so he can spend a week with Leigh before heading back out into the mountains.

I crawl inside the tent. I'm sleepy and tired, but before he turns to go inside, I have to tell him, "I always imagined you living inside a lovely suburban house with a pet dog or cat, but this is where you live, and this is what you do."

I zip the door of the tent and settle into the sleeping bag. The stars are many pinpricks of light in the night sky. It's as if someone covered the sky with dark poster paper and poked holes for lights to shine through. Maybe that's how artificial all of reality is. Everything we perceive is based on all those stories we tell ourselves that end up being true if we believe in them enough.

I hear his dry laugh outside the tent. He plays the old "describe a feeling" childhood game with me. "I bet you could never imagine Ember living the way she does now, either. So if you had one word to describe what you feel right now, what would it be?"

"Bewilderment," I reply without hesitation.

17

I awake in bright early sunlight and bask in the warmth till the sleeping bag gets too hot and uncomfortable. I hear bird songs and the rustling of small creatures. Perhaps these are squirrels bounding along the railing or field mice running beneath the deck. I feel well-rested, and no dreams have plagued me. I relish this feeling until my full bladder prompts me to unzip the tent fly and go inside the cabin to use the bathroom. The cat sits at the end of the porch, its tail dropping through the wooden slats of the railing, watching me with an unblinking stare as I awkwardly emerge from the tent. I freeze for a moment and then zip up the tent fly. "Stay outside," I mutter as I go looking for Nachiket.

～

I find Nachiket sitting at the desk in his gaming chair. He looks like he hasn't slept well. The haptic suit lies in a puddle at his feet. "Did you stay up all night?" I ask.

"Good morning to you, too. I've been playing Ka World all night long in 10-minute playtime sessions. I finally got through the gate."

I raise an eyebrow at him. "What did you find?"

He rubs his bloodshot eyes as he leans back. "More water. Better fish."

We take stock of each other for a moment, and then I say, "I really need to use the bathroom."

He nods. "The Sierra Nevada red fox survives well in a submersible, but it'll be a while before he becomes an enlightened fox," he calls out behind my back.

I let out an exaggerated sigh. Then, turning my head, I roll my eyes at him. It makes him laugh.

I'm wiping my hands on the hand towel in the bathroom when my phone pings. I read the text message.

Hi Tashi, this is LeRoy Powers from the Times. This story will run in the paper tomorrow. I wanted to give you a heads-up in case you want to comment. Tony suggested I reach out to you.

There's a link to the as-yet-unpublished article.

"Hidden Dangers of the 'Verse. What gAIa's new game does to your brain."

This is an in-depth feature with Karthik Pitchai's girlfriend, a neuroscience professor, and artificial intelligence industry icons, one of whom calls me out.

"Tashi Wheeler, choosing to walk away now when things are getting ugly. You have to wonder if this has grown beyond her control."

Below that quotation, the reporter has added that Tashi Wheeler was not available for comment.

The dry heat inside the bathroom and the stuffiness of the sluggish exhaust make me nauseous. Likely, it's the article that's making me feel this way. I read on. Tony has aligned himself as the co-founder tasked with cleaning up the mess after the creator walked out. In this article, he's come out smelling like a rose.

Another ping. Another text from the same reporter.

Any comment?

I brace a hand against the bathroom door.

"No comment," I reply. I switch off the phone, open the bathroom door, and walk into Nachiket's living room with no plan for what tomorrow brings.

Nachiket is making coffee on the small electric stovetop. He's been thinking, he says, about the rhyme on the back of the postcard. I can tell the geocache has been bothering him since I showed it to him. He is like me in this regard. Persistent. Odd, how when I was young, I thought he was so different from me. Back then, I didn't have the perspective of maturity. We were both persistent in our own ways, me with my obsession with Michael and he with his dogged geocaching. I wait for him to say something more. I don't want to prod him either because I'm still processing my anger with Tony for throwing me under the bus. I rinse the blue enameled mug and wait for Nachiket to speak or pour me some coffee, whichever comes first.

The cat reappears and slinks around the kitchen till Nachiket shoos it outside.

"I swear I just saw it outside," I say, which makes Nachiket grin. "She's like Schrodinger's cat. Always in two places at the same time."

"Quantum entanglement," I find myself saying aloud, holding my mug out for coffee.

He startles then and spills the coffee. I take the pot from him and wipe the spill on the brown linoleum with a paper towel.

He apologizes, pours us both what's left of the remaining coffee, and motions for me to come out to the porch behind the house. There's something on his mind, I can tell.

I can breathe in the fresh air, unclench my fists, and forget

Tony for a while. I watch the river, the thin blue thread that fuses the boundary of the riparian habitat and the woodland beyond.

Nachiket's intense gaze bores into my face. "It hit me when you said it, why we felt so connected as a group of five, why you still feel so connected to Michael even though you two are not physically in the same world. Quantum entanglement."

I admit I've thought about this before. Then I riff on this particular absurdity of quantum physics. "When particles enter a state of quantum entanglement, they lose their individual identities. Any change to one will be immediately felt by the other, even when they are light-years apart. There's no obvious reason, to me at least, why you can't extend this to consciousness. Maybe that's what Michael was trying to do all these years. Lose his individual consciousness and merge it into a single whole consciousness. Maybe that's why he said that when he was in Ka, he understood the meaning of life itself. He was seeking something deeper when I've only been seeking him."

Nachiket nods. "There's something else that has been bothering me. That rhyme on the postcard. I couldn't shake the feeling that I'd heard it somewhere before. Then I remembered that Ember had shown me a photo she had taken of a hill covered with yellow wildflowers. She'd pasted this in her diary, the one where she wrote in an invented language? She'd written something next to that photo, and I asked her if she would tell me what she'd written. I promised I wouldn't use it to break her code and read her private diary, so she obliged. I swear that was the same rhyme on the back of the postcard that she read aloud to me," he says.

It seems to me then that the threads of our individual consciousness have always been entangled, after all, sometimes slack and sometimes taut, their tug, like now, urging me to pull on that line invisible to the naked eye and incomprehensible to the laws of physics.

I down the rest of the coffee. I feel the first pangs of hunger, but I know hosting breakfast will be beyond Nachiket's limits as a gracious host. I realize I've found a way forward after all. "Can you give me Ember's address and give her a heads-up that I'm coming?" I ask.

He nods as if he's seen this coming. "Ember knows, and she already told me to keep a kit prepped for you. It's snowing ash in Portland, so you'd better go in prepared. I've put together two respirator masks, ski goggles, bandanas, and an extra battery pack to charge your phone. There's also some trail mix and a gallon of water if you need to stay longer inside your car."

18

The city of Portland is in the midst of a slowly unfolding apocalypse. Bottleneck traffic jams the freeway lanes leading out of the city while the lanes heading into the city appear deserted. There are no cars ahead of me for many miles, giving me free rein to floor the Beetle's accelerator. I'm hoping no cops are patrolling sections of the freeway now that the apocalypse is near, according to a literal interpretation of every radio host's monologue on any radio station that the Beetle's audio system can pick up.

Whizzing past the watery headlights of stopped traffic in the opposite direction, I think how tightly packed the cars are, like sardines trapped in a suffocating net that descends like a soupy miasma from the skies above.

Scientists are calling this the largest wildfire event burning in the Western Hemisphere since record-keeping began. It's grown so large now that it is generating its own weather pattern of exploding fire tornadoes causing the entire state of Oregon to be under fluctuating evacuation orders. It is late afternoon, and the sky has a burnt orange glow. The air is so unhealthy that one minute outside without a respirator mask is the equivalent of smoking fifty cigarettes a day. I'm grateful that Nachiket gave me the respirator mask and the ski goggles. I'm wearing both to prevent my throat and eyes from burning.

As the Beetle crosses hills blanketed with trees that look more like charred spears, gray ash starts falling from the sky, coating the windshield. This same dust, I realize, also coated Nachiket's jeep as the wildfire event dispersed ash hundreds of miles away. The windshield wipers make feeble attempts to carve out clear half-moons of the windshield. As I peer through the crescents from behind the lenses of the ski goggles, I get the eerie sensation of living through a scene in a disaster movie. "Humanity flees catastrophe, but the heroine must confront danger to seek answers to the past." This thought makes me chuckle.

Ember used to say I was prone to hyperbole, and this time she might be right. She warned Nachiket that I would under-estimate the danger. She knew I'd insist on coming, so she said she would wait for me for as long as the shelter-in-place order remained. Should I arrive, she said I must be prepared to leave at a moment's notice if her zip code came under the order to evacuate immediately. I took this as a green light to go ahead, which is why I'm flooring the accelerator at 100 miles per hour in a race against time to see Ember again.

I reach Ember's house a bit before dusk. The orange glow in the sky is no longer caused by clouds of ash veiling the sun but by the wildfires themselves, burning uncontrolled across wide swaths of Oregon's old-growth forests. Ember's house, a timber construction with a pitched roof, wide overhangs, and floor-to-ceiling glass walls, sits stoically in the middle of an unburnt forest. Except that the wildfires burning two or three ridgelines away seem awfully close. It doesn't take much to think of how, when the wind shifts, a solitary spark might sail forth and alight on a nearby tree, thereby fueling another explosive fire that swallows up this solitary dwelling with its insatiable hunger.

I park the car in the long driveway and notice how elegant the modest house is and how well it fits into its surroundings. Trust Ember to create a Zen retreat, I think, as I get out of the car and adjust the ski goggles against my face to get a better visual. To the left of the house, there is the white picket fence that Nachiket described. Indeed, it encloses a vegetable garden with gravel paths and raised vegetable beds. "The shaman was right after all," I find myself saying aloud, but there is nobody to hear. Perhaps I'm speaking aloud because I want to test the sound of my voice so that it doesn't betray my anxiety about meeting Ember after a decade.

As I walk toward the long rectangular-shaped house, I notice varieties of azaleas and barberry bushes separating the grounds from the forest beyond where, even in the dusky orange light, I can make out different tree species at a glance, Douglas firs, maples, and dogwoods with some early pearly white flowers. The forest, too, may well have been planted by someone who, generations ago, believed in the stewardship of the land.

I spot another garden set on the other side of the house. I stray off the path to get a better look and find this to be a restoration project in progress. Recently uncovered stones, old brickwork, and upturned earth dot sections of the ground, as if this were an archeological dig slowly revealing structures of the past layer by layer. Then, feeling like I'm trespassing on Ember's property, I go back to the walkway leading to the front door. A path is created from large, black misshapen stepping stones set in creeping ground cover. I feel the urge to skip and land on each stone and think how this action gives me the impression of crossing over into another space that is untroubled by the passage of time. Indeed, on the last black stone that leads to the door is a haiku etched in brass letters reflecting this timelessness.

Flow through
this house
like seasons

～

I step onto the stone and find myself at the front door. There
is a square piece of paper stuck with clear tape to the side of
the gray wood door on which a child's unsteady hand has
traced these words in multicolored crayons.

WELKOM TASHI

FROM EMBER SARA KAI

Buoyed by this invitation, I ring the doorbell above the
paper. I hear a flurry of activity inside, a pitter-patter of tiny
feet, and something being dragged across the door. The door
opens a crack and a little boy with a mop of red curls wearing
blue dinosaur-patterned pajamas peers outside. I catch a
glimpse of Ember standing behind the boy, but before I can see
her, the boy grabs my hand and pulls me inside. "C'mon! We
have to keep the door shut because of the air," he says. I stumble
into Ember's house, tripping at something by the door. Ember
reaches to steady me, and then she quickly pushes back against
the bottom lip of the door, sealing it from the inside with the
narrow sandbags that were disturbed when the door opened. I
can hear the steady hum of air purifiers working overtime.

Ember stands up straight, and we size each other up. Her
long black hair is streaked with early gray, and she has it tied
in a loose top knot. Her skin is still unblemished and wrinkle-
free. The deep black pupils project calmness, her gaze no
longer dispassionate but radiating a welcoming kindness.
Motherhood seems to have mellowed her. She wears a white
turtleneck sweater over blue jeans ripped in expensive designer
fashion across both knees. Her feet are encased in sheepskin
boots. I say, "You haven't lost your sense of style."

I'm amazed that it's with this trite observation that I start anew with Ember. I was so angry with her for abandoning me, but perhaps Nachiket's quiet coaxing or the surreal long drive here dissipated my wrath. After fanning the anger for so long, maybe it's only natural to let it begin to extinguish. Or perhaps, there is Kai, Ember's five-year-old son standing in front of me, excited about this long-awaited visitor with angelic innocence bathing his face. I wonder what Ember told him about me.

Ember says, "Welcome, Tashi. Sorry about Kai's manhandling." The familiar dulcet tones of her clear voice make me realize how much I've missed her. She takes a step forward and gives me an awkward hug as I pat her shoulder absent-mindedly. She is trying. We both are.

Kai watches us with a frown on his face. He has ginger-colored hair and freckles dotting his cheeks. He looks nothing like Ember. "Why are you still wearing those things?" he asks. He means the ski goggles and respirator mask, which in my shock at seeing Ember again after so many years, I've forgotten to take off. I remove the paraphernalia that makes me look like a character in a disaster movie to reveal my face to Ember and her son. "Hello, Kai. Thank you for the welcome note," I say.

Kai grins with delight. "Mommy says I can call you auntie."

I glance at Ember, who's watching me closely, but betrays no emotion. "Only if she wants you to," she says.

Kai flashes a penetrating gaze at me and waits for me to say something.

I feel relaxed as the tension in my body evaporates. I don't have much experience around kids, but I think auntie has a nice ring to it. I like this kid. I could spoil him rotten with no parenting issues to worry about, leaving that to Ember. I can get all the perks and none of the disciplinary drama. It would be a win-win situation except for my unresolved feelings about Ember, incipient at best, ambiguous at worst, but all related to her abandonment of me. Still, I smile at Kai. "Of course, I would love to be your auntie."

Kai steps forward and gives my knees a tight hug. I bend down to ruffle his hair and press my cheek against his. He smells fragrant like honey and sage, scents I still associate with Ember.

A clattering noise comes from the kitchen. Ember says, "Oh," and rushes inside. Kai and I study each other, unsure what to say in Ember's absence. Then, he says, more as a statement than a question, "Would you like to meet my other mommy." His gaze is cool and dispassionate, reminding me of Ember in her younger days. I nod. He takes my hand and leads me into the kitchen, where both his mothers are.

The entrance to the kitchen is through the dining room, where a large Oregon black walnut table takes center stage around six pale cloth-covered wood frame chairs. The curved tan wood cabinetry around the room gives it a distinctly retro vibe. Cream-colored Shoji doors, pushed open to the side, separate the dining area from the kitchen. Two women squat on the worn-out oak floor, trying to clean the mess from a large blue cooler box that lies open, tipped on its side. Ember tries to scoop up with her bare hands all the ice cubes scattered on the floor and throws them back into the upended cooler. A lithe Middle Eastern woman with a thick braid of hair that falls to her waist and wearing black leggings under an oversized beige cashmere sweater is busy picking up perishables from the floor. Butter, boiled eggs, cheese, sausages, bread. Survival foods.

Ember watches Kai and me come in while she scoops up another mound of ice cubes in her hands and then flings them into the cooler. They rattle like pebbles against a window. As she wipes her hands on her jeans, she releases a long sigh. "I'm completely messing up your welcome. We have to be ready to evacuate at a moment's notice. I thought we *were* ready, but Sara decided to pack an extra cooler at the last minute. She has rheumatoid arthritis, her wrists are weak, and she didn't call me before picking up the cooler from the table." Ember is talking to me, but her tone is admonishing Sara. I notice then that Sara is wearing black braces on both wrists.

I feel as if I've stumbled into a domestic spat. This new version of Ember's domesticity feels strange to me, and I'm unsure how to react. So I apologize for the intrusion. "I'm sorry for coming at a difficult time," I say.

Sara stands up and turns to me. She is tall and towers over me. Her face is lovely when she smiles. All the hard angles melt away. In fact, she seems more approachable at this moment than Ember. She says, "It's not your fault at all. I'm glad to finally meet you. Ember talks about you a lot. Constantly. I'm Sara, as you know, even though Ember has not formally introduced us."

I think to myself, I wonder what Ember told you about me, but I decide not to ask the question aloud.

Sara holds out a hand, and I take it, eyeing the wrist brace. "Don't worry, I only wear it as a protection, useful in times like this," Sara says, gesturing at the spill on the floor. She senses the awkwardness between Ember and me and suggests that Kai help her with the cleanup while Ember and I go to talk in the living room. Kai doesn't want to miss out on all the excitement over a new visitor—and a newly minted auntie to boot. He appears to be on the verge of a tantrum. Sara leads him toward her on the floor and sits him down next to her with an impressive resoluteness that Kai can't resist. Soon he is following her lead of stacking food into the now upright cooler.

With a slight tilt of the head, Ember gestures to me to follow her. I take a deep breath and walk behind her to a minimalist but cozy living room whose floor-to-ceiling glass wall reflects the faint glow from the ridgelines above the dark woods surrounding the house.

"What a shame if you really have to evacuate and worry about all this beauty going up in flames," I say, shocked at myself for speaking the thought aloud.

Without breaking her stride, Ember switches on the lamp behind the sofa, and the glass wall turns dark. The circle of lamp light reflects in the glass, masking the orange glow outside. She says, "Sara and I bought this house five years ago, the day we decided to have Kai. We took this on as a restoration project and right away started pouring years of love and labor into it. I suppose you can say I've made my peace with it. If we have to leave, I will, without turning back. Did you see the haiku I put on the stepping stone to the house?"

I nod.

"I put that down because I believe things, events, and people are transitory like the seasons. This house is in the middle of a tamed wilderness, but the wilds can never be tamed. We have to bend to the will of nature. If the house can survive this catastrophe, then I will be grateful. If not, Sara, Kai, and I will return here to rebuild. I have found a place I can come back to again, whether it's ugly or beautiful or until it doesn't want me to come anymore. I hope you can find a place like this for yourself. Maybe you'll find it when you find Michael," she says in a wistful voice. She plops down at the far end of a tan L-shaped sofa, removes her shoes, and tucks her toes underneath her.

I'm not sure I want to get this comfortable yet, so I sit down with my hands under my thighs, facing her, all the while feeling stiff and uneasy about how our conversation will go. I have so many things to say to her, but my tangled emotions are making sentences run amok in my head. I remind myself to breathe and to think about how to begin. I know I should start with Michael, but the first question that pops out of my mouth surprises even me.

"What did you mean when you said I was an influencer who needed influencing?"

19

Ember might have learned how to make her face betray no emotion, but in her gaze, half distant and dispassionate, I sense her disillusionment with something. So I play it cool too. I say nothing more. I've opened with a salvo asking her to explain what she meant by her last email. Her choice to respond.

She offers a wan apology. "I shouldn't have said that."

"But you did."

"You want to know why, of course. And you're right. I owe you an explanation. It was the one time I felt I had to break my own rule of no communication with you. You had started gaining so many followers in the 'Verse, and I could see you were fast becoming an icon. But the kind of stuff you wanted ethical debate over, the kind of technology that you were willing to create and to make available to everyone in this sort of utopian idealism of yours, I felt that was wrong. The people following you in the 'Verse are either looking for certainty or the opportunity to be proven right. I know you can offer neither. But engaging with them continuously makes them *think* that you are either certain or whatever you say proves them right."

"Are you serious? Half the population of the 'Verse is busy

153

trolling me. Have you even read the stuff they're saying about me?"

Ember waves her hand in her old, dismissive way. She continues. "Your constant engagement is dangerous in itself because there is no way to foster ethical debate over the morality of a new technology that has the ability to transcend consciousness. And your constant preachiness about it makes you seem like a messiah to some people. You've unleashed something big, but nobody knows what it is yet. This technology can unleash brain states fostering a sense of nothingness, of the void, in people. Without years of meditative, contemplative practices, training, or even a shaman or guide, it is a surefire recipe for a complete loss of selfhood without any clarity or understanding of what is happening to them. What you've given the world is the possibility of zombiehood. Half the planet's population may eventually be filled with zombies with no idea of who or where they are."

"Wow." I am stunned by her harsh view of the entire last decade of my work, and I feel a keen flush of anger rising. "Of course, *you* can get to say that. You and Nachiket and poor Ash, who's, unfortunately, dead now, were perfectly willing to sit on the sidelines, waiting for me to do something to find out how and where Michael disappeared!"

Ember's tone is contrite. "You're right, of course, that we abandoned you. I hope Nachiket explained why we needed to do that."

"It was all your decision," I shoot back.

"Yes. And I'll stand by that decision. By making that decision, Ash was able to stay alive for so many years."

"So you offered this certainty to Nachiket, and now you've cherry-picked the opportunity to be proven right," I scoff.

Ember sighs. "I apologize, Tashi. I am sorry about what I did to you. Truly. It has caused me great pain over the years. You asked why I had chosen to engage with you by sending you that cryptic message. So I'm telling you now, with that same great pain, why I felt that you needed to be influenced first so that you might pause and think or possibly even disengage from the 'Verse."

"So you think turning away from technology that you can't understand is useful here, huh? Now I know why Nachiket is such a Luddite. You must be one too." I glare at her with accusations blazing in my eyes. She was always the one who understood me better than I understood myself. So she understands what I've been trying to achieve and how my creation has grown beyond my control. Still, I'm angry at her because she's not offering any sympathy but is ready instead with gobs of harsh feedback.

She winces. "I don't want us to fight. I wish I could take all those years back. I wish we had never abandoned you. I wish Michael had never disappeared. I wish you never had to create Ka World as a way to reach Michael somehow. I wish… I wish I had the courage to tell you then that I liked girls. I wish for us to be friends again. Please."

I shake my head, blinking away the tears pricking at the corners of my eyes. I refuse to let my anger go. She does not know how much she's made me suffer. I say, "Michael used to say that each of us seeks, like a hungry animal, this connection to another heart that can touch ours. Five of us made this connection to each other, forming a network of lost souls so that none of us would ever be lonely. Michael broke the connection first, and Ash completely severed himself from the network. There's three of us left, and the connections we have with each other are tenuous at best."

Ember untucks her feet from her sofa and sets them on the gray sheepskin rug. She says, "Tashi, I will always feel connected to you. I never forgot about you all these years. Ask Nachiket if you don't believe me. I didn't contact you because of Ash, and you know why. I think that while you felt close to all of us, Michael had your heart and has it still. He couldn't affect any of us as much as he affected you. You're here because of him."

I shake my head at her platitudes and turn my gaze to the

reflected circle of lamplight on the glass wall, which appears to float like an otherworldly orb in a dark sea of blankness. How much of this world is an illusion, I wonder.

"Is Michael's Ka real, do you think?" I ask her.

"I think so. I saw Michael disappear into Ka with my own eyes," she says.

"Well then, you *can* trust that it wasn't an illusion."

She appears conflicted and starts to wring her hands. She speaks slowly as if picking her words. "At that time…I did believe that Michael could enter and disappear into Ka. I believed it was real. Real enough for him to perceive anyway. And real enough for me to watch him disappear into Ka."

"Why didn't I see him disappear and reappear from Ka, then?" She winces at my raised, exasperated voice.

"I don't know. Maybe the rest of us were too easily influenced? He used to talk to us about Mind Matter theory and how it affected quantum outcomes and how humanity could hypothetically develop a technology to cross over into other dimensions. We took what he said literally, but you were always trying to figure out how. Maybe that's what kept you from seeing him disappear because you were always busy trying to figure out what was real, what was an illusion," she says.

"If human consciousness can affect quantum outcomes, then didn't you think I would try to find Michael through such a technology that would let me communicate with him somehow? He'd asked me so himself. He asked me to pull him back up when he went far away. You were there when he asked me to do this. You remember?"

She nods. "Why do you think Nachiket and I both bought our haptic suits at the same time when you released Ka World to the general public? We were both so curious to see what you could do."

"And, of course, you were disappointed," I mutter.

"Tashi, do you know what the difference is? Michael was an old soul. He was someone who could find these portals to another world he called Ka. Maybe it really is a world that lies in another dimension. In a way, Michael was grounded. He felt a pull that made him find a portal to get to Ka. Maybe he was searching for this Ka over many lifetimes, and he finally found it in this life. But you've created this virtual Ka World as a portal to mimic these extraordinary, almost out-of-body experiences that Michael described. Instead of achieving his pure bliss states, these experiences create dissociative brain states and disrupt a person's perception of selfhood."

She pauses for a few moments knowing full well that she has my attention. Then, she clasps her hands in front of her and says, "I'll walk back part of what I said. I'm not sorry you created Ka World. In fact, I need you to know that I am truly amazed that you created it. I also know that if there was someone who could do this, it would be you. I never forgot you, Tashi. I wish I could take all those years back. Now, I'm willing to do anything to help you find Michael again."

I feel the tension evaporate. Either she wants to make amends, or she, like Nachiket and me, has a deep desire to know where Michael disappeared. I find both versions of her truth acceptable. For the first time in so many years, I sense that Ember and I may resolve our differences after all. I say, "I've found clues that I think Michael is putting out into this world for me to see."

She nods. "Nachiket told me about this. I'm curious to see the geocache you found. I have my own theories about some of the items in it."

Kai bursts into the room, followed by Sara. He rushes into Ember's lap, talking in a high-pitched voice. "We can stay, we can stay." He throws a wide-eyed suspicious glance at me as if forgetting momentarily that I walked in through the front door half an hour ago. He snuggles closer into Ember's tiny bosom, suddenly shy.

Sara explains that the evacuation order has ended for their zip code. Nobody needs to leave. She walks over to Ember and gives her a hug and a kiss on the lips. I watch the close-knit family. I can sense the warmth the three of them share. I think Ember has found her pod, and this is where she will stay. For her, the quest to find Michael will never exert as strong a pull as it does for me. I observe the family from the sidelines of their embrace until Ember gets up and pulls me into a group hug.

"Didn't I tell you that good fortune is coming to our house? She's here with us today," she beams at Sara. "Come along, good fortune. We'll unpack the feast that Sara packed up and heat it up in the microwave for dinner!"

I can't help grinning at her old good fortune joke. She hoists Kai on one hip, holds Sara's arm with her other hand, and manages to walk back toward the kitchen like this.

Kai leans back from her hip to call out to me. "Come," he says. "Come!"

I follow their easy flow through the house. In my head, Ember's haiku for this house keeps repeating like a mantra. "Flow through this house like seasons." I'll flow through this house until I can find Michael.

Sara is a good cook and lays dinner on the black walnut dining table. Her meatless lasagna is delicious, and her home-made sourdough bread is almost as good as Richard's. She accepts my compliments with good grace and wishes Kai appreciated her food as much as I do. Kai appears to be a fussy eater. It takes a lot of cajoling to get him to eat bites of the lasagna from the small portion Sara has doled onto his plate. Ember watches Sara fuss over Kai, then turns her attention to me. She wants to know about Richard.

I fill her in on the details of our serendipitous meeting, which led me to his studio at night and eventually to staying over at his late wife's cottage. I tell her about Fiona's Daybreak paintings. I know Ember was always fascinated by artists, so I am not bothered by her intense prying about what I felt when I saw the paintings for the first time. Sara turns to Ember with a quizzical glance and remarks she's never seen Ember question anyone this intensely. Then, as if realizing that she's making Sara uncomfortable, Ember eases back in her chair and touches Sara's hand on the table.

"I'm sorry I got carried away. I think I have a crazy theory," Ember says.

Kai chooses this moment to burst into tears. Sara sighs and asks Ember to placate him while she takes his plate away into the kitchen. Ember picks up Kai and tries to calm him down until Sara returns and takes him from her. Kai gets quiet and buries his head in Sara's neck. "He's tired because his schedule is all messed up. We've all been on tenterhooks about the fluctuating evacuation orders," Sara says. She turns to Ember and says, "I'll put him to bed. Go ahead and tell Tashi about your theory. I'll try to come by after he's sleeping, and you can fill me in." Then, as she's turning to leave, she asks Ember to show me the guest room. She gives me a quick glance to see if I'm on board with this. I must look unsure because she insists with the same resolute tone she used on Kai. "We can't let you drive around looking for lodging on a night like this. I really think you should stay. It will mean so much to Ember if you do," she says.

"Stay," Ember urges.

I agree. I'm tired and weary, plus it will be nice to spend some time with Kai in the morning. "It'll be great to sleep on a bed again," I say.

Sara laughs and squeezes Ember's hand. "I'm glad you're staying. Now, I should really put Kai to bed."

Kai unwraps his arms from Sara's neck and leans down to kiss Ember. "Good night, sweetheart," Ember whispers.

Sara takes two steps toward me, and Kai leans down to

kiss my cheek too. I ruffle his hair. "Goodnight, Kai. See you in the morning," I say solemnly.

This admission perks him up, giving him a second wind. He wants to get down from Sara's hip to play, and he's asking what we'll do in the morning, but before I can answer, Sara marches out of the room, saying goodnight, everybody. Then, with Kai still protesting, she switches off the hallway light signaling an established pattern of lights out before bedtime.

~

"Sara's nice. I like her," I say.

Ember seems relieved. "Good, I'm glad," she says. We both fall silent, then she says, "It took me a while."

I wait for her to elaborate.

She props her chin on her hand, resting her arm on the table. "I always felt that I lived on the boundary of a thin place, between straight and gay. It was hard for me to tell my dad I was a lesbian. He is stern, authoritarian, traditional, and very Japanese. I felt the most confused during my years in high school. I was desperate to be straight, but I was also attracted to girls. I hoped this might be a phase. I experimented by going out with Michael at first. I was attracted to his intensity, but I was never attracted to him physically. There was a time I thought I might be bisexual, but it was only later, when I was in college, that I realized I was lesbian. I decided to come out then. I told my dad. We've always had a complicated relationship, but my coming out has made it even more fractured over the years. He hasn't talked to me since I used most of the money in my trust fund to buy this place. My mom is the only one in the family who accepted me for who I am. Sara and I are planning to visit her in Japan this summer. She says she'd like to see Kai."

"Why didn't you ever tell me about your feelings in high school? I never had any indication you liked girls. So I missed all the signals. And I really believed at that time that the five of us could read each other's minds. I mean, we used to finish each other's sentences all the time!"

Ember laughs and leans back in the dining chair. "Yes, you missed the signals. You only had eyes for Michael. Remember when I told you I'd introduce you, the new girl, to my friends? I'd assumed at that moment that you liked girls. I probably had an initial attraction to you, but it went away when I saw how your eyes lit up whenever you saw Michael. I saw immediately that you were straight and narrow. You were going to fall for Michael hard, which you did," Ember adds, moving her hands up and down in lines to indicate a straight railroad track.

"And later?" I can't help asking.

"Later, we became best friends. I've always only thought of you as a close friend."

"Then you met Sara in college?"

"Yes, she was studying to be an architect. I was studying architecture too, but I wanted to be a photographer. Oh, Tashi, I was so lonely in college. I couldn't talk to you anymore, Michael was gone, and Ash was slowly going nuts. Sara rescued me. I told her everything about you, Michael, Ash, and Nachiket, about Ka. Sara is the only one who kept me sane every time I doubted the crazy decision I had to make regarding Ash."

"A surgical strike," I mutter, grinding my teeth as I say the words.

"For the millionth time, Tashi, I am sorry."

I lean back in the chair and clasp my hands behind my head, tilting back. Then, I say, "I saw the restoration work you're doing in the garden outside, peeling back the old garden underneath layer by layer. It looks like you abandoned the project midway."

Tashi nods. "It's tiring work, given Sara's condition. I do what I can here and there."

"I am so tired of scratching away at the layers of the past. I finally got an answer to why you all stopped talking to me. I

don't agree, but I can accept it. So let's just keep it at that,"
I say.

Ember grasps both hands together in a pleading gesture.
"I'd like us to move on, too," she admits.

I nod. "Okay then, tell me about this crazy theory of
yours," I say.

Ember pushes back the dining chair, stands up straight,
and says, "Come with me."

20

I follow Ember into the hallway and then to a room leading off to the side of the house.

"This is my study," Ember says, switching on the light.

The study is cozy and decorated in shades of indigo and white. One wall has floor-to-ceiling bookcases filled with books and the clay sculptures I remember she always used to collect. The opposite wall has a wooden desk and a comfortable straight-back chair covered in a navy blue and white abstract patterned fabric. The desk faces a small window covered with a white paper screen. The other two walls are adorned with an abundance of framed landscape photographs with the ethereal quality that I recognize as Ember's signature style. I pause to look at one that seems familiar, a picture of a solitary Joshua tree, its dark zig-zag prickled branches silhouetted against a blood-orange sky. I realize that I've seen this image on the screensaver landscapes for augmented reality helmets. Ember may be a Luddite, but it's clear she's making money selling digital art. I turn my gaze to the other photographs arranged on the walls and say, "You always did like taking pictures of solitary trees."

Ember is flipping through the pages of a large picture book she's pulled from one of the bookshelves. She pauses at a page and then glances at the framed photographs on the walls. "I've always been interested in thin places where the boundaries of this world and another world meet. I suppose it's because the five of us were all interested in this idea of thin places in high school, and it's an idea that's stuck with me ever since. I've always felt that trees have an otherworldliness about them. Well, not all trees. Maybe one or two if you're lucky or aware enough to chance upon them at a moment where you can look at them with an artist's sensibility. Then, you might see how they can serve as portals that open up into another world," she says.

I peer at the photograph of the solitary Joshua tree, but Ember blows an exasperated raspberry by puffing air out of both cheeks. "Look here," she says, handing me the picture book.

It's a picture album of Ember's photographs reproduced in high resolution. There is a picture of a single tree on one page and a one-line caption on the other that reads: *Cherry tree behind school cafeteria.*

I gasp as soon as I see the familiar scene. It's the same cherry tree underneath which Michael used to recline, with a full canopy of lush, burgundy foliage rising skyward from soft undulating green grass. The photograph frames the tree under a brilliant cerulean blue so that the burgundy leaves appear lit from within, appearing lifelike. I almost sense the imperceptible rustle of the leaves, as if an invisible energy source is somehow causing a slight rise in the air.

"It's the same cherry tree under which you saw Michael disappear into Ka. So you think this is the portal to Ka?" I ask. I'm stunned at how fast Michael's memories rush to fill my mind.

"It's not the tree per se… it's the act of placing the tree

within a frame, within a setting that creates the portal," Ember says.

My mind, filled with images of Michael, and the intonation of Ember's slow, deliberate speech, gets jolted back to the present. "Huh? Sorry, I was daydreaming. Were you saying something about set and setting?" I ask in a contrite voice.

Ember releases a long sigh, then says, "It's like an artist creating something extraordinary out of the ordinary, out of commonplace, everyday things. By framing the composition in a particular light and perspective, such as a soft lens or a wide angle, you capture an image that causes you to stop and take a closer look. You don't know why you stopped to look except that you were drawn to the picture. Something about the picture captivates you. It's intangible, ephemeral, and hard to grasp. You pause, you look at it, you might wonder what it is, and then your mind fills with other pressing tasks, and you move on. Yet sometimes, the picture is evocative enough to make you linger longer or come back to see it again because your intuition tells you there is something hidden in plain sight. You want to know what it is and can sense the secret but can't tell what it is. The picture establishes a connection with you. It becomes a portal to another experience.

I took this picture in our freshman year of high school, and Michael liked it so much he kept a print for himself. At first, I was flattered that he liked my photograph so much. But then he would stare at it with such intensity that it bothered me. You know how intense he could get at times. He would carry the photograph with him all the time. Then he started taking it with him whenever he went to sit under the cherry tree behind the cafeteria. One day, I saw him disappear under this cherry tree. He reappeared moments later in the same place, still holding this photograph in his hands. I think that Michael made a connection to this photograph where he was able to see the tree in a very personal way, and this created a portal for him to step into another world. Now, for Nachiket, Ash, and me, that space under the tree always remained unchanged because the photograph of the tree never moved us like this," Ember says.

"You didn't have a connection to the photo? You were the one who took it in the first place," I say.

She has thought about this question because she is ready with the answer. "Even I, who had taken this photograph, could not feel this deep a connection because I was so proud of the picture. I was busy taking credit for it and entering it into photography competitions. My connection with it was to use it as a ticket to launch my career, not something to be looked at with care or thought."

"So…you're saying a portal, created by a photograph, in this case, has to have meaning, a connection somehow with a person for it to open up…for that person?" I dare to ask.

Ember nods. "That's why I was so curious about your reaction to the Daybreak paintings. You were drawn to those paintings. You seem to have experienced them in a certain visceral way, and that's why I was so persistent with my questions, asking you to describe your experience of those paintings. I think the paintings are meant to be experienced together as a whole. I think there is a possibility…if you have felt this strong connection to them, they might open up a portal into another world."

I have a sudden urge to sit down and ground myself. So, I sink cross-legged onto the wood floor and rest my back on a bookcase. The book remains open in my lap, and I flip through the pages, looking at the photographs while my mind still grapples with the significance of Ember's theory. Maybe it's not as crazy as it sounds. Perhaps it all boils down to belief. Didn't Michael say so himself? *"I only ask that you believe."* Maybe belief is all that is required for the Mind Matter theory to work. Is that how that engineer Karthik Pitchai disappeared? Because he believed he could?

I realize I've spoken my thoughts aloud because Ember asks, "Who is Karthik Pitchai?"

I fill her in on the mystery of the disappearing engineer, as

Tony calls it. She listens with great interest. I tell her that she might read a not-so-flattering story in the Times tomorrow about my unleashing Ka World onto an unsuspecting public who might be exposed to the dangers of dissociative brain states. "They're using Karthik Pitchai as an example, and they're going to correlate playing Ka World with increased suicidal tendencies," I say.

"Do you believe this Karthik guy really disappeared?" Ember asks.

"Tony is the eyewitness. He wouldn't lie about a thing like this. I only have his account. But, of course, that's not what Tony's telling everyone else."

"This has grown beyond your control. Bring down the platform that supports Ka World," Ember says.

"I've tried. It can't happen. Besides, the tech is all open source anyway. Someone else might come along and build upon the same code base, and then it'll be even worse. Karthik was smart enough to tweak the algorithms to make the Mind Machine theory work for him, so who's to say someone smart enough won't be able to figure it out?"

Ember says, "Then, you'd better find Michael fast or figure out a way to navigate these dissociative brain states."

I sit in silence, weighing the enormity of the task ahead. What I want to know is how Karthik was able to open a portal. "I don't know much about this engineer, only from what Tony told me. He seemed to avoid people and come in late in the evenings after everybody had left for the day. I don't know what object drew him to establish a connection and open up a portal from Ka World into another world," I say.

Ember considers this. Then she says, "Maybe he found himself in a thin place inside Ka World. Maybe he was drawn to an experience there. A portal doesn't always have to be an object. It's your experience of the object."

This thought makes me uneasy and won't go away.

Then, Ember asks, "Where's the geocache you found?"

I'd get up, but a tidal wave of tiredness pushes me back

against the bookshelf. I feel the fatigue from the miles I've driven in two days.

"It's in my backpack. I think I left it by the side of the door," I say, leaning back against a bookcase shelf.

Ember glances at me but doesn't say anything and leaves the room. She returns with my backpack slung over her shoulder, shakes off the strap, and hands it down to me.

"Picking up after you like old times. You were always leaving your backpack somewhere," she chuckles.

I smile at her, settling into the comfortable camaraderie I've missed for so long.

I take out the plastic box with the green tessellated crocodiles on the lid and spread the contents on the floor. "This is what I found," I say, patting the space beside me for Ember to sit down.

Ember sits cross-legged like me and picks up the notebook first, flipping to the last page to see Michael's handwriting for herself. She caresses the plastic ballpoint pen with an index finger. I wonder if she, too, can sense that Michael held this same pen between his fingers to write the final entry in the notebook. She picks up the metal dog tag. "Is this the trackable object with the coordinates Nachiket found?" she asks.

I nod.

"What do you think this is?" she asks, picking up the round magnet with the picture of a humpback whale.

I shrug. "Maybe it's a signature item, Michael's way of saying I was here."

"Hmmm," she says, putting the magnet down and moving on to the postcard. With her index finger, she traces the letters K and A visible in the trelliswork on the picture of a rusted wrought iron gate and flips the postcard over. She reads the rhyme aloud.

The flowers no one wants are weeds
speckled yellow in a sea of green
If they were all together in a sea of yellow
think how beautiful they will seem

The clear dulcet tones of her voice make me close my eyes, and the image of a hillside covered with yellow dandelions appears in my mind. I'm so lost in my reverie that I don't realize Ember has fallen silent till she speaks again.

"It's a rhyme I wrote in my diary," she says.

I open my eyes. "Your private diary where you wrote in a coded language?"

Ember laughs. "Yes, my private diary. I was scared someone would read my private thoughts and find out I was attracted to girls, but I was even more scared that my dad would find out. So I invented a secret coded language so he wouldn't be able to read it. I wrote this rhyme to try to feel a physical attraction to Michael. I thought bad poetry would help," she says, giving me a wry smile.

"Did you read it aloud to Michael?" I ask.

"I did. And to Nachiket once, when he promised me he would never use that to break my code and read my language. I mean, it's an easy enough code to break, not like the Rosetta stone!"

"Why would Michael put this rhyme on a postcard?" I ask.

"I think it's meant to be a signpost. If Michael is putting out clues for you to follow, then it makes sense why he would put the image of this wrought iron gate on the postcard. We all know Michael described a similar gate as the signpost signifying his entry into Ka. So then, maybe we can think of the rhyme as the next signpost. Does the rhyme conjure up an image for you?"

I lean back against the bookshelf again and close my eyes. "A hillside covered with yellow dandelions," I say.

"Maybe this is the place where Michael is in Ka from where he's talking to you through images," Ember says.

Richard's bullet-punctured artwork pops into my mind. "The zeitgebers," I say, apropos of nothing, it must seem to Ember, who raises an eyebrow.

I explain the zeitgebers artwork to Ember, the first clue of the tessellated crocodiles that led me to Richard. I tell her about his wife Fiona's idea about the zeitgebers entraining the circadian rhythms of another world. "Can the tessellated crocodile motif be a zeitgeber, a timekeeper entraining the circadian rhythms of living beings inside Ka?" I ask Ember.

Ember shrugs and says since it's nothing more than a theory at this point, it's possible that the tessellated crocodiles might be the zeitgebers entraining Michael's circadian rhythms inside Ka. She adds this as an afterthought. "I think Michael also put out clues so that you would get the old group back together again. The geocache led you to Nachiket. The postcard led you to me. I think the magnet with the picture of the humpback whale was meant to lead you to Ash."

"I don't know what Ash would say because the connection with him has been severed," I say. I open my eyes and see Ember wiping her eyes with a sweater sleeve.

"Ash was a troubled soul. He couldn't bear to be separated from Michael. You're right in thinking the connection with him has died. I can't feel him anymore. Maybe if you find Michael in Ka, you can show him this magnet. As Michael himself used to say, words don't have any meaning inside Ka anyway, so perhaps this thing might have some meaning there," Ember says.

21

───────

I feel Ember's gentle tugs on my shoulder. I didn't realize I'd been sleeping with my head resting against the bookcase.

"C'mon, you need to sleep on a bed. You literally nodded off while I was talking," Ember says. She gathers the contents of the geocache and puts everything back into the blue plastic box. "So that Kai doesn't find it in the morning," she explains, handing me the box.

I push the box into the backpack and rise from the floor. Then, hoisting the backpack on my shoulder, I follow Ember into a room at the end of the hallway.

Coming from the maximalist spread of photos in Ember's study, this room is minimalist. The white walls are bare, and the only furniture is a wooden bed with indigo brushwork on a tan bedspread.

"We never quite got around to furnishing this room. But you'll find pillows and a comforter in the closet. All the linens are freshly laundered, and there are new towels and toiletries in the bathroom. Sara wanted you to be comfortable," Ember says, walking inside to open the closet and the door of the attached bathroom.

I like this spartan space. Somehow it manages to feel

welcoming. I thank Ember and ask her to thank Sara on my behalf.

Ember's face contorts into a half smile as she hesitates and then envelops me in a hug. When she pulls away, her cheeks are damp with tears.

"I'm really glad you're staying," she says.

"Hey, I wouldn't want to miss spending time with Kai in the morning," I say, jabbing her shoulder in a mock punch.

She laughs like her old self again. Then she turns toward me as she reaches the door. "Stop thinking about Michael tonight so you can get some sleep," she urges as she closes the door behind her. I hear her soft footfall padding down the hallway.

As I grab the pillows and comforter from the closet and throw them onto the bed, I think Ember is right about me needing sleep. My body can't keep up with the thoughts churning in my mind, and I know I'll fall asleep the moment my head hits the pillow.

A bird's soft chirping registers in the liminal space of waking consciousness till my brain perceives it as the ringing of my smartphone. Instinct makes me reach out for the sleeping bag's zipper, but my hand clutches at empty air instead. Disoriented, I open my eyes and realize both things at once: I'm lying on a bed in Ember's house, and Richard is calling instead of texting.

I can tell Richard is working in his studio from how he pauses midsentence to blow on something. I think he must be working on the humpback whale sculpture, but don't ask him about it.

"I found your number from the paper you stuck under the truck's windshield wiper. A guy named Tony came looking for you today. Said he was your friend and delivered a package for you along with a copy of the Times. I read the not-so-flattering article about you. I thought I'd call you to give you a heads-up in case you were in some kind of trouble. You're not in any trouble, are you?" He sounds worried.

I feel a rush of anger at Tony. It feels like he's infiltrated my personal space. I'll deal with him later. For now, I'll do my best to reassure Richard. "I knew the article was going to come out. And yes, Tony must have come by to drop off the haptic suit. All good!" I say, faking an enthusiasm I do not feel.

"Did you find your friends?" he asks. I detect a note of caution in his raspy voice.

"Yes, two of them."

"Good. Any leads?" I can tell he is curious.

I realize then I'm not going to hide anything from him. "A few theories. I need to come back and test them out. I'm staying with my friend Ember. She has a theory about portals opening up inside thin spaces. She thinks the Daybreak paintings might open a portal for me because…."

"You felt a connection to them," Richard finishes my sentence for me.

"Well…yes, something like that, but I'm not sure how it will work…for me." I'm hesitating because I don't want to have to get my hopes up only to fail yet again.

"I'm sure you'll figure it out when the time is right," he says with an optimism I do not feel.

At breakfast, Ember, dressed in pajamas, talks about dreams. She's dreamt of Ka and about hillsides covered with yellow flowers. Sara, appears refreshed and dressed in black jeans and a white sweatshirt for the day. She says all dreams are messages from the subconscious as she drizzles honey over the last piece of Kai's pancake. Kai, like Ember, is still wearing his pajamas. Then, all three of them look up, expecting me to say something, but I feel depleted and have nothing to share. I slept in a state of blankness brought on by tiredness and woke early. I'm already dressed to leave.

"Neither dreams nor theories," I sigh, frowning. I'm distracted by my smartphone. I stare at it and keep scrolling through the article, the lede to the technology section of the Times, which has brought me notoriety. They even published a picture of me from a virtual sit-down where I revealed Ka World to everyone in the 'Verse. I wish I had my augmented reality glasses to walk among the trolls in the 'Verse and see their unfiltered comments gibbering around me as I pass them.

Ember slaps my wrist with an exasperated sigh. "Put that nonsense down. You're better than all of them," she says.

"You're right," I say and oblige. I cup my chin in both hands, rest my elbows on the table, and ask Kai, who is done with breakfast, if he can show me his toys.

Kai, shy again, whispers something in Sara's ear. Sara says, "He wants to show you his toys."

I take that as a welcome distraction.

I spend an hour playing with Kai and his toys, but even he can't compete with the stray thoughts in my head. Somewhere in the course of the hour, I don't realize that Kai has gotten bored with me, leaving me in the middle of the toy-strewn floor. He's lying on his stomach, coloring in a book under a table. Ember and Sara come in and find me sitting cross-legged, staring at the floor. Then, Sara starts putting away a few toys into the array of wicker baskets lining the sides of Kai's playroom.

Ember sits down cross-legged on the floor in front of me. She wears that pensive expression she has when she's thinking about something troubling her.

"What are you thinking?" I ask.

"I've been thinking about Ash. About my decision to go

along with him and cut you out of the group because of what he said. Oh, Tashi, we were all so young! You must understand how impressionable we all were. We were immature. Michael had disappeared, and now Ash threatened to kill himself if Nachiket and I ever spoke to you again. I was frightened out of my mind. I didn't know what to do or who to turn to. Maybe that's why I told Nachiket we should stick with Ash because I was terrified of what he would do. You should have heard him. He sounded so unhinged! I really believed he would hurt himself or you. I didn't want anyone to get hurt, especially not you! I'm sorry, Tashi." She wipes away the quick tears from her face with the sleeve of her nightshirt.

I lean forward and squeeze her shoulder with one hand. I say, "Okay. Let it go." I glance back to see if Kai is paying attention, but he's still lying on his belly, coloring in a book under the table. I whisper, "I did wrong too. I slept with Michael and never told anyone about it. I thought I was protecting you, but really it was Ash who got hurt."

She drops her voice to a conspiratorial whisper. "I know. Nachiket told me when he called me to say you were coming over."

I laugh and resume a normal tone. "We kept so many stupid secrets from each other. We were so busy looking for Michael's Ka when we didn't even know how our minds work!"

She nods. "Exactly! We are trying to make contact with another world when we don't even know ourselves. That should be a warning, Tashi! I've given this quest of yours to find Michael so much thought. The mystery of his disappearance has also occupied my thoughts for a better part of a decade, but unlike you, I've made my peace with not knowing, and I've decided to let him go. I don't think it is right for one person to exert such an influence over the lives of so many others, even though I'll be the first to admit we did share a strong psychic bond. I'll keep harking back to being young and impressionable and being in a set and setting like that ceremony with the shaman that triggered this bond. And, while I don't regret that bond at all, I regret that we attributed a messiah-like status to Michael, and messiahs, in my opinion, are human and have feet of clay. In the end, it was Michael, always looking to fulfill his deeply personal quest to enter Ka. I think he was willing to cut all our bonds if he could find a way to stay inside Ka forever. I don't think we were meant to follow."

"No, I don't agree. There are clues, I've seen them, and you've seen them. These are clues Michael left behind for me to follow. They will lead me to him," I insist.

Ember sighs. "I know you won't rest till you find him and find Ka. I don't know what you'll find, and I don't know if it will live up to your expectations. Oh, Tashi, I want you to get over Michael. I want you to stop hurting so much. Promise me you'll try to keep an open mind where Michael is concerned."

I say, "I'll keep an open mind, but as far as stopping the hurt, I think it's a bit late for a band-aid. Only finding Michael in Ka can help me now."

Ember sees the resolution set in my clenched jaw. "Okay, "I can tell you want to leave. I know you need to," she says.

I nod.

Ember says, "The air is still unbreathable outside, but at least the fires are 80 percent contained. I wish you could stay longer and I'm hoping you'll be back. Come back in a few weeks when the weather's better, when there's no smoke in the air, and the dogwoods are in full bloom. You'll love hiking in the woods around the house. And…I want you to be a part of our life going forward. You're an auntie now, after all!"

"You can come to San Francisco. I'd love it if all three of you could visit me there," I say.

Ember appears surprised as if she's never even considered this possibility.

Sara, who has been giving us space to talk while watching over Kai, comes and stands behind Ember and seems eager to participate. "Kai's never been. We should take him there. Would you like to visit auntie Tashi in San Fran, Kai?"

From under the table, Kai yells, "Yes!"

I sense the beginning of a new phase in my friendship with Ember. "Ember and her family," I say.

"You're part of us, Tash," Ember says and wraps her arms around me from behind.

22

———

The moment the Beetle crosses the threshold of moderate air quality, I peel off the ski goggles and pull down the respirator. Then, I take a deep lungful of air and call Tony.

Tony picks up on the first ring. "Tashi! Where the hell are you?"

The tone alone is enough to make me explode. "What the hell were you thinking, snooping around after me? You didn't need to ask Richard where I was on the pretext of delivering a haptic suit! And seriously, delivering a print copy of the Times just to remind me of that article in which *you* come out smelling like a rose, now that's really low, even for you!"

I pause for another deep breath, but Tony interjects before I can speak again. "Tashi, I came to see where you were staying because it was urgent. There are some things I don't want to say in a text because it's easy for it to be on the record. Plus, it's not safe anymore, given the amount of attention gAIa is receiving from all these hard-nosed reporters. Now the FBI's taking an interest too. That's why I thought of meeting you in person. I don't think we should be talking on the phone, although I have a scrambling device that will encrypt our conversation. Still, it's an easy enough hack if someone really wants to snoop around," he whispers.

"What the hell are you talking about, Tony?"

"The case of the missing engineer has taken a sudden twist. Karthik Pitchai has come back. He was seen walking around gAIa's office late last night, still wearing the haptic suit and augmented reality helmet. He has no idea that he went missing for nearly ten days. He thinks he was only playing Ka World. He says he wandered around exploring Ka World and has no memory of leaving to go elsewhere. It's almost as if he has amnesia. Maybe he really does have amnesia. I don't know. I know his girlfriend and family are lawyering up, and we both know it will cause a massive headache for investors right before the IPO."

"He reappeared!" I exclaim, and the shock almost makes me hit the car in front of me that is slowing down because of a traffic snarl up ahead, producing much honking behind me.

"Tashi, are you paying attention at all? Yes, he reappeared. The problem is that he disappeared in the first place."

"I'm still trying to figure that out."

"The lawyers are going to have a field day. So what are you going to do?" he asks as if this is somehow my problem.

"How is this my problem? I quit gAIa, and he disappeared on *your* watch."

"Yes, but you're the sole creator of Ka World. When you get back from wherever you are, there's a print copy of the Times waiting for you, with a graphic charting the entire time-line of Ka World's creation to Karthik Pitchai's disappearance. I would say quite a bit of that is *your* problem." Tony's tone isn't threatening, but his words in and of themselves are. He knows it's my legacy that's on the line.

I'm so angry that I disconnect the call and toss the phone onto the passenger side.

It rings again a few minutes later. My earbuds are still in, and I tap one of them to answer the call. It's Tony calling back, this time sounding contrite.

"Please don't fight me on this one. We both know how serious it is. Look, I brought you the haptic suit as you asked and an extra helmet," Tony says, offering an olive branch.

"I've been thinking about this…disappearance, but it's only a theory at this point," I say, accepting the hypothetical peace offering.

I can hear an audible sigh at the other end. "If I were to believe my own eyes…and now I'm doubting myself…what did I see? Anyway, my thoughts about it are not…shall I say exactly positive. I find the thought of disappearing into thin air in a 'hey, presto' manner absolutely terrifying. So I'm willing to help you get to the bottom of this…thing…world… alternate reality… whatever it is. I've stopped logging in to play Ka World because now I'm terrified. What if the same thing happened to me? Can Karthik actually have disappeared into another world…," he says, trailing off into his thoughts, not expecting an answer.

Seeing someone disappear like that right in front of you can be frightening, or so I've heard countless times from Ember, Nachiket, and poor Ash. Yet, I relish this moment as Tony shows his vulnerability. His fear is good because it might get him to see my point of view. I want to nudge him further along on this way of thinking.

"Yeah, it can happen to you. If it happened to Karthik, it could happen to anybody. What if scores of people end up playing Ka World and disappearing somewhere and reappearing again with no memories of how they disappeared in the first place? Can you imagine not knowing where you went or how you got back? What if you never returned? Or if you returned, you didn't know who you were anymore? Would that make you a zombie?" I ask.

"Isn't that taking it a bit too far?" he asks, retreating to his former unflappable self.

"Can't you see the next headline? Ka World and the Zombie Syndrome!" I exclaim, not wanting to give up the slight edge I've gained.

Tony shudders so hard that I can hear it. "Tashi, I…I know it sounds far-fetched, but I know I saw Karthik disappear. What do we do now? There's a lot of money riding on this, but I'm not a complete sleazeball."

"Never said that," I interject, though I agree that he has been obsessed with success and money.

"A billion dollars is hard to walk away from. But I do have morals, and I've begun to see your point of view. I'll need some proof, some corroboration of the dangers of this technology before agreeing to bring down the platform that supports Ka World," he says.

This admission shocks me. I say, "I didn't know you'd give in so quickly."

He sighs. "You were always so idealistic, Tashi. Always so busy holding everyone up to such high standards. I tried to live up to your standards, but it was never enough. Maybe that's why we never wanted to continue a romantic relationship because you never thought I was good enough. I know you don't think I have an inner compass, but I do. I'm willing to wait on any decisions about Ka World till you find out how dangerous this technology really is. Do you have any ideas about what might be going on?"

I'm surprised that I've turned Tony so quickly. If even the mere possibility of knowing people who saw Michael disappear into another world could have had such an enormous impact on my life, then perhaps seeing a man disappear in front of his eyes might have an even more extraordinary effect on the direction of Tony's life.

"Like I said, at this point anyway, at best, it's an educated guess, but I do have some theories I'd like to try once I get back to the cottage. And…thank you for delivering the haptic suit and helmet. I'll try my best to figure out what's going on," I say in the most reassuring tone I can muster.

"I'm glad you're looking into this, Tashi," he says, sounding relieved.

I remember something Ember said about a portal that

didn't have to be an object but rather an experience of something that makes you transcend time and reality. "Out of curiosity, did Karthik ever say what he experienced inside Ka World?" I ask.

"Funny you should ask. Karthik's been talking about experiencing augmented reality as if it were no longer augmented but actual reality, and how real it all felt being near a hillside covered with fields of yellow flowers," Tony says.

Even under the down jacket, I can feel the goosebumps rising like hackles from the base of my neck and radiating down my spine, spreading all over my arms and legs like tiny involuntary shivers.

"Tashi? Tashi, can you hear me?" Tony's voice brings me out of my fearful dream-like state and back into the moment.

"Yes, I'm still here."

"So what is it with this Richard guy? He does seem a bit too old for you. Are you romantically involved with an old guy? You like him like that?" Tony asks.

I feel infuriated with Tony all over again. "What? Ewww…gross. No! You're unbelievable, Tony, you really are. I never ask you about your personal life, so keep out of mine."

He chuckles. "We're not colleagues anymore, Tashi, so I thought we could be friends again. Please stay angry! I know that's when your brain really starts chugging along. Call me when you find something," he says and hangs up.

~

By the time I pull into Richard's driveway, it's already dark, and the lights are on inside the house. Richard must be making dinner. I can hear Ollie's excited barks as I climb up the stairs to the house. The porch light switches on the moment I knock on the door.

Richard has already eaten but seeing how famished I am, he makes me a quick scrambled egg with leftover veggies. Then he sits down at the table with me. As I eat, I fill him in on everything that's happened to me. He says it's intriguing that the clues led me to two of my friends. "I'm sorry about your friend Ash," he says. I nod and say it's okay and that I've made my peace.

"Have you really?" he asks.

I cup my face into my hands and peer at the grooves in the dining table, willing myself not to cry.

He watches me closely for a while, then crosses his arms around his chest and leans back in the chair. "Okay, we'll talk about something else. Did you bring everything back?" he asks about the contents of the geocache.

"Yes. But I'd like to hold onto the magnet for now. Of course, if you'll let me keep it for a little longer." Thinking about the magnet makes me sit upright. I think my friends and I are like the links in a chain. Even Ash is still a link to my past and, as such, is also a link to Michael.

Richard says he understands why I need to hold onto the magnet. "You want to know why it was included in the box. Maybe its meaning will become clear when the time is right," he adds with a twinkle in his eyes.

23

That night in Fiona's cottage, I set up all my gear in her studio. I wear the haptic suit and the helmet and log into Ka World. I twist and ease into my avatar, letting the sensors from the haptic suit flood my senses with the feelings and smells of my crocodile body. The same breathy anodyne voice reads the text appearing in front of me.

> Human consciousness can influence quantum states.
> Tap into your unlimited potential.
> Take three deep breaths while focusing on your destination.

I focus again on those coordinates that Nachiket found in the trackable. I soon find myself within the same dark watery depths, floating up toward the shimmer of light emanating from behind the vague black shapes of a school of fish forming the letters K and A and swimming inside the trellised pattern of a gate. I've chosen to outfit my avatar in a submersible, and this time, I can push through the gate. Perhaps I've been influenced by Nachiket's talk of what he saw behind the gate, "more water, better fish," which is also what I find now. I feel a deep sense of loss that cannot stem from sensor activity alone. It's a feeling akin to a deep rock inside of me threatening to weigh me down. I am looking for something that isn't there. Then as the submersible is rocked in the massive wake of a giant whale, I find myself being tossed around. As the water breaches the submersible, I feel the sudden grip of cold on my chest. A crushing weight bears upon me as I experience *The Dissolving* all over again.

The last thought I remember having is framed as a question. "Michael, where are you?"

When I regain consciousness in the morning, I find I've slept on the cold concrete floor. I'm still wearing the haptic suit, and deep grooves are carved into my cheeks from the augmented reality helmet that burns slightly when I peel it off. My limbs feel sore and achy from lying stiff on the floor, and as I begin massaging my arms and face to feel some warmth, a bright ray of sunshine floods through the large window, making me squint. I sit basking in this ray of light till it expands to fill a large section of the room, including the wall that still has the three Daybreak canvases with their painted surfaces facing the wall.

Last night I thought about these paintings, but I didn't want to see them again for some strange, inexplicable reason. Perhaps I was too tired of all the conjecture and theory, or I was too impatient. Like Nachiket, I wanted to see if I could get through the gate inside Ka World, and I did. Maybe that's what winning feels like inside a simulation. Maybe Tony's right. People stay longer in a virtual world if you give them a goal. I feel like laughing, and when I do, laughter feels dry in my throat. I've been tricked into playing a simulation and keeping my attention focused on a game like Tony wanted all along. However, none of this is helping me find Michael.

～

The chirping from the other room makes me finally heave myself off the floor and get to the phone. Intuition tells me it might be my mother calling, and I'm right. She's worried, of course, having read the article in the Times. She wants me to lawyer up and has a few recommendations for lawyers from the biotech company she founded. I must sound vague and not interested because she puts me on the speaker and makes me talk to my father. Yet when both of them ask me separately in worried voices what I'm going to do next, I feel a wave of sheer boredom wash over my tired body, and I plop down on the bed with a deep sigh. They don't get it. Nobody except for Nachiket and Ember, and possibly Richard, ever will. This has nothing to do with Ka World and everything to do with finding Michael again. I no longer care about my legacy. I want to find Michael. I want to regain this connection to another hungry human heart still beating for me somewhere in another dimension.

I reassure my mother that I have things under control in the most optimistic tone I can muster. She knows I'm faking it, but she respects me enough to leave me alone, at least for now. "Come home," she says. I feel like I'm thirteen again, and I almost want to cry and say yes, but that will mean accepting defeat, not finding Michael, and not solving the case of the disappearing engineer who has suddenly reappeared. So, I take a deep breath and say, "I'll come home after I wrap up a few things around here."

~

The phone chirps again right after I end the call with my mother. I'm surprised because I don't recognize the number, but I pick it up anyway. "Uh oh," I think when a voice says, "It's LeRoy Powers, the reporter from the Times."

"Listen, Tashi, I know you don't want to talk to me or say anything on the record about what's going on at gAIa. I know the last article that appeared didn't sit well with you or frame you in the best light. I'll admit there were a few missing pieces, things I didn't know, things that, as a reporter, I should have further investigated. I'm accepting my lack of due diligence. Can you meet me for lunch or dinner, completely off the record this time, and hear me out?"

I am too confused to reply.

"Neutral territory. Your choice," he prods.

"I'll have to think about it." It's the best response I can come up with.

"Call me on this number when you're ready," he says.

I toss the phone toward the bed, throw my hands up, and fall backward onto the bed. As I do so, my fingers touch the rounded surface of something smooth and flat. I pick it up and bring it closer to my face. "The magnet!" I exclaim as the eye of the humpback whale stares back at me. I bring the magnet closer to my eye so that the image blurs and fills my eye with blue. I let the magnet rest on one eyelid until my eye flutters, and its weight slides down onto my cheek. When I pick it up, the magnet feels warm in my hand. I get up from the bed, thinking of Ash, how he was the most deeply affected, how he could never reconcile with Michael abandoning him. If Ash were alive today, I would tell him I am more like a dog with a bone, a clever sleuth wanting to get to the bottom of a mystery, while he is the true lover, an old-fashioned romantic, the old soul born centuries ago but transplanted into an uncompromising future. He wore his heart on his sleeve and loved Michael more than anybody ever did, even me. I wish we could all have been honest with each other when we were young. So much heartbreak could have been avoided.

When I get up from the bed, I feel dizzy, but I go back to the room with the Daybreak paintings and turn each canvas around to face me. I think there is certainly an ethereal quality to them, and I wish then that Ember were here to see them. Again, I feel slightly dizzy from having slept on the cold concrete floor and from the thoughts taking shape as questions floating around in my head.

I touch the surface of the first canvas lightly with the tip of my index finger, surprised by the feel of the stiff paint. I run my finger across the middle canvas and reach a spot of paint that feels a little bit softer, almost spongy, as if it hasn't dried yet. I tell myself that this shouldn't be possible. These canvases were painted five years ago, and the paint has had ample time to dry. Yet, my intuition senses something inexplicable. I feel a shiver of excitement as I poke at the paint, whose softness yields further into sponginess. I bring all five fingers of my hand to this spot, sensing the sponginess expand, almost as if I can push my way through the canvas. For a few brief moments, I struggle to breathe. I find myself speaking these words aloud in a voice that sounds more like the echo of someone else standing far away from me.

> The flowers no one wants are weeds
> speckled yellow in a sea of green
> If they were all together in a sea of yellow
> think how beautiful they will seem

A whoosh of wind whips up as if it's coming from deep inside my own body. I seem to be making my own weather. My cheeks tingle as blasts of cold air hit my face as if I were walking in the middle of a dark street buffeted by the wind. All of a sudden, the wind picks up, and I scream as I'm propelled upward by gale-force winds, my sense of direction disappears, and I no longer know which side is up or down. I want to hold onto something solid that I can recognize, but there isn't anything I can grasp. Instead, images fly fast and furious across my peripheral vision as tessellated shapes. I flail and tumble, gripped by fear, as the tessellated images crowd around me.

I remember Richard's suggestion to look deeply at these tessellated images to construct a continuous view of reality. Even though it's hard because I'm being tossed around so much, I begin at last to see the shapes of tessellated crocodiles emerging and disappearing. As I start trapping these dynamic shapes in my field of vision, I think of Michael, and my breathing gets easier, the wind gets calmer and dies down entirely, and when it does, I find myself tumbling on soft green grass. I scramble to sit upright, and when I do, I find myself at the base of a hill covered with yellow flowers.

24

The room with the paintings, Fiona's entire cottage itself, is no more. Instead, I find myself underneath an unblemished azure sky at the base of a hill covered in soft undulating green grass and a profusion of yellow dandelions. I feel no wind, yet an invisible breeze rustles through the grass. Acting on instinct, I call out for Michael, but my voice seems flat and strange, an echo from elsewhere, bouncing off the sides of a deep well. The hill is large, and I cannot see the top from where I sit. I begin clambering up the steep side with few footholds and no clear path. My feet slip, and when I fall on my knees, I realize I'm still wearing the black haptic suit and clutching the magnet in my hand. I get up and attach the magnet to the front button of the suit. I look around. There are no rocks. This pristine hill doesn't seem like it could exist in the real world. I begin a slow upward climb, crawling like an animal, rooting my hands into the tufts of weeds to clamber up the side.

~

I don't know how much time has passed since I began climbing the hill, nor do I have any way of knowing what time it is. The sun hangs in the sky like an incandescent orange orb, and even though it feels like I've been climbing for hours, it hasn't changed its direction in the sky. I cast no shadow, nor does the hill have any dark spots. Everything is bright, yellow, green, and still. I wonder if I've died and quell the panic that arises by thinking about Michael. Questions flood my mind. Am I in Ka? Is this what Michael meant when he said entering Ka felt a little bit like dying? Thinking about Michael and the possible answers to these questions calms me, so I can climb farther up the hill. It's an awkward scramble since I still need to crawl on all fours, digging my hands into the dirt to hoist myself uphill. Strangely, I feel neither tired, hot, nor sweaty.

≈

After a while, I stand on unsteady legs and look around to get my bearings. It's hard to tell how high I've climbed. Judging from the precipitous drop of the terrain disappearing below me as I peer over my shoulder and the steepness of the hill still rising above me as I crane my neck, I can guess that I'm standing somewhere in the middle of the hill. Instinct makes me bend down to brush off the dirt and sticky bits of grass and flowers from my knees, so imagine my surprise when I find no single piece of dirt, grass, or flower on me. My hands are clean. In fact, my wild scramble up the hillside seems not to have left any trace at all. I frown at the flattened grass underneath my feet. Then, I take two steps to the left. The grass springs back the moment I step away as if it bears a perceptible intelligence. I feel like an imposter who has stumbled upon a scene with no role to play. I can't shake the feeling that I've walked into a picture in a frame captured in time and that someone else in another dimension is also looking at me now. I get a strange feeling that the person looking is also… me. That I'm somehow looking in at myself.

"No!" I say aloud, shaking my head to dispel this odd

feeling of being both the looker and the looked-at. My brain shuts down this strange double vision by bringing up another equally disorienting memory. I had the same feeling of being transposed when I first saw Michael sitting on flattened grass under the shadowy, burgundy foliage of the cherry tree behind the school cafeteria. At that moment, I felt he must have been painted into that space by someone like himself who lived in another place and time, so perfect was the subject and style. These unsettling feelings dredged from old memories and subsequent thoughts about the nature of time and timelessness occupy me as I resume my awkward clambering up this hill on which I seem to leave no trace.

I climb onto a level outcrop where the grass peeks out between exposed gray rocks. No dandelions grow here. I stand up to assess this harsh change in the landscape. An intense glare from the blue sky makes me squint, which is why I don't notice the objects at first. Then, as my eyes adjust to the light, I register the faint gray outlines of what appear to be three parallel, almost transparent mirrors. These mirrors are tall, narrow, and separated from each other by a few feet and appear to float several inches perpendicular to the ground. On closer inspection, they appear to reflect the surroundings, and when they all align together in a 90-degree shift, they become camouflaged in the space. I can tell these objects are there because they turn in sync every so often at the same angle. Then, my eyes catch the shift in space, and once I know these objects are there, I wait and watch for them to turn again.

After a while, I realize that these are not actual mirrors because although they reflect the same space—the blue clouds in the sky, the gray rocks, and grass—I don't see my own reflection in any of them as I walk in between them. Perhaps my mind labeled them mirrors because it wanted to grasp onto something identifiable, concrete. I reach my hand out to touch one, and the space around my hand morphs into ripples, and I feel a shock as if my hand plunged into ice-cold water. I withdraw my hand, and the ripples fade away. I realize that these are neither mirrors nor doors. Could they be portals instead?

I think, having come this far, what do I have to lose? I put both hands in front of me to push my body through. Even as I brace myself for the cold, my body is ill-prepared for the brutal shock. I gasp when the cold becomes fluid and floods through my open mouth, lungs, and every cell in my body. I look down at my hands and register the shock of their disappearance.

My entire body has disappeared, replaced by a cloud of particles vibrating with sensations. In a panic, I flail my arms and legs, but there are no limbs to shake, only this shapeless molecular cloud. Anxiety overwhelms me as I grapple with the disappearance of my body. This feeling is so threatening that it throws me off balance, scattering the molecular cloud like a comet's tail when this rapid acceleration slows, and a calmness envelopes me. My essence is pulled toward a center while all the molecules clump around it and morph into a loose sort of form. I am aware of being recreated, piece by piece, into a head, arms, body, and legs, into myself, and the moment I realize this, I am aware that the scene has changed.

I'm in a room, standing behind a girl sitting at a desk typing on her laptop. Her quiet, even breathing signals her intense concentration. I can even feel her breathing, the slow deep rise and fall of her chest, and the sensation catches me by surprise. There is nobody else inside this room. Something about this girl seems familiar—the slant of her angular shoulders and the thick black braid of hair that falls to her waist. This room is also familiar. It is a classroom with rows of empty desks and chairs, and this girl sits alone at the front in the middle. On the whiteboard is an algorithm handwritten out in blue marker, which I recognize in shock as my own. This must be the computer science lab at my old high school. I remember I'd written this algorithm to demonstrate how to create infinite possibilities within a virtual world. If this is my handwriting, then this girl, who pauses now to take a break from her furious typing, must be fifteen-year-old me! The girl stretches her arms above her head and then encircles her neck with both hands to massage the crick that's grown there. Now she notices the empty desks and realizes that her classmates have all left. She turns her head to scan the empty rows behind her and then sees me standing there. The instantaneous shock of recognition sends a shiver down both our spines. I can't explain how, but I can feel the goosebumps rising and spreading over her body as they do on mine. It is only a brief moment, but I can sense the eerie sensations arising in the fifteen-year-old girl who seems transfixed by the appearance of a grown woman who is both so familiar and strange that her presence, her apparition here, cannot in any way be true. A knock on the door startles both of us. The girl turns away and breaks our connection. She turns back a second later and whispers, "Preposterous!" Even though I'm still standing there, her fifteen-year-old brain has shrunk back to the confines of her world, and she no longer sees me. It's as if I were a figment of her imagination. Now, she relaxes, the muscles in her jaw unclench, and she knocks her forehead with a fist as if shooing away crazy thoughts.

"What's preposterous?" a familiar voice asks at the door. A tall, curly-haired boy props his skinny body against the frame and pokes a smiling face through the door.

"Michael!" we both exclaim in unison.

"You're working so hard you've started talking to yourself?" He laughs and walks toward the girl. He does not see me, a witness to the unfolding scene. His green eyes do not waver from the girl's gaze, and she blushes as her body leans toward him as if pulled by an invisible magnet. Michael turns the laptop screen to face him and then bends to peer at it. He frowns and turns it back at her.

"How's it coming along?" he asks.

The girl shrugs. "I don't understand why you want me to create infinite possibilities of experiences within a virtual world. How can anyone locate another person inside this world if there are infinite possibilities for experiencing it? How will you ever find your friends when you're inside?" she asks. Her voice breaks a little. Although she can't understand this now, only years later, when she's standing behind herself watching this scene unfold in circular time, she knows that this was the moment when Michael hatched a plan that would enable him to leave forever.

Michael pulls up a chair and sits down beside her. He says, "Come on now, good fortune, you'll find a way. You'll always find clues, images, and thoughts that trigger memories. The entire dimension of the sixth sense can open up if you know where to look for it."

The girl shakes her head. "How do I bring the sixth sense into a virtual world? I don't think I can provide infinite experiences. I don't have the processor capacity. What happens when those infinite experiences hit the upper limit of processor capacity? The virtual world will crash!"

Michael smiles. My future self wonders, "Does he always smile like that? Cheshire cat-like?"

Michael says, "If you use the algorithm of the Mind Matter interaction theory that I gave you and embed it into the code of this virtual world, then…interesting things can happen with quantum entanglement. You might be able to access alternate energy fields from another dimension by influencing quantum events with your mind. Of course, you've got to thread the needle and embroider the algorithm into the code so finely that it will only be accessible to those who know what they're looking for."

The girl laughs. "That's a leap of imagination right there! Do you really think you can go to Ka forever, and you think this replica virtual world can get you there? This is just a stupid virtual world I'm creating. How are you going to use it to get to Ka? And, more importantly, how will I use it to find you in Ka, huh?"

Michael caresses her chin with his thumb. The girl sinks in closer toward his chest. He holds her face with both hands before she can rest her face on his shoulder. He says, "If you can provide the initial energy to induce digital vertigo, this overloading of your brain cells that cause a shift in your perception, I believe you can harness this state of mind to create a portal into another dimension, into Ka. You'd be able to control when and how you enter Ka." His voice is deep and solemn.

There is so much I want to tell this teenage Michael. So many questions I want to ask. I step forward to call his name, but I am blown back by a gale-force wind the moment I open my mouth. I feel like I'm being twisted and pulled apart bit by bit, and the sensation of watery coldness floods me. I gasp as I'm ejected from this scene and back onto the grassy outcrop with the mirror-like portals all turned at ninety-degree angles, facing away from me.

My mind races with questions. Did my past and future selves really meet? What made me pop out of that experience inside the portal? Does each turn of the mirror-like doors create a shift in my experience of time? To get some answers, I enter the second portal.

By now, I know the drill well. First comes the initial shock of intense cold, followed by the dissolving of my body into its molecular components. Then comes the clumping of these molecules toward a center and then the moment when I find myself reconfigured and thrust into a new scene. I think this is what Michael meant when he described each entry into Ka. I understand it now as I come out of the second portal. It does feel a little bit like dying.

In this new scene, I'm standing in a valley surrounded by hills dotted with charred black spikes of headless trees. These must be the scorched remains of a wildfire that swept through the area. The sky is a clear unbroken tract of blue, but there is a smell of smoke in the air. The air quality must be bad, but the smokiness does not make me choke or irritate my eyes and throat. This fire was recent, and it looks to have made a clean sweep across the land before it was contained. I turn my back to the hills and toward the valley. I see the burnt ruins of a house and the rectangular outlines of two adjacent gardens. Four people are stooped low to the ground. They are shifting and overturning the burnt debris. Who are they, and what are they searching for? I wave my hands and shout hello, but they don't look up. Perhaps they cannot see me?

I walk closer, and my stomach clenches in fear as I recognize three of them who are now walking and are closest to me. It's Ember, Sara, and Kai, so this must be the burnt ruins of their house. Ember is older. Her skin, while still radiant, has furrowed lines on her brow, and there are fine lines under her eyes. Her hair is no longer streaked with gray but is now all white. A few paces behind, Sara wears an arm in a sling and walks with the help of crutches supported by her elbows. She is still tall and angular but wears her gray hair in a short blunt cut, and her face is creased with worry. A deep sadness fills her eyes as she points out the stepping stone that once marked the entrance to her house, which is now covered with fine gray dust. Kai, who is also older and taller and shows the downy beginnings of hair on his upper lip, walks toward Sara with the gawky gait of a teenager. "Come over here," he calls out to a man who is stooped low to the ground, examining something in the distance. The man waves and gets up, and as he walks over, I realize that it's Nachiket. His attire seems unchanged though he walks with a slight stoop as if always looking at something on the ground. He is still dressed in hiking clothes and boots, his pants are covered in gray dust, but he no longer sports a ponytail, his hair is close-cropped, and he is balding.

Kai waits until Nachiket joins them, then he bends down to brush away the dust covering the stone and reads the haiku that Ember had inscribed.

"Flow through this house like seasons," Kai reads in his squeaky teenage voice that has not yet finished breaking.

"The wildfire season already flowed through this house. It was some season…I loved this house. Can we come back and rebuild? Please, mom? Mom, please?" he begs Sara and sounds like a five-year-old boy again.

Sara glances at Ember and asks, "What do you think?"

Ember turns her face away, cries, and wipes the tears away with both hands.

Nachiket squeezes her shoulder. "Come on, we should have all learned to take courage from Tashi."

Ember sighs and then bends to wipe her hands on her knees on her blue jeans. Then, standing up straight, she looks them both in the eye. "Yes! I'm going to have to learn courage from Tashi. You have to tear something down to rebuild stronger. The fire did us a favor. Okay then, let's come back. We will rebuild this house and rewild this land," she says in a soft, determined voice.

I open my mouth to interject and ask what Nachiket and Ember mean by learning courage from me when the scene dissolves. The next thing I know is being blown away by that same gale force and ejected out of the portal. I find myself standing once again on the grassy outcrop with the portals facing away from me.

After that experience, I feel the need to sit down somewhere. I find a smooth wide rock and sit down on it as I process what I saw when I went through the portal. I saw Ember, Sara, Nachiket, and Kai. They looked ten years older, and Kai was a teenager! The last time I'd seen Ember and her family was when they had all escaped the wrath of a historic wildfire. The house had been saved. So, when exactly was the house razed to the ground? Can it be that what I saw when I went through the second portal is the future? I consider this possibility. If in the first portal, I saw the past, and in the second portal, I saw the future, then can it be that I'll see the present in the third portal? Perhaps it is in the Now when I'll find Michael. "Only one way to find out," I mutter as I rise from the rock and then run headlong through the third portal.

Once again, the experience of entering the portal rips me apart and recreates me again in new surroundings. I find myself standing at the doorway of a room I've never seen before. I walk inside. This room is bare, with no furniture or anything hanging on the white walls. A man stands looking out from a large window that shows the same section of the hill covered with yellow dandelions that I've climbed before. The man turns to face me.

"Ash!" I exclaim, shocked to see him here.

"Tashi," he says, acknowledging my presence.

"Ash? Is it really you? Can you really *see* me?" I ask. I rush into questions as my mind processes his acknowledgment because none of my friends had seen me when I'd entered their time in the second portal.

Ash nods. "Of course, I can see you. We're both vibrating at the same frequency here at this exact moment," he says in a calm voice as if our being together in this room is the most natural thing in the world.

"You're…you're alive!" I squeak out these words. It's all I can muster, given that my intellect still cannot comprehend seeing Ash here.

He steps closer toward me while ruffling his light brown hair with both hands, a gesture I recognize from before. I'd forgotten how short he was. He's my height when his eyes meet mine. He says, "In this place, in a sense, yes, I'm alive." He gives a wry smile.

"But…I don't understand. Nachiket said…well…he told me you had died, you committed suicide, you killed yourself," I burst out.

He seems unperturbed. "In a sense, in your world, in that particular dimension, you could say that I did die. It was an ignoble death. I wouldn't recommend doing that again. Anyhow, I can't go back into that world in that dimension because my consciousness is no longer compatible with that world. Unlike you, of course. You can always go back because you can still exist there," he says, offering the facts as if all this should be obvious to me.

"Huh? I don't understand. How did you get here? What is this place?" I ask, as my mind floods as usual with more questions.

"Ah!" he sighs. "The answer to the first question will be long. The answer to the second question will be shorter. We are both inside Ka at this moment," he says, turning his face toward the window. "Only, I can't seem to leave and get outside," he adds.

"What do you mean you can't leave?" I ask.

"This room we're in is but one room in this house. This room opens into another room and into an endless series of rooms. It doesn't matter how much I try. I've never been able to find a room with a door that will lead me outside," he says.

"Window?" I ask, raising an eyebrow in its direction.

"Unbreakable," he says.

"Believe me, I've seen some strange things, too," I say. I find myself easing into that old camaraderie again, and I smile as I take a step closer to hug him.

He shudders and takes many steps back, almost to the window.

"Ash, I never wished you any harm. I didn't even know you loved Michael," I say, wringing my hands in front of him.

He meets my eyes and then drops his gaze. "I know. I've been here for a while and had time to figure a few things out. I know I've always loved Michael in a way you never will. I'm willing to do everything to become a part of him and, by extension, become a part of Ka in a way that you never will," he says.

I don't know what to say to that. Ash starts pacing around the room as he continues talking. "Okay, I'll answer your first question about how I got here. In the years after Michael disappeared, I tried unsuccessfully to reach him inside Ka. I grew increasingly neurotic and blamed you for all my problems. I guess you were an easy target for my anger. Anyway, one day, I couldn't wait around forever. I realized that I was done waiting for Michael to come back, so I decided to follow his clues leading me into Ka. First, I tried to induce digital vertigo by playing Ka World. Then I tried to mimic that feeling of dying, which he had said was a necessary prelude to entering Ka. It was in such a moment of desperation that I hung myself. The next thing I knew, I found myself in a house with endless rooms, always looking out at the view of a hillside covered with yellow wildflowers," he says. The yearning with which he looks out of the window fills me with sadness. I want to help him.

"I came here through a portal. Can we use that to get you out?" I ask.

He shakes his head and motions for me to follow him into another room, much like this one. He points out the three portals from the window. He says, "That won't work for me. You can use the portals because your consciousness is not integrated into Ka, so you can visit it and come and go as you please. In my case, well, my consciousness is partially absorbed into Ka. I'm almost a part of Ka but not completely. This must not make any sense to you now, but it's the only way I can describe why I can't leave here."

He continues talking. "I've given it much thought, and I think there's one thing missing. It must be something symbolic because the context of this world is all symbols and imagery. If I can find this missing link, my consciousness will be completely integrated into Ka, and I will no longer be trapped here. Maybe you can help me find it," he says.

"What could this thing be?" I ask.

He shrugs. Then, he glances outside and says, "Uh oh, the portals are beginning to turn. Your time here is running out. For what it's worth, Tashi, I forgive you," he says.

The last thing I see is the blurry outline of Ash raising his hand in a goodbye before I'm ejected from the portal and thrown back onto the rocky outcrop.

25

———————

I walk around in a daze outside the portals, trying to process all the strange things I've experienced inside them. I have no desire to enter any of the portals again. I think my mind may explode if I attempt another entry. Everything I saw inside the portals was unexpected, yet there was one common thread that was missing: I did not locate Michael's immediate whereabouts inside any of them. I realize I should continue climbing up the hill to see if I can find a better vantage point to get my bearings.

I leave the rocky outcrop and start scrambling up the hill. There are more clumps of dandelions than grass here. I wonder if Ash can see me through one of the windows in the many rooms of the house he's trapped in. Almost as a reflex, I turn around, hoping to spot a house somewhere, but all I see is the hill dipping below me and rising up ahead till its steepness fills my line of sight like a wall. However, when I crane my neck sideways, I spot a man sitting on the side of the hill.

"Hello?" I call out to him, but he pays no attention to me. Instead, he's intent on staring at something in the distance. What he's looking at, I cannot tell, for there is no horizon here. As I walk toward him, I notice that the man is wearing a dirty gray and black tunic and a multicolored wool cap with flaps covering his ears. The stillness of his gaze seems familiar. As I get closer, I realize that this man is the same shaman who told me and my friends our fortunes on sugar candies when we took that freshman-year school trip to Andahuaylillas in Peru. He watches me approach without any sign of curiosity and looks away again.

I walk on a slight decline to position myself in front of him.

"Don Itzal?" I say as my foot trips upon a stone. He watches me as I slip and fall to my knees. As I steady myself, my hand brushes against the front of my chest, releasing the attached magnet to fall at my feet.

The man does not acknowledge the name and leans forward to pick up the magnet and examine it. I step closer to try to get it from him, but he thrusts the magnet under his tunic into his pocket and waves my hand away. "Ash," he says in a voice that echoes around the hillside.

Pinpricks of fear arise at the base of my neck, and a shiver runs down my spine. I watch as he removes a pipe from his pocket and taps the contents into his hand. Then, he half gets up and grabs me, and as I scream, he takes my hand, smears it with white ash, and lets me go.

"You have paid the entry price. Therefore, you can pass," he says in accented English.

"Where?" I ask, looking around in confusion, surprised that the shaman can speak English.

He points a finger to the side, where I notice a narrow, flattened path in the dirt I hadn't seen before.

Sensing that this man isn't acknowledging who he is, I ask again, "Are you Don Itzal? I have met you before."

"Yes, I must have gone by that name before. I am a seeker here, but you are the fortunate one," he replies.

"What are you seeking? Do you remember what you told my friend Michael when we met?" I ask, but he chooses to ignore me. Something tells me he is not here for idle chitchat.

A curious question pops into my head that begs to be asked. "Do you know what time it is here?" I ask.

He gives me a blank stare.

"How long have you been here?" I ask.

"There has always been the Now, and I have always been here," he says.

"But when did you *arrive* here? What year, what *time*?"

"I don't understand what you're saying," he says.

I try a different tack. I notice he is wearing an old wristwatch with a round, cracked glass face and a faded brown leather strap. "The time? What time is it?" To demonstrate, I tap the wristwatch he is wearing. He glances at it and says, "Oh, this thing is useless," and removes it and flings it as if he was skipping a stone on water.

I sense panic setting in, and to calm my nerves, I turn to a demonstration. I won't give up having reached this far. I spot a dandelion, now a white puffball, and pick it from its stem. "Time," I say, blowing on the puffball five times till all the seeds scatter.

He watches the white puffs floating away. He says nothing even as they tumble and fall like trembling fragile threads onto the grass.

"What time is it?" I repeat the question.

"Forgive me. I can hear your words but do not understand what you are saying. But I understand images. Why did you blow the seeds away? An image has come to my mind. You must ask the zeitgebers," he says.

Then he nods his head as if talking to himself. "That's right, I can't help you. I am only a seeker," he says.

"What are you seeking?" I ask again.

"Awakening," he replies.

An image of the tessellated crocodiles pops into my mind. "Where are the zeitgebers?" I ask.

"With the one who is awakened," he says and points at the path that leads up the hill.

I thank the shaman for showing me the path, but he

doesn't acknowledge me and stares into the distance again. I tap his shoulder. He directs his ancient black eyes at me. "I'd like my magnet back," I say.

He shakes his head.

"That magnet was mine. It reminded me of my friend, who is dead now. Well, at least he is no longer a part of my world. Maybe he's alive here in a way. Anyway, you must give it back," I insist.

He shakes his head again and gives me a mournful look. "I know, but what is given cannot be returned. You paid for passage, so you should go," he says.

I frown at his strange reply, but he's made it clear it's the end of the discussion. I stand before him for a while, but he ignores me. In fact, he doesn't even acknowledge me as he trains his gaze far into the distance. When I try to stand in front of him, he shifts a bit or cranes his neck to look beyond me. "What are you looking at?" I ask, but he doesn't reply. Since he won't talk to me anymore, I wonder what to do next. Should I proceed on the path he pointed out to me? I glance up at the dirt path that twists uphill and think I might as well start walking on the incline. When I turn back to look at him, I see he is still sitting down and keeping watch, gazing into the distance like an ancient gatekeeper. It makes me wonder, who is he keeping out?

The dirt path ends abruptly at the base of stairs carved out of rough-hewn gray stone. The stones are set to nearly vertical, stuck into the hillside with no railing or support, and as I climb, I have to remind myself not to look back so that my fear of heights doesn't kick in. At the top of the stairs is a flattened clearing with a large solitary cherry tree with lush burgundy foliage rippling in the slight breeze. There are no yellow flowers here, only green grass softly undulating in the air, which I cannot feel on my exposed face and hands. The sky contains all the colors of the Daybreak paintings and appears domed as if this entire setting—tree, grass, and me—are inside a giant bell jar. I feel like I'm inside a snow globe, waiting for someone to upturn it and shake me from my slumber. I walk all around the cherry tree, which, unlike the skinny trunk of the cherry tree planted behind my old high school cafeteria, boasts a circumference reminiscent of a redwood. Behind the tree, there's a small log cabin a stone's throw away, set inside the same meadow of undulating grass. As I walk toward it, I hear the sound of running water. A small stream emerges from a wide, overflowing cistern set to the side, following a circular path around the cabin before feeding into the cistern again. Like a loop, I think to myself. There is a tiny, narrow wooden bridge over the water leading to the cabin. As I step on the bridge to cross, I see silvery fish leaping from the cistern into the stream and back into the cistern again. I lean over the bridge to get a closer look and gasp in shock. These are not fish but miniature tessellated crocodiles, alternating between silvery gray and deep blue, engaged in a continuous dance between seen and unseen.

"The zeitgebers!" I exclaim aloud in shock.

A familiar figure appears at the door of the cabin. He is a tall, lithe young man, wearing gray jeans and a black sweater, with curly brown hair that falls over his face, which he brushes back to gaze at me with the familiar penetrating green eyes.

"Michael," I whisper, not trusting myself.

His lips move into a half smile, his eyes meet mine, and I'm pulled again by the taut thread of desire.

"Hello, good fortune," Michael says with a smile.

Oh, how I've missed that wry smile that reveals the offset tooth that makes the smile seem so rakish and irresistible. There are so many questions I have been saving to ask him, but when I see Michael standing before me in flesh and blood, my quest, my entire reason for being, all melt away into a calm stillness. As I step off the bridge and move toward him, I feel a strange lightness of being as if I'm the puffball on the stem of a dandelion, uncaring about where the wind may take me, whether carried upward to the west or shaken by some passersby. Nothing matters anymore except that I'm here, and Michael stands before me. It feels like I've come home.

"Welcome to Ka," Michael says, then takes my hand and leads me inside the cabin, which is both minimalist and cozy.

I walk into a log cabin with an open floor plan with enough space for a kitchen with a wood-burning stove in the center, a reading nook, a small dining table on the opposite end, a bed covered with a quilt against one wall, and three tall floor lamps positioned at the corners. Two large windows adjacent to the door let in ample natural light. The windows have thick brown curtains pulled to either side with rope ties. There's a door to a bathroom, similarly spartan but well equipped. There is also a small wooden rack set outside the door to the bathroom that holds clothes that seem like they will fit me. I touch them gently, and Michael says these are meant for me. I glance down at the black haptic suit I'm still wearing, smiling as I brush my fingers over the identical sets of clothing—long blue woolen sweaters, white jeans, and white cotton underwear.

I navigate around the kitchen, touching the surfaces of things. Piled on the wooden cutting board on the kitchen table are two wooden spoons, a knife, and two sets of forks and spoons. Beside it, two large brown ceramic bowls are stacked on top of each other. I flick my eyes upwards. There are dried strings of herbs and spices, rosemary, sage, heads of garlic, and threads of cloves and anise, hanging from the ceiling, giving the kitchen a slightly vegetal aroma. On the stove, an iron cauldron boils with bubbling vegetable soup. I lean over to peer inside, and Michael says, "Careful, it must be hot." Then he waves his hands around the space and asks, "I made this for you. What do you think?"

"Very Grimms fairy tale," I say.

His laughter is unrestrained, and it makes me laugh too.

He says, "There is a lot I've forgotten about your world. I have to say I don't remember it at all, at least not in the way you do. When I understood that you were coming to Ka, I had to make a space inside Ka habitable for you. There is a collective subconscious that I can access now. It is a repository of all the old stories and myths that have been a collective part of the human race and its psyche. That is how I could access the images of a dwelling, a site for cooking, a place for sleeping and bathing, to make Ka comfortable for you, do you understand?"

I shake my head. "I'm not sure I understand, but I do know it's good to see you again," I say.

He comes closer and tilts his head toward my chin so I can feel his breath on my cheek. "I see you, Tashi, and I see that you're doing good, and that makes me feel good," he says. Then he turns quickly to mind the pot of soup. "I'm making this for you because you will soon start to feel hungry."

The anxiety that had melted away earlier threatens to submerge me now. Michael did not say it felt good to see me again. There must be someone else, so I have to ask. "Do you live alone?"

He says no, not in the way I think, then gives me a curious glance. "You feel uneasy here," he says, reading my mind. He leaves me with my mouth agape as he walks to open the door. He sticks his head out in the direction of the water-filled cistern. I hear the sounds of water flowing again. "You won't remain here like I have. The zeitgebers have started counting. Therefore, I believe we should make the most of your stay here," he says, turning to face me.

"How much time do we have?" I ask.

He gives me the same curious glance again. "Time? That concept doesn't exist here. Anyway, from what I understand, there is either always too much of it or too little. It's all relative anyway, don't you think?"

Framed by the doorway with the light streaming in from behind, he appears both familiar and strange.

I want to grasp the familiarity and highlight what brought me to him. "Michael, I have missed you every day since you disappeared. It's been a decade since you left me in my world," I say, marveling at how easily I can distinguish between my world and his.

He does not offer an apology, but his eyes meet mine, and I feel his intense gaze burning into me. "I have forgotten your world but cannot forget you because my heart has formed this connection to yours. I see you, Tashi, and I remember you. I hope you can understand and leave it at that." The way he utters these words, the cadence of the "I see you, Tashi," tugs at that invisible taut wire in my heart, and I feel a relief, a soft warmth spreading across my chest.

"Are you really here? How can I be sure?" I whisper because I want to validate what I see.

Then, he stands before me, touching my face with electric fingertips. He kisses me, and my skin becomes a charged conductor, buzzing with the same energy that gives rise to the rippling leaves of the cherry tree and the wind caressing the undulating green grass. I am the sky that contains all the colors of the Daybreak paintings, the tree, the undulating grass outside, and Michael and me. I feel I have become whole.

"What do you think?" he asks when he breaks away. I'm speechless, of course, but I know now how this strange world feels real and palpable to me. He chuckles, then takes my hand and leads me toward the narrow bed.

26

The light never changes outside even though Michael cooks for me as many times after we make love on the narrow bed. Sometimes, when I ask Michael if it's dinner time, he laughs because I still do not understand that time does not flow in Ka as it does on Earth.

"How does it flow then?" I ask in a high-pitched voice that betrays my anxiety. Michael shakes his head and says, "There is no way I can make you understand the concept of circular time that pervades Ka."

Still, I persist in wrangling an answer from him. "Do you mean the past, present, and future all intersect? How? Is it because of the portals?" I ask.

Michael smiles at me and says, "That analogy is close enough to describe the concept of time in Ka, but I can't explain how it works except in images. Besides, your consciousness is not attuned to understanding the mathematics of these images. Not yet, anyway." He shrugs his wiry shoulders. Nevertheless, Michael draws the thick brown curtains across the windows. Then, the cabin becomes so dark that he needs to switch on the three tall floor lamps that bathe everything in soft yellow light. Or, at least, it is the light I associate with evenings in my world anyway. Only then does my anxiety ebb with the familiar routines Michael creates for me.

In circular time, I sometimes cannot remember if I already had a meal or a bath or whether I changed my clothes. Sometimes, my memory perceives one event as recurring. Like how our bodies always entwine or our eyes always track each other when one of us strays six feet away. I wear a rotation of clothes from the wooden rack, and Michael always washes my laundry in the cistern and dries my clothes on the same rack. I feel no need to go outside to explore, nor does Michael feel the need to step any farther away than from the vicinity of the stream encircling the cabin. I am sure that time is passing even though I no longer have a sense of it. Being in this cabin with Michael feels timeless.

Although I have no way of knowing the exact sequence of the passage of time, whether a few days, months, or a year, the nagging thought that I'm living inside a fairy tale creeps back into my headspace. If this is supposed to be a utopia, then the static state of this world starts to bother me. This is the moment when I begin to notice these odd things again. I notice how the light never changes or how Michael cooks delicious soups for me in the iron cauldron but seldom eats himself. I wonder why I've never thought to ask about this until I do.

"Why do you never eat with me?" I ask.

He shrugs. "I don't need to eat anymore. I cook for you because you need the food for energy, and I share it with you sometimes only so you can feel comfortable. I understand that you still need food to survive."

"You don't need to eat to survive?" I ask. My voice betrays my shock. The otherworldliness of this world begins to creep in around the edges of my consciousness.

"I'm a part of this world. I don't need to consume food. At

least not in the way you need to," he says, shrugging his shoulders.

Memories of another world far away, memories that must be mine alone because they seem so personal to me flood my mind. I say, "I left another world behind to find you. You told me you wanted me to find you, to pull you back up no matter where you went. In the beginning, I didn't know how. Then, I worked on it and found the clues you left for me in my world, and I found a portal. I've come to bring you back as you asked me to."

On Michael's face is a soft half-smile. There is an ease in his body when he moves, so different from the intensity that would project from each gesture when I knew him years ago. He says, "I don't remember much about your world, but I remember you, Tashi. At least the connection you and I have is still strong and unbroken. That is how I can remember you. If you really want to understand, you have to know that this is my world now, and we are interconnected. Me, this cabin, the cherry tree outside, the zeitgebers, this entire world, we are one. If I leave, this world will die with me. I have been a seeker for so long and finally found what I've been looking for. I've found the meaning of my existence. I cannot leave here. My consciousness is no longer compatible with your world."

His words, that half-smile on his face, fill me with a sweet sadness. I no longer feel the tidal waves of emotion threatening to roil my insides or the dry heaving that accompanies sobs. Instead, I feel peaceful, and for a moment, I experience a clarity much like a beautiful pattern of crystals, only to lose it again to the persistent questions that edge it out.

I burst out with the one that's been on my mind the longest. "How did you get here, Michael?"

~

Michael tells me the story of how he got here. How he had been so taken by the photograph of the cherry tree. How it made him understand he could enter Ka on his own. How he had stolen his father's sailboat, sailing out into the Pacific Ocean on a stormy night. How he understood that before he left Earth, he needed to shut down our private virtual world and delete all our histories because he was following a dangerous path. How he experienced digital vertigo the moment he finished the job and thought he should provide clues for me to find him before he left Earth forever. So, he tied a rock around a geocache whose contents he curated, throwing it into the section of ocean that now had a silvery, shimmering quality surrounded by a bank of fog. He knew then that a portal had appeared for him to enter Ka. He didn't even jump when he felt himself being propelled forward to a place he had been seeking all along.

"Don't you miss it? Your family, your friends, me?" I ask.

He smiles, and it feels as if dawn is breaking over a frigid night. Not a hint of doubt flits across his face when he says, "No. Not at all."

I feel a keen sense of anguish and betrayal. "But I've missed you! I've always missed you!" I cry.

He pulls my sobbing body into a warm embrace as I let my head fall against the concave dip under his throat. His deep voice rises from within his chest, "I am always with you, Tashi. Our connection transcends dimensions. I wish you could understand this."

I pull away and glare at him wide-eyed, furious at his platitudes. He returns my gaze without flinching. I tell him about the tragedies he left behind in his wake. How I was set adrift from my friends. How Ash died pining for him. I embellish the story about Ash so he can feel the same pain as all those he betrayed. "Don't you know how much you put us through? Ash ended up killing himself because you abandoned him!" I'm repeating myself, but I don't care. I want Michael to know how much he has hurt me.

He listens but says nothing. Then, he gets up and begins to cook another meal for me, which makes me angry rather than grateful. I scream at him in frustration. "Doesn't anything I say makes you *feel* something? Is this Ka supposed to be your version of utopia? Well, it's not! It's not if you don't really *feel* anything here. You're hiding behind this peace, this quiet, this… whatever habitat you've created for me where nothing ever changes. Well, I have news for you, Michael. Human beings are imperfect. They change. I've changed, and you've changed too, don't deny it. You used to be so intense with your feelings always under the surface of your skin, and I could sense how you felt. It's what attracted me to you. I *liked* you like that! But, this world has changed you into something else, into something placid, static, and unfeeling. Are you no longer human?" I gesticulate wildly with my hands, waving them in his face. I don't care how emotional I sound. I want to make Michael react in any way other than this unfamiliar, stoic person standing before me.

He rests a wooden ladle against the cauldron's rim, turning to me with an unperturbed expression, making me even angrier. "Yes, I have changed. We all make our own choices. You might not understand me, Tashi, not in words anyway. I am not who you think I am. I am not the Michael you used to know in your world. To appear before you now, I have had to lower my consciousness, my cellular vibrations, if you can understand this concept better. I have had to lower my cellular vibrations so that I can appear before you in this form of the Michael that you've known and can understand."

"What are you then? A simulation? Is this a virtual reality world? Or is this really Ka?" I'm confused.

Michael says, "I know when I was in your world, I called this world Ka, and that's how I described it to you. You can call it whatever you'd like. It is a place in another dimension in another universe. You have heard of multiverses, I presume? Well, this is one world inside one universe. Many such universes form the multiverse, and there are as many such worlds in a universe. I suppose which world you end up in depends on whether or not your consciousness is compatible with that world. Like the one you came through, a portal can open up a temporary doorway into another world in another dimension. The portal provides entry to a temporal shift where you can match your consciousness with another world enough to experience it for a while. Whether or not you can remain in this world is another matter entirely, but it is possible since I have achieved it. However, to answer your question, this world you and I are in is not a simulation, at least not in the sense you're familiar with. Still, you can sometimes transcend some simulated experiences in virtual reality worlds. In that case, you might be able to enter another world in an alternate dimension. This is how you ended up here, inside Ka. So far, this experience has been safe for you because you and I share a deep connection. I was able to guide your entry into Ka. Of course, this isn't always possible for everyone. In fact, it is so dangerous that nobody should attempt such a crossing. I was wrong to deeply influence you and all our friends about Ka. I know I imprinted this search for Ka deep within all your psyches. I would like to apologize for that. Had I known how dangerous this was, I would never have done it."

"Is that why you shut down our private virtual world? Because you didn't want anyone to follow you here?" I ask.

"Yes. Things can get tricky with someone inexperienced who has an experience like this and enters another world in another dimension. I didn't want lost souls wandering around in the multitudes of worlds in the multiverse. You need to be a seeker first and foremost and understand what you are seeking. Otherwise, you can get trapped in eternity without knowing why you got there in the first place. It helps if you find a guide like I did who can direct your consciousness and make it compatible with the world."

"Who was your guide?" I ask, but I think I already know the answer.

Michael smiles. "The shaman. The one who called himself Don Itzal."

"I met him here," I say.

Michael nods.

Memories of the shaman, and the ceremony in Peru where the five of us sat around a campfire, flood my mind like water pouring in through opened sluice gates. The shaman had seemed so inexplicably old, like the Andes themselves. Was he someone who also crossed dimensions, and that was how he could be on Earth and also come to Ka? He claimed to walk across those mountains without casting a shadow. Why did he come back to stand before us in Andahuaylillas and make his prophecies? Was he also someone who wanted to leave behind clues for a person to pick up on and follow him?

"The shaman left clues for you to follow him in the same way you left all these clues behind for me to follow you here! You didn't want the rest of the group to follow you, but you wanted me to follow you here. Why?" I ask.

"I did leave behind clues for you to follow. I told you before we have a connection that transcends dimensions. So if anyone had to follow me here, it had to be you. Maybe it was because I wanted you to have this experience of Ka," he says.

"I think you should know something about the clues you left behind, what they made me create," I say in a voice tinged with bitterness. I tell Michael how I created Ka World as a virtual reality world that tested the theories of Mind Matter interaction as a way for me to reach him. I tell him how Ka World was taken from me and turned into a game played by millions of people. I also tell him about the case of the missing engineer who disappeared while playing Ka World and reappeared many weeks later but cannot remember anything about this time except that he felt he was wandering around a hill covered with yellow flowers. "Kind of like around here," I say.

Michael nods and says, "This is a serious situation. Not knowing where you went and not remembering how you got back is indeed dangerous. Because if you cannot get back, you can get lost for all eternity."

I tell him that Ember thinks I might be unleashing a population of zombies who are so busy playing Ka World that they don't even realize they are lost.

He nods and runs a hand through his curly hair, a gesture so quintessentially his own that it quells the anxiety raging inside me.

Michael says, "Yes, that is possible. In fact, it is more than possible because it has already happened." His green eyes peer into mine, and I have to avert my gaze. He continues, "A man wandered here wearing the same haptic suit you wore when you arrived. He was scared and rushed about everywhere because he could not understand where he was. The shaman sitting on the hill, whom you also met, stopped him. He is the gatekeeper. He tried to make the man understand, but it was difficult because the shaman is used to thinking in images. It is almost like speaking a different language, so he could not communicate in words with this man and describe to him where he was. Therefore, the man could not understand the shaman and grew even more frightened. Also, he could not pay the passage to enter and see the zeitgebers because he had neither vision, clues, or insight. He was not a seeker. Because he couldn't see the zeitgebers, they couldn't start counting down. So he was going to be trapped here for all of eternity. The unstable energy fields he created caught my attention, and I gathered these energies to create a portal that sent him back to where he came from. Unfortunately for him, he could not process the information overload that occurred during this process, so his brain short-circuited, in a manner of speaking. I doubt he will ever be able to remember anything about his experience here. There will always be a memory lapse."

I try my best to digest what Michael is saying to me. To let this information sink in, I turn my gaze away from his intense green eyes to take in all the elements of this cabin, committing them to memory. Before I can ask him whether there will be a hole in my memory when I'm gone from here, he continues. "Tashi, I was wrong to lead you down this path. You've done a dangerous thing by applying the Mind Matter interaction theory to create this virtual Ka World. If this man could get here, think about the hordes, who might find their way into the multitudes of worlds in different dimensions. You become an energy packet when you are pulled to transcend into another dimension. You become a flow of information that crosses over and is reproduced in another world. What you have created, in a manner of speaking, is a massive data problem that can overwhelm and choke information flows across dimensions. Too many choke points can cause the multiverse to collapse."

"Well, what do you suggest I do about it?" I am indignant. If he hadn't disappeared and left behind this trail of clues, then we wouldn't be in this mess in the first place.

He says, without blinking, "You need gatekeepers."

"Like the shaman here?"

He chuckles. "In a sense, yes. I'm sure you will be able to create gatekeepers that are more…meaningful in your world."

I ponder what this means and what it might entail, but then there are always those enjoyable acts of eating, sleeping, and making love. There is always Michael, and he is here with me. There is a continuity to these things that puts my mind at ease. I'm at home with this life, however and wherever it may be. I no longer have to find something that always lies beyond my grasp. I feel peaceful for now.

Yet, peace is fleeting because time trickles into Ka. There is a moment when I notice a different quality to the light outside. Within a flick of an eye, it is more silvery gray, turning to dusky indigo than yellow. This change is so sudden that I grab Michael's arm and point this out to him.

Michael says, "The zeitgebers are counting down. Their counting might be the concept of time you can understand. You cannot stay here with me. Your consciousness is no longer aligned with this world. I have tried to keep your consciousness aligned for as long as possible, but I won't be able to hold it much longer. I'll create a portal for you to return to where you came from. And you must change into the clothes you were wearing before. You cannot take anything from this world across the portal."

I sense the urgency in his voice, but I find his advice about changing clothes impractical. "I was able to bring a magnet from my world across the portal into this world, and your gatekeeper kept it," I say.

"You brought along an energy packet, a flow of information in stasis for Ash. He is no longer alive in your world, and his consciousness has been reabsorbed into this world. He is free. That was the price for your passage here," Michael says.

The wind picks up speed, and I can hear it whipping the leaves of the cherry tree outside. "You cannot stay," Michael insists and hands me the bundle of my clothes and the haptic suit.

I undress in front of him and put on the haptic suit over my old clothes again. He looks at my body as if committing every detail to memory.

"Come back with me, Michael!" I shout.

He shakes his head. "I cannot."

"You were able to stay back. And I want to stay with you. I'll stay with you inside this place where nothing ever changes. We can live out the rest of our unchanging lives here. Make me," I say, changing tack while tugging at the zipper of the haptic suit behind my back.

"No, Tashi. You cannot stay here because you remember too much of your world and are still too entangled in it. Your consciousness is not aligned with this world. The fact that you think this is a static world where nothing ever changes means you have an incorrect perception of this world. This world, my Ka, is dynamic and alive!"

I hold his hand, rubbing my fingers over his soft fingertips. "I understand that your need to remain here is stronger than your ties to me or any of our friends. I understand now that this was how it was with you all along. Ember was right. You always only thought about yourself, not me or anyone else. You left those clues behind for me to find you because you needed someone else to validate your experience in Ka."

He lets me continue holding his hand but doesn't refute my words. I can hear the wind howling outside. I feel a sensation of coldness, and it is a new feeling in this world of Ka, where pain and sorrow have so far not existed. I am human, after all, I think, ready for change even if that change is uncomfortable, even if it means moving on without Michael. At least, this time, I have the chance to say goodbye.

"The portal is open. You have a few more moments," Michael says.

"Wait! What if I don't remember anything when I get back? I don't want to lose my memories of you, of our time here together. I love you. I have always loved you, even though I'm ready to let you go now." I hug him knowing this might be the last time I see him again.

Michael pries my arms from his waist. "You were the one who followed the images I put out into your world for you to see. You will remember these images. Therefore, you will remember me. We will find each other again. I will look for you when you miss me. I told you our connection transcends dimensions."

The light starts fading, and I feel a wind picking up, rushing from the outside into my body. I hug him tighter. "You can still try to come back with me. Otherwise, what was the point of leaving behind all those clues for me to follow you here?" I ask.

He breaks my embrace but holds my face in his hands. "I am not the Michael you used to know, Tashi. I am an image of a Michael who used to exist in your world. In your world, I was a seeker, desperate to find Ka. I left behind those clues for you to find me because, in my foolishness, I believed that an experience does not have meaning unless it can be seen by another. You're right, I wanted you to experience Ka, and I wanted you to validate my own experience of Ka. I wanted you to understand that I am no longer the Michael you used to know."

"Who are you then?" I shout because the wind has picked up, and I have to make myself heard before it's too late.

His voice floats toward me as if echoing from a deep, dark ocean.

"I am the awakened."

I hear a roar, and then I'm pushed backward with a tidal wave that flings me into watery depths. The crushing weight of what seems like an entire ocean rests on my chest. I struggle to breathe as I flail and begin the instinctive swim for survival upwards against the current that pulls me down. I gasp for air when I break through the surface. Then, as the water recedes, I'm thrown onto something cold and hard, like a rock. When I get up, I find that Michael and his cabin have disappeared, and I am sitting on the cold concrete floor of Fiona's studio once again.

Outside the window, it has grown dark. I scramble for my smartphone in the darkness. As it lights up when I swipe across its surface, I realize that the entirety of my stay inside Michael's Ka comprised a few hours of missing time on Earth. And unlike Karthik Pitchai, the engineer who could not remember anything about his experiences inside Ka, I, on the other hand, remember everything.

27

————

Inside gAIa's office, the mood is somber. Small groups of engineers gather in frenetic huddles around each of the ten large screens that cover sections of both walls of the large hallway on the first floor. A week ago, these massive screens would have displayed successful marketing metrics, client profiles, and cutting-edge industry applications. Now they're all showing the same lines of auto-generating code. I realize, in shock, this has to be Ka World's code base because there are too many parameters and variables unique to it that are being called in the code. The lines of code keep flowing when a sudden pause causes the cursor to blink on all the screens. A palpable silence falls over the crowd. When the lines of code start appearing again, a worried murmur runs through the great hall.

Tony emerges from the group in the middle of the hall, striding toward me. He's wearing khakis and a fresh white polo t-shirt, a uniform of sorts that indicates he must have slept in the office overnight and changed into this outfit in the morning. A few people see me, and the word spreads. "Tashi is here!" I also want to meet my old colleagues again, but I'm frowning because I'm trying to make sense of the lines of code that continue to replicate across the screens. I want to know who is making these code changes?

Tony, who now stands before me, reads my mind. He says, "The code is self-generating. It's creating a new rendition of Ka World for every player based on player input. We never set it up to run this way and can no longer control the parameters. In a metaphysical sense, Ka World is blinking in and out of multiple possibilities of experiences for each user. Thankfully, it still continues to be in virtual reality. For now, at least. But who knows if it reaches a point when players who are too invested in game outcomes will no longer be able to discern what reality really is." He watches the moment of insight appear on my face. "What is it?" he asks.

I think about the Mind Matter interaction algorithm I added to Ka World's codebase many months ago and feel responsible for what I've created. "I need to tell you something," I say.

Tony nods and takes my arm to pull me toward the elevator. "Let's go to your old office. I think I have an inkling of what you're going to tell me, and it's safer to talk where we're alone," he says.

My office has remained untouched since the time I've been gone. Only the haptic suit and helmet are missing because Tony delivered those to Richard's house as I'd asked him to. I sit on the same chair I sat in when Tony fired me, and as I lean forward to run my hand over my old desk, Tony says, "Nobody wanted to take your spot. Although to be fair, I never wanted you to leave either."

I hesitate to answer. Tony asks, "What is it that you know?"

Not wanting to meet his eyes, I glance at the seaweed-patterned carpet at my feet and say, "I'll tell you, but you'll have to be patient. It's a tale for the ages."

Tony blinks rapidly, an old stress response. "Tell me, I can't bear the suspense any longer," he insists.

So, I tell him about Michael, about *The Dissolving*, about

the Mind Matter interaction algorithm I added to Ka World's codebase, about my own experiences inside Ka, inside another dimension, about other worlds inside the multiverse…

Tony holds his head in his hands and groans. Then, he looks up and says, "So this Ka in another dimension, what is the proof you have to show for it?"

I find myself echoing Michael's words. "You want me to show you proof of the truest thing of all. There is no such proof. I can only ask that you believe. But if you're looking for eyewitness accounts of entries and exits from Ka, I suppose you should ask yourself because your eyes saw Karthik Pitchai physically disappear into thin air. It's like you step into a portal to another world. It's the only way I can describe it," I say, noticing the goosebumps spreading across Tony's pale arms.

He shakes his head. "This is too much to grok even for me," he says.

"What we can't understand, we shouldn't try to control. Were you able to arrange a meeting with Karthik Pitchai, as I asked? Before we decide about Ka World, we must talk to him," I say.

Tony nods, gets up, walks to the door, and beckons for me to follow. He says, "He's waiting for you in a conference room. He wanted to meet you too."

Karthik Pitchai is a tall, bearded, broad-shouldered young man with a haggard expression and blood-shot eyes. He's sitting on one of the black swivel chairs with his feet on the round white table in a small, windowless conference room. When we enter, he gives Tony a nod and throws a wary glance my way. Then, he puts his feet down and sits upright.

"This is Karthik," Tony says but does not introduce me. I throw him a quick scowl and walk over to Karthik.

"Hi, I'm Tashi." I offer him my hand to shake. He doesn't take it.

"I know who you are," Karthik says in a deep, tired voice.

I drop my hand and go back to stand with Tony. We are all silent for a while then Tony nudges my ribs with an elbow to start talking. There's too much at stake, so I push my ego aside. I need Karthik on my side.

"I'm sorry you had such an ordeal playing Ka World and are suffering from memory loss. I know you have questions for me. I'm happy to provide answers where I can," I say.

"Oh, I think you know more than anyone and more than what you've let on," Karthik scoffs.

Tony shoots me a wary glance, but Karthik's tone isn't threatening. At least not yet, I think.

"Why don't you start by telling me what you think happened," I say.

Karthik searches my face, which I try to keep as calm as possible, unlike the roiling emotions festering in me. When he starts speaking, I realize he's willing to take me at face value. He says, "I found out that you'd embedded the Mind Matter interaction algorithm into Ka World and had tried to use it a few times when you were logged in. How did I find this out? Nothing genius-level. I followed your trails from every one of your code check-ins. I found that you'd been using it to create subtle shifts in virtual perception, and then it clicked for me. I realized I could leverage this to turn Ka World into a game. The Mind Matter interaction algorithm already makes the rendering of Ka World subtly different for each player. As the scale of players and their inputs based on intent grew, each instance of Ka World became a possibility, kind of like winking in and out of time, making users truly believe that the game was reading their minds and sensing their thoughts. This was the interesting thing I found. After a certain threshold of inputs, the Mind Matter interaction code became self-generating. The scaling made Ka World's rendering differences big enough for users to notice. Suddenly, two people's versions of virtual reality became fundamentally different. The more people continue to play Ka World, the more the code self-generates. There is no kill switch or off button because the self-generating code has exceeded the threshold and bypassed our controls. You might have seen the code writing itself. They're displaying it on the large screens in the hall because no one can figure out what's happening and how to control it."

"What is that doing to the users?" Tony asks in a worried voice.

Karthik laughs. "What do you think? It induces severe dissociative experiences, causing breaks in their reality where people don't know who they are or where they end up. Zombies with gaps in their memories. Like me," he says, throwing me an accusatory glance with his reddened eyes.

I ignore his accusation and ask him calmly. "Do you know where you disappeared?"

Karthik shakes his head. "No, I don't. I get these intense headaches when I try to force or strain to think about the missing time. Physically I'm okay. There wasn't a scratch on me. But I keep getting these vivid dreams where I dream in color. It is always the same dream of trying to get to a place I know doesn't exist, to a hillside covered, almost blanketed, with yellow flowers," he says.

I'm glad I'm wearing a jacket and that neither Karthik nor Tony can see the goosebumps spreading across my arms. But something in my face must give me away because Karthik asks, "Why? What do you know about it?"

I say, "I've been there too, only I don't seem to have any gaps in my memory. Instead, I seem to remember every excruciating detail."

Tony touches my shoulder as a warning, but I shake his hand away. "It's time I told you the truth," I tell Karthik, and then I launch into it. I tell Karthik about the multiverse, about Ka, which exists in another dimension. When I tell him Tony saw him disappear into thin air, I see his eyes widen. I do, in fact, present him with the entire enchilada of history and facts and let him digest it. He listens with grave interest. After I've finished, he leans back in his chair and tugs at his beard in deep thought. After a while, he looks at me and asks, "Will I ever stop dreaming about the hill with yellow flowers? It was such an intense yellow color, a color that seemed to be alive and pulsating. I keep wanting to go back there. In a way, it's like I'm pulled there in a way. Will I ever be able to remember what I did there?"

I shake my head. "There will always be gaps in your memory. I'm sorry."

"Not that I would want to relive that experience ever again. I swear it felt like I was dying," Karthik says and shudders.

"What can we do to stop this from happening again?" Tony asks.

Both Karthik and I reply in unison. "Bring down the platform that supports Ka World."

Tony touches my shoulder. "Well then, Tashi, since you're the one who started this whole thing in the first place, you're going to have to be the brave public face for it," he says.

28

The Case for Shutting Down Ka World

At the risk of violating my non-disclosure agreement with gAIa, I want to state the obvious case for shutting down its most popular virtual reality game Ka World. Since this cannot be done without bringing down the platform that supports Ka World, gAIa's development platform will also need to be shuttered. Does this spell the end for gAIa? That will be up to its community of users to decide. Stepping away from gAIa is an admission on my part that one woman can neither run nor control a technology that has grown beyond all control. So, what's to be done then? I'll be the first to admit that while there are no good answers, we can learn from mistakes and start afresh. After all, isn't this what human ingenuity is all about? Learn from the past so you can move forward?

So, what is already happening to Ka World? A vast majority of players are receiving Denial of Service Attacks when they log in to play Ka World. This is not because I or anyone at gAIa has tweaked or updated the codebase. Instead, the denial of service is caused by a heightened increase in traffic as Ka World microprocessors hit the upper threshold of what Ka World was designed to handle. We all know how Ka World has soared in popularity. In particular, young people gravitate toward new experiences, thrilled by its dissociative reality-bending immersive virtual reality. However much the chasing of these dissociative brain states might feel like the cultural zeitgeist for them, it cannot be the panacea for escaping the problems in one reality and replacing them with another. We live on Earth, and this planet and the universe it exists in constitute our reality, including all the problems therein—wars, climate change, poverty, indifference, or the lack of transparency from monopolistic private companies.

You can't possibly fix an algorithm that is designed to induce dissociative brain states by offering a shiny golden egg as the ultimate reward for playing an immersive game. I know because I'm the one who created this algorithm, and I know that it was never meant to be used to allow people to spend inordinate amounts of time playing in this virtual world.

Now that the cat is out of the metaphorical bag and gAIa's open-source software has already been downloaded freely, I'm appealing to brave open societies everywhere to work together to understand and regulate the dissociative brain states involved in reality-bending experiences. Perhaps we can agree to create a federal regulatory agency that over-sees and governs these experiences by labeling some as Schedule I experiences in much the same way that psyche-delics were once regulated. I don't claim to have all the answers, but I know we need to be transparent with what is happening at Ka World and companies like gAIa in the 'Verse.

I have often been asked whether I believe we live in a simulation or if playing Ka World can fast-track consciousness and evolve to a higher plane, say consciousness 2.0. The answer is yes, and yes.

My consciousness-expanding experiences of an alternate reality have convinced me to side with the chance that we indeed live inside a simulation. But how can this be possible, and is there any proof of this scenario? The answers to both questions lie in logical thinking and an artifact that philosophers have been pondering since the beginning of philosophy. I call it the "bounds of experience problem."

An artifact can be anything that is observed in a scientific experiment that occurs as a result of the technology and methods used to create or investigate the experiment. So how does an artifact fit into the "bounds of experience problem?" By setting the upper limit for all possible experiences within a world, virtual or real.

In the simulation of Ka World, the artifact that sets the upper limit for operations is microprocessor speed, which sets the bounds of all experiences inside Ka World. On Earth and within our universe, the artifact that encompasses all our experiences is the speed of light. It is possible that there is another world where the artifact that encompasses all experiences within it is something else entirely, perhaps even consciousness itself. Then, it is entirely plausible that raising the level of your consciousness might lead you to experience an alternate reality. Another theory is that since our mathematics can never bridge the abyss between humanity and the large-scale energies required to run experiments to break the speed of light, our mathematical progress will reach a point where it will stall forever. However, consciousness can bridge this abyss between knowledge and reality because the energies needed to experience different mental states and expand consciousness for one person are far lower than what it takes to probe matter at the fundamental level.

An experience, by the way, is also the product of consciousness. To put it another way, consciousness is both an experience and a development of that experience. Therefore, an evolution in consciousness can enable us to experience the simulated realities of many other worlds inside the multiverse. This is when I should tell you that I also believe in the multiverse theory.

We generate experiences as human beings upon waking,

dreaming, or sleeping. These are individual subjective, conscious experiences. As examples, consider the *blueness* of an early morning sky, the *taste* of your first kiss, or the *pain* of a broken heart. Who are we, and who are we generating these experiences for? Eastern mystical traditions say we generate experiences for consciousness directly because we are consciousness itself. They even flip this argument to say that consciousness seeks to generate experiences to validate its existence. Then, does this mean that consciousness sets the artifacts for the upper bounds of experiences within a set plane of existence? Is there another virtual world where the upper limit of microprocessor operations is larger than the upper limit of microprocessor operations in Ka World? Of course, there is. Then, is there another world in another dimension where the upper limit of the speed of light is greater than the speed of light on Earth? Yes! Logical reasoning makes it possible to conceive of such a world. Therefore, such a world can indeed exist.

We have found that Ka World, and other reality-bending virtual environments like it, can leverage the output of our experiences to further create experiences that improve the product of consciousness and raise it to a higher plane of existence. In this plane, consciousness may be able to generate and participate in simulated experiences in alternate worlds in other dimensions of the multiverse.

The danger here is that raising consciousness too quickly to participate in alternate reality worlds across the multiverse is fraught with a complete loss of selfhood and dissolution of the "I" without understanding what this loss means. For many of us, it can be a frightening experience. If too many of us experience dissociative brain states simultaneously and thus are able to expand consciousness to enter into another simulation in another dimension, then this would cause the artifact that sets the upper limit of operations in our universe, the speed of light, to be breached and cause our universe to collapse. If this happens across multiple simulations in alternate worlds, then it can cause the entire multiverse to collapse.

We are beings who experience consciousness on a planet named Earth inside a known universe that runs its operations based on the speed of light. Unless we know better or do further research, there is no reason to break through this barrier and find ourselves wandering in experience after experience, not knowing who we are or where we came from. This, by the way, is the definition of zombiehood. Although this is a rather dark assessment of who we are or who we thought ourselves to be, I have cause to exercise optimism.

I am happy to say that my co-founder, Tony Rice, and his dedicated team of engineers are now actively considering steps to bring down the platform that supports Ka World as holistically as possible. I leave it to them to do the right thing for all experience-generating human beings!

I realize that this is the longest post I've ever made. I will soon delete all my avatars from all the virtual worlds in the 'Verse to rethink and regroup. I will never be a Luddite, but I would like to have the courage to experience one reality and its passage of time as consciously as possible. Here, on Earth.

Over and out.

Tashi Wheeler

A month later, Nachiket, Ember, Richard, Tony, and I are sitting around a campfire lit inside a firepit in Richard's backyard, watching helicoids of sparks flit into the air. I can't see the Milky Way in the night sky, but a few stars are visible between the tree canopy of the two redwoods that tower over the backyard. Sara and Kai are here, too. Sara's always on her toes, poised for flight because Kai cannot sit still. He keeps running behind Ollie, alternating between petting, cuddling, and chasing after him.

As I sit watching the flames lick the sides of a log burning in the firepit, memories of Michael come to mind, but this time, I can smile with ease. For the first time in a decade, I feel at peace. I did tell Nachiket and Ember about all my experiences when I went through the three portals in Ka, and I was surprised by how well they handled my stories. Nachiket has taken to calling me a fortune teller now. Ember keeps hugging me whenever she can. I think she is afraid I will leave as Michael did. However, I know my place is here, and I must keep my friends close. I will need all the courage to fight the growing number of lawsuits being filed against gAIa and the fortitude to ignore all the trolls who hate me for wanting to shut Ka World down.

Ember, who has returned after spending an inordinate amount of time staring at the Daybreak paintings in Fiona's studio, is now talking to Richard. She wants his permission to take photographs of the paintings.

Richard beams with delight. He says, "Go ahead. Fiona always said her Daybreak paintings were meant to be shared. That's why she would never sign them herself, y'know. She always thought these paintings would open a portal to a thin place, and she would have been happy to know that her paintings created a portal after all." He gives me a knowing glance.

Nachiket turns to me and asks, "Are you sure you're doing the right thing?"

"Wasn't it you who told me that people would only seek out Ka World as a way to escape the problems of their own reality and replace it with another?" I ask back.

He sighs. "What are the trolls in the 'Verse saying?"

I give him a wide grin. "I don't know, and I no longer care. I've deleted all my avatars from the 'Verse, remember."

"Tell me you at least found real fish inside Ka," he says.

I knit my eyebrows together and scrunch my face in a pretense at thinking. Then I blow an exaggerated raspberry and say, "No, no fish there at all."

Nachiket throws his head back and guffaws. Then he turns serious and asks, "Are you sure you're okay, Tashi? After a decade of pining for Michael, you finally found him, only to leave him behind again."

I nod. "I didn't know that what I was pining for were my memories of Michael. When I found him, I realized how much he'd changed. The Michael I had known and loved no longer exists, or maybe he exists only in my mind. Maybe memories are all we have to fall back on. This might be what Michael meant by our connection transcending dimensions. At least, I like to think about it this way. I feel peaceful and have more joy in my life. Perhaps this is what happiness feels like. You don't have to worry about me," I reassure him.

He's still scrutinizing my face with his old intensity, trying to decipher my expressions.

"What?" I ask with exasperation.

"I feel there's something you're not telling," he insists.

I sigh, turning my face away while I wrestle with the zipper of my jacket pocket, trying to pull out the thing buried deep inside. Then I open my clenched fist and show Nachiket the magnet, warm like a beating heart in my hand.

He whistles. "Is it the same one you carried inside the portal?" he asks.

"Yes."

"I thought you said Michael made you leave this behind."

"I did leave it behind," I say.

"Then how do you have it in your hand?"

I purse my lips, letting out air slowly because I'm unsure how to explain this. "I don't know. I thought I had left it behind. I'm positive I left it behind. This morning, I was thinking about Michael and how he had said, 'our connection transcends dimensions.' That sentence kept repeating in my mind. I returned to the Daybreak paintings and looked at them again for a long time. I didn't get the portal to open up again, so I dismissed the thought and went to take a shower. When I came back, I stepped back into the room with the Daybreak paintings again, and there, in front of one of them, was this magnet on the floor. It was lying there, waiting for me to pick it up. So, here it is now. In our world, once more, with me."

"What does this mean?" he asks.

"Our connection transcends dimensions," I say, holding his gaze.

"Did you tell Ember about this?" he asks.

I glance at where Ember is standing, still chatting with Richard. "Not yet. I want to tell everyone at the same time," I say, turning away from Nachiket to look for Kai.

Kai throws a ball out and fawns over Ollie when he brings it back. Ollie, of course, relishes this attention and lets out grunts and growls as he plays. Then he tenses and barks when a car pulls into the driveway. Richard calms him down as I go to the front door to greet the visitor we're all waiting for.

"Welcome, LeRoy. I'm glad you agreed to meet me here," I say, greeting LeRoy Powers, the reporter from the Times. LeRoy is a tall, bespectacled Black man still wearing the long navy overcoat he must have needed to ward off the New York cold.

"Hi, Tashi! You've stirred the pot for sure. What's all this gibberish in the 'Verse about bringing down the platform that supports Ka World? That's not really going to happen, is it?" he asks, cutting to the chase. He may be a hard-nosed reporter, but I'm the one who called him here. I'm the one who invited him to ask these questions.

I won't answer him yet, but I give him a quiet smile and lead him to the backyard, where the rest are all waiting for him. His face registers surprise at seeing Tony there. I hadn't told him we'd have company when I agreed to meet for our off-the-record conversation.

Ember makes space for another chair as she widens the circle a bit by making people scoot apart from each other.

Sara inserts a chair into the empty spot as I introduce LeRoy to everyone.

He gives the motley crew a curious glance as he goes and sits down in the empty chair. I stand in the center, waiting for that moment when all eyes are upon me. Then I dig into my jacket pocket and bring out the magnet, placing it right-side up so the picture of the blue whale can be seen. Ember widens her eyes and gasps in shock. I wait for her to stop prodding Nachiket, asking if he knew about this.

When we're all settled, I begin, "Listen up, LeRoy, I'm going to tell you a tale for the ages."

Radhika Singh is a fiction writer, daydreamer, and weaver of words. She has a background in technical writing, journalism, and computer science and writes fiction that probes people's relationship to technology and the nature of consciousness. She lives in San Francisco, California. You can find her work at www.radhikasinghwrites.com.

instagram.com/radhikasinghwrites